Witch Killer

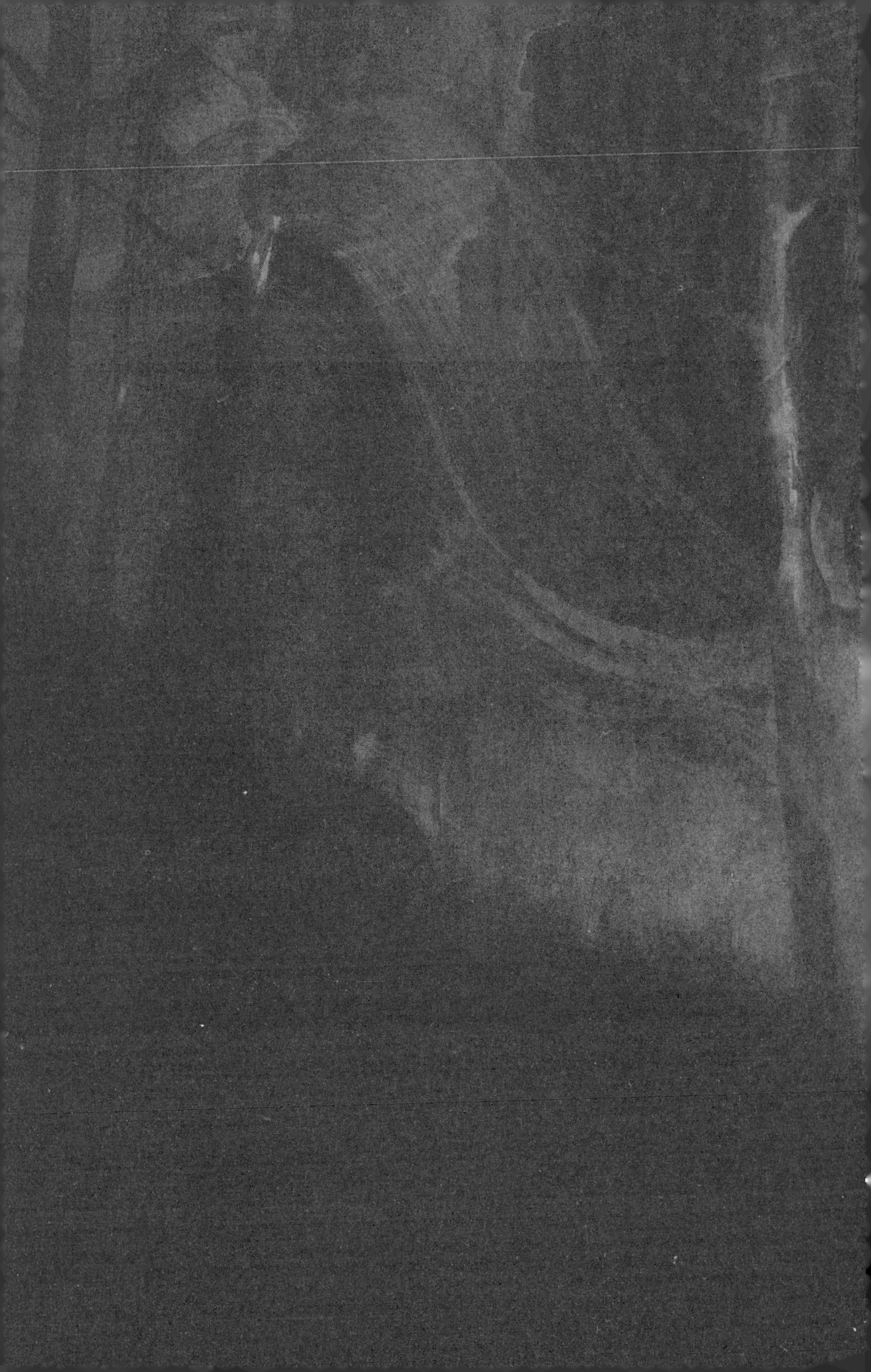

Witchkiller

ASHLEE LATIMER

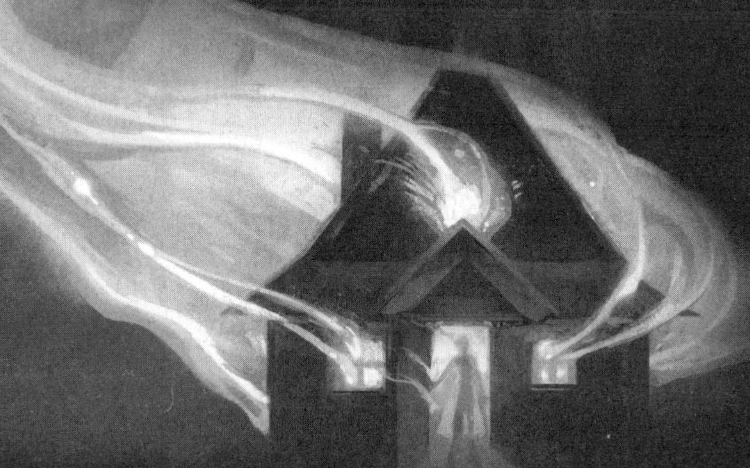

SCHOLASTIC PRESS
NEW YORK

Library of Congress Cataloging-in-Publication Data available

ISBN 978-1-5461-3768-9

10 9 8 7 6 5 4 3 2 1 25 26 27 28 29

Printed in Italy 208

First printing, October 2025

Book design by Maithili Joshi

For the girls whose first monsters
were fought at home.

Prologue

Hansel Henoth had not thought much or often about his death, but he was determined it not happen at the hands of a witch. She met him blow for blow, blocking each strike with precision. Almost as if she knew him better than he could have ever imagined.

He could not drown out the whimpers of the mewling heap in the corner, or their sobs and gasps, which were both distasteful and distracting to him. He redoubled his efforts. The witch had overtaken his sister, but he would not allow himself to meet a similar fate.

"Watch out!" For one moment, he looked toward the source of the rasping voice behind him.

That choice cost Hansel everything.

CHAPTER ONE

I awoke with my hand pressed over my mouth to muffle my screams. After five months, the nightmare still haunted me. Every morning, I awoke to the sound of steel ripping through flesh. The stench of blood—mine, my brother's, the Wood Witch's—filled my nostrils. Each time, I had to remind myself why I didn't feel the scratchy wool of my worn blanket, didn't hear the snoring of our father, Ansel, across the small sleeping room we all shared in our cottage.

I killed the Wood Witch.

I *had* to kill her to save Hansel.

Now we were part of the nobility because of it.

I remembered her raising her sword overhead. I remembered his blade clattering to the ground, too far away for him to reach. I remembered blacking out. Hansel claims I took up his weapon and ran the Wood Witch through.

I stopped her from killing us, but I wasn't able to stop Hansel as he ransacked her cottage and stole her hoarded jewels, all stacked up in the corner like firewood.

The light scraping of tree branches against a glass window

startled me, pulled me back to the present. I was still getting used to the sound, one of the many new experiences of living in a castle. We didn't have any paned windows in our old cottage. I curled my knees to my chest and reveled in the brush of soft cotton against my skin. The sensation grounded me as my eyes adjusted to the darkness of the predawn. I still felt small in the center of my too-large bed. Even stretched out, my fingers and toes couldn't reach any of the edges. A feat, since I stood a head taller than all the other girls my age in our former village.

I lived my life on an emotional tightrope, caught between appreciation for the luxury we now enjoyed and guilt over how it was acquired.

I yawned, the sound echoing through my cavernous bedroom. Though I feared and longed for it in equal measure, I needed to go back to sleep. I closed my eyes and made myself lie back on the down-filled pillow. I willed myself to ignore the cold sweat drying on my skin and drift off once more, hopefully to a dreamless place.

Sleep did not answer my summons, though I lay completely still until the morning light warmed my closed eyelids. My governess must have paid off the sun to push me from my bed as early as possible. Tonight, all of Polly's hard work would be put to the test. I needed to get up and find her. She would not relish the possibility of being rushed through our final preparations.

I scrambled out of bed, untwisting myself from the splendid bed linens, visions of Hansel bearing down on the Witch still filling my mind. His dishonest narrative was beginning to work on my subconscious.

But no, the images were a lie. One meant to protect me.

I had defeated the Wood Witch.

Though no one other than Hansel would ever know my shameful secret; my brother had told everyone that *he* was forced to kill the Witch to save *my* life after the Witch lured me to her cottage.

Imagining the sound of her flesh ripping apart as I pictured myself thrusting Hansel's sword through her shoulder made me nauseous, but the image had bloomed and lodged itself in my mind as soon as my brother had told me, in detail, how I took her down.

"I had no choice." I whispered the words like a prayer and a plea every time my chest grew tight beneath the pressure of my guilt.

I just wished I could actually remember what happened to lead to so much blood pooling on the wooden floor. Everything just before the fight was nonexistent, a void in my mind. Everything during, a tangled muddle of memories and lies that I struggled to unravel into coherency. I relied on Hansel's recounting, the way I had always counted upon him to be my shield and support.

I took tentative steps into the rest of the room as the sun stretched out its rays to disperse some of the gloom. Behind me, the four-post canopy bed loomed, larger even than it felt when I was sitting in its middle. The frame alone took up more space than an entire room in our cottage.

My suite was decorated with elegant, hand-carved furniture placed in every possible nook or cranny. No expense had been spared. But I still hadn't brought myself to add anything personal. Worry stood over my shoulder at all times, reminding me not to grow too comfortable. Our security rested entirely upon the strength of Hansel's lies. If anyone were to uncover the truth, it would all disappear in an instant.

You know what people would do if they found out you *were responsible,* Hansel had told me after he first laid out the cover story he would tell.

He didn't need to elaborate. I understood our world as well as he did. A man with a sword was a hero—a woman with any weapon, even her own voice, was a threat. So I had sat there, meek and mild, and memorized the tale he'd soon spin for anyone else who would stand still long enough to listen.

Witchkiller, they now called him, reverence coating every syllable of their whispers. I knew the tone would have been different if the title were draped upon me. Knew that no one would have taken kindly to our newly acquired wealth if they'd had reason to suspect I was responsible for it. No one liked a girl who could lay claim to a living of her own. The single common thread shared between common girls, ladies, and witches alike.

The silence grew more unsettling the longer I stood there. In our village, there was always a sheep bleating or a parent scolding a young child that could be heard through the thin cottage walls. Before my brother's theft, our family would never have been able to afford so much as a single night at an inn as lavish and remote as this castle, removed from the everyday intrusions and noises you learned to handle when living around other people in small spaces.

I needed to find Polly.

Heedless of the fact that I was still wearing no more than my sleeping shift, I left the room and tiptoed down the hallway in search of my governess. She wouldn't be pleased that I was flouting decorum, but she'd be *less* pleased if I wasn't ready for the prince's birthday ball in time. I was surprised she hadn't already shown up in my room of her own accord.

"Polly!" I whisper-shouted, wary of alerting my brother or father to my presence. I was not ready to face Ansel's relentless criticism—or to navigate the labyrinthian, ever-shifting personality that Hansel had developed these last five months.

After all, wealth had not saved me from my father's temper. Once upon a time, my brother stood as a shield against it, but of late he joined our father's side more and more often. Still, Hansel protected me from the outside dangers of the world. He could have left me after I defeated the Wood Witch. Or chosen to tell everyone my sins. Ansel would never have considered anyone's safety but his own. But Hansel had fought for me when it mattered. I could not hold my brother in complete contempt, but that did not mean I wished to run afoul of him, unplanned and unprepared.

After no luck in the first two corridors, I steeled myself and returned to the staircase that I'd neglected when I first began my search. I'd hoped to find Polly without going anywhere I wasn't allowed; I didn't want to risk a scolding from our housekeeper, Mrs. Chambers, for breaching one of her many rules. She didn't like when I used the servants' stairs.

It isn't appropriate for a lady of your station, Miss Gretel.

I rolled my eyes. She was just another voice of reproach in my life. I tried my best to respect her authority, when possible, but given the choice between facing my father's wrath and our housekeeper's derision, it wasn't really a choice at all.

I placed my hand against the wall to guide my way down the dark, cramped steps. I should have brought a candle. The farther I went, the louder the chatter that wound up from the hub of the castle's operations. At the bottom step, I pressed my ear against the door, fingers wrapped tight around the handle so no one could open it without warning. None of the voices on the other side belonged to Polly.

Maybe she would be waiting in my room for me by now. I turned and climbed up the stairs with increased boldness, eager to get back where I belonged before I was caught. When I reached the landing, I flung the door open without hesitation and barreled through the door, toward the main stairs.

Right into Hansel's chest.

"Hansel!" I forced my tone into lightheartedness as I tried to gauge his mood.

Hansel held me at arm's length, his face twisted by an irritated sneer with which I was growing too well acquainted. "What are you doing, roaming about in this state?"

I blinked at him, trying to reconcile the image of the person before me, so different from the disheveled and kind brother I once knew. It was still a shock to my system every time he went in this direction.

As opposite from my current appearance as he could be, Hansel looked resplendent in his well-tailored waistcoat and trousers. His white-blond hair was parted and coiffed, tamed with such stringency not a single strand was out of place. He even appeared taller, though maybe that was owed to the fancy heeled riding boots he wore.

Suddenly self-conscious, I took a step back, my heels grazing the edge of the step behind me. I crossed my arms tight, covering my chest.

But hobbled though I was by cowardice, I would not flee. That would only invite a chase.

"Apologies, brother, I was looking for Polly to complete our preparations for the ball tonight."

Hansel's laugh was sharp, hollow. "That eager to be paraded about, are you?" He gestured to my untamed curls, which pointed in every direction. "You cannot manage a hairbrush on your own, and you think you could run a household?" He stepped closer, forcing me to take a step back up the stairs.

"But—I—I—" I stuttered. He knew I wasn't allowed to dress myself anymore.

He grabbed my arm and locked his eyes on mine. "Perhaps it was a misstep on my part to take responsibility for your mistakes. I wouldn't be surprised if you one day forget to mind your tongue and accidentally reveal your transgressions in a fit of gossip."

I drew myself up to my full height and squared off my shoulders, the way I had done when facing our father so many times. "I know what is at stake, Hansel. I'm not in danger of telling anyone what I did."

Dark storm clouds rolled into Hansel's eyes, replacing mockery with anger. "This is precisely what I mean, sister. *You* did not do anything of consequence, save putting yourself in danger with your reckless wandering. Remember?"

I lowered my voice. "But you know—"

"I know that *I* killed the Wood Witch. *I* am the reason we have all of this wealth now and live among the nobility, instead of in that hovel some had the nerve to call a home." He began stalking me up the steps. I grabbed the railing to keep from falling as I walked backward, but I did not bow my chin. Looking away for only a second could have dire consequences.

"If it hadn't been for me, you'd be dead in the Witch's decrepit cottage. Instead, you live here and so does Father." His mouth curled into a threatening sneer. "You sleep in a bed I paid for. You eat food won by my hand. Your entire life is now my choice."

As we reached the top of the stairs, I mapped out an escape route in my peripheral vision. My focus shifted and he pounced upon my mistake.

Hansel snatched a handful of my nightgown and pushed me to the ground, leaning over me so his body formed a cage. "The very clothes upon your back are thanks to me, Gretel. So you will listen to me when I speak and you will not question me when I tell you your reality. Going forward, it would behoove you to at least *attempt* to keep my words tucked somewhere in the echoing cavern of your skull. Am I understood?"

I nodded, silent.

"Splendid." He brought his mouth to my ear. "This is the story you must commit to, even within your own mind: Five months past, I rescued you from the Wood Witch. I killed her just before she ran you through. Isn't that so?"

I searched Hansel's bright blue eyes. The same color as my own. The one trace of our mother that we both carried. His expression shifted from one of anger to near pleading, as if he wished to communicate something with me but could not speak it aloud. My own icy fear began to thaw; how many times had my brother and I been forced to communicate in code, circumnavigating our father's tempestuous moods together in a language only the two of us understood?

Of course!

This must have been one of those times. How foolish I was not to recognize sooner. I would worry about translating Hansel's message later. For now, I would prove to him that I could play along.

I breathed a sigh of relief and smiled up at Hansel. "Ah, yes, brother. You are so kind to remind me. I will do better to remember this time."

In an instant, Hansel's face softened fully into the dear companion I loved and remembered. He helped me stand and gave my hand an encouraging squeeze. "I have no doubt that you will."

He was unrecognizable compared with the snarling terror that had held me hostage only moments ago.

"This new life of ours is still strange to me," I admitted.

"Yes, but we all have our part to play, including me."

Once again, I detected hidden meaning and unsaid words in his tone. His reaction a moment ago was surely due only to the pressures of his new role. We had been allies in our house for as long as I could remember. He was my best friend. No witch alive or dead could change that.

After an awkward silence, Hansel cleared his throat. "Now, go make yourself presentable and I'll send up a breakfast tray. No doubt, you'll need all afternoon to prepare for the ball tonight."

His face was impenetrable. But his instructions steered me back to my original purpose.

"I need to find Polly," I reiterated.

Hansel frowned. "That girl is never where she's wanted. It is shocking how difficult responsible maids are to come by."

"She is not a maid." I spoke before I could stop myself.

"The particularities of a female servant's title hold no interest for me. What matters is that she is clearly not fulfilling the duties of her position."

I didn't understand how Hansel could condescend so about the staff; less than half a year ago, we were lower than they in both esteem and rank. Guilt twisted in my stomach. It was my fault that Hansel's derision was turned toward Polly. I should have made up a reason for being in the hallway. I needed to turn his focus elsewhere.

I rolled my shoulders back and smiled prettily at my brother, doing my best to imitate the ladies I had seen strolling through the stalls of the market where my family and I had once sold vegetables alongside our neighbors. The ones Polly had trained me to emulate. "Brother, would—"

"Miss Gretel, there you are!" Polly declared from the other end of the hallway. She held a breakfast tray.

"Polly! I was just—"

Hansel cut me off. "My sister has informed me that you were not ready at her door to help her prepare for the ball, Polly."

Polly was unflappable, her even-keeled nature honed by years of poor treatment from previous employers. "Begging both your pardons, Lord Hansel. We must have just crossed paths, Miss Gretel and I."

Hansel raised an eyebrow, a tactical, silent gesture meant to ruffle her.

"I altered my routine this morning to fetch Miss Gretel's

breakfast." Polly smiled, undeterred. "She must have slipped right past me."

"Are her maids no longer capable of carrying trays?"

"They're readying her dressing room, sir."

Hansel's eyes narrowed, but he relented. "I see."

"I'll take Miss Gretel with me, if that suits you, sir."

It was in both our best interests for her to defer to Hansel, but it still pricked me to be talked about and around, as if I were a child or a piece of furniture.

Old enough for the marriage market, but not to organize my own morning. The dichotomy of being a seventeen-year-old girl. The absurdity of it all made me sick.

"Yes, quite. See that she is ready."

"Of course, sir." Polly bobbed a curtsy so smooth, even the teacup on the tray she held didn't clatter in its saucer.

Hansel appraised me with cold eyes, a hint of challenge emerging from their depths. "You must take pains to be perfect, Gretel. If you perform well, our family is sure to be the talk of the evening."

"Yes, brother." I echoed Polly's curtsy.

As I straightened, I smiled wider and pressed my hands against my stomach, willing away the brewing fear that bubbled there. My mind tumbled adrift on a fierce river of all that I needed to remember, all that I would have to prove I had mastered to be a proper lady, worthy of her position in this fine household.

Hansel kissed me on the forehead and disappeared back down

the stairs, taking them two at a time. I resisted the urge to claw at my own skin and kept smiling until he was well out of sight.

"What if no one asks me to dance?"

Polly plucked one of the leftover plum slices from the breakfast tray I'd barely touched. "Then I will likely lose my position and you will be responsible when your father turns my mother and me out loose amongst the elements."

Annika and Frida smirked as they laced up my bodice.

We were freer with one another in the privacy of my rooms. Since we'd moved into the castle, the three of them were my only source of comfort and safety.

I frowned at Polly. "I need you to be serious."

She rose from her seat and came to stand next to me. "And I need *you* to have more faith in the education I've provided you. You know the answer to your question: When you are without a partner, you must mingle with the young ladies and their mothers."

"The other girls have trained their entire lives for this level of scrutiny."

Frida popped her head around my waist and addressed our reflections in the mirror. "So have you, miss, in a way." Her brown eyes were wide, fervent with belief.

If only I could bottle some of her optimism.

Annika did not share my enthusiasm for Frida's outlook. A full head and shoulders taller than her counterpart, she glared down at the shorter maid from where she stood preparing my hair for braiding.

Frida's gaze lowered as she bobbed a curtsy. "Forgive me for speaking out of turn, miss."

"Frida, you know I do not think like that." However much Ansel and Hansel may have forgotten about our former lives, I remained aware that not too long ago, I held a lower station than the girls currently dressing me. "You may always speak openly when we are alone."

"Say what you will," Polly said encouragingly, goading Frida on.

Frida straightened, fiddled with a strand of dark hair that had escaped her bun. "It is only that Lord Ansel and Lord Hansel are very—" She paused, looking to Annika for guidance.

Annika kept her hands to the task of plaiting my crown braid as she finished her counterpart's sentence. "Particular."

"And they never scare you, Miss Gretel! No matter what they say," Frida chimed in once more.

She was wrong about that. I had merely learned that to flinch before Ansel only invited more cruelty. It pained me that I was beginning to apply the same techniques to my brother.

Polly squeezed my shoulder. I shifted to face her in the mirror. We could have been sisters; she was a few inches taller than me, almost Hansel's height, but we had the same ruddy-brown waves and broad, curvy build.

"Gretel, trust that you can do this."

"Can she?"

I startled at the sudden sound of my father's voice from the doorway, smearing the rouge that Annika was dusting on my cheeks. It was my first time seeing him all day. Ansel Henoth had been fearsome enough as a farmer, with his towering figure, quick hands, and sharp tongue. Cloaked in his new identity as a nobleman, however, he appeared lethal. Assumed power radiated off him in waves, thick and foreboding as the stench that wafted from the cow pies in our former neighbors' fields during high summer.

"Hello, Father." My maids and I dropped quick curtsies. The moment he entered the room, all our individual personalities disappeared. We became a uniform regiment of subservience.

Father sneered at me as he crossed the room and I instinctively froze, looking up at him from beneath my lashes. It was a strange comfort that, despite his expensive clothes and more diligent hygiene, his general constitution remained unchanged. I appreciated knowing my enemy.

He stopped a few feet away from me, running over my appearance with a piercing gaze. As a small child, I had often wondered if he possessed some magical ability to see through things, through people.

"We leave in three-quarters of an hour and yet you haven't laced up your bodice."

I sighed internally. This was an old battle between us. One that had begun when he'd first forced me to start wearing a corset a year before even my most precocious classmates. Long before we'd acquired our newfound wealth and higher station, he'd nurtured grand fantasies about what a proper match might bring our family.

I chewed the inside of my cheek, weighing the cost of pushing back. The expectant silence that hung in the air told me that if I didn't, Ansel would simply find something else to berate me about. I would move forward, then. Better an evil I was prepared for than one more new thing to learn.

"It is laced, Father."

Behind me, Frida gave the smallest squeak, whether of disapproval or fear—or a mixture—I couldn't be sure. I pressed on.

"The laces are meant to be supportive, Father, not restrictive. Tight lacing is dangerous. Some women have died from it." Never mind that he didn't care about my reasoning; the longer I continued speaking, the more time I bought myself. "Besides, I do not wish to be so revealed in front of the queen and the prince."

The slap came without warning.

My body had barely a second to tense just before his broad hand made contact with the full side of my face. The blow crossed me with such force that I stumbled on my voluminous skirts and lost my balance. For the second time in one day, I found myself on the ground at the mercy of a male relative.

I braced for my father to restrain me the way Hansel had, but he instead fell back several paces, holding his ground from the center of the room.

"You have a responsibility to this family to secure an excellent match."

I pushed the hanging half-finished braid out of my eyes. "And if I die for my efforts along the way?"

Ansel shrugged. "Your dowry will be one less expense for me to worry about."

I knew better than to respond this time. When Ansel was in a striking mood, no amount of stubbornness could contend with or persuade him. Once, Hansel would have leapt between us and taken the blow himself. But no matter the accord of fragile peace I had reached with my brother earlier that morning, I felt in my bones that the days of him defending me from Ansel were behind us. Now I was alone.

"Good," he said, pronouncing my retreat the correct choice. He produced a handkerchief from his pocket and wiped his hands, cleansing himself of his contact with me. More than perhaps anything about this new life, I was always staggered by his transformation into someone so externally refined.

He turned his attention to the maids. "Now, tidy my daughter up and make sure that her assets are *arranged* appropriately. We're putting her on the market to fetch an offer of marriage, not sainthood."

"As you wish, sir. I'll see to it myself," Polly promised.

Frida and Annika mumbled words of assent, bobbing in alternating curtsies all the while. The terror on their faces matched my own, though I was careful to keep mine locked up tight inside, where Ansel could not see.

My father took his leave.

In due time, I found myself seated in a gilded carriage across from Hansel and Ansel, feeling as trussed up as any venison I had ever prepared for roasting. When I had descended the staircase, I feared that I would topple over. Uninterested in finding themselves on the receiving end of an attack from Ansel, poor Frida and Annika had cinched my corset so tight, I thought surely even my father would admit my bosom was too much on display.

But he'd said nothing, and now I sat before the pair of my harshest critics. The cold stare with which Hansel regarded me confirmed what I had earlier suspected. Despite whatever appearance of kindness he'd performed after our confrontation, he was no longer the friend I'd once known. I could convince myself that he was playing a game, carrying out an elaborate plan of sneak attack against our father, the details of which he would soon no doubt illuminate for me. Or I could accept the truth: Sometime in the interval between our venture to the Wood Witch's cottage and this very morning, my brother had switched sides for good.

I watched the blazing autumnal landscape roll by our carriage and wished my brother had abandoned me one choice sooner—that he had condemned me to death at the hands of the Witch, rather than this half-life beneath the thumb of our father.

CHAPTER TWO

I had to admit that the palace was beautiful. It almost quelled the morbid thoughts that drifted through my mind whenever I had to spend prolonged periods of time with my brother and Ansel.

The spiral towers and grand staircase appeared out of the mist as our horses trotted over the drawbridge and down the long entryway, like a fairy tale made manifest. I had never seen such grandeur up close before. Arrangements of pumpkins, tapers, and garlands of preserved leaves decorated every available surface in a vision of seasonal transition.

The calendar shift wasn't the only change on the guests' minds. The halls leading to the main ballroom reverberated with unfiltered gossip.

We joined the queue to enter the palace. The crush of people jostled me into the path of two middle-aged noblewomen who were dressed like green and gold copies of each other.

"I heard the queen thinks the prince too young to ascend," said the green.

Gold made a sympathetic sound. "No, I was told she simply does not wish him to bear the weight of the crown alone."

I locked eyes with the girl my age trailing dutifully behind them. A living memory of what her mother and presumed aunt must have looked like in their youth.

Her gaze scanned over me before she turned away with a curled lip.

I trotted to catch up with Hansel.

"A stable boy told one of my maids that Prince Wilfried must take a wife by year's end."

"Will it be a love match?"

"—doubts about his ability to lead—"

"—seeking a particular sort of girl—"

"—eager to stabilize the line—"

On and on their speculations went. I once assumed I had nothing in common with the prince, but maybe he felt as trapped as I did. Offered up for consumption. Relegated to being an object for the strategic advancement of others.

To bear the burden of responsibility for a kingdom in addition to the rest of it? A horrifying prospect. Pity stirred within me for this boy, though I did not even know what he looked like beyond rumors that had drifted far enough to reach our old village.

We wound our way through the halls. Generations of royal portraits lined the walls, but one caught my eye. A boy about my age, with pale skin, honey-blond hair, and warm brown eyes that were tinged with sorrow. Prince Wilfried, I was sure of it. He must have sat for the painting shortly after his father's passing last year. Before I had the chance to draw any closer, the crowd jostled us along and I turned my attention back to those around me.

Our prince was not the only one drawing the attention of his subjects. Criticisms of me soon joined their conjectures about him.

"How shameless." A jab at the neckline of my dress.

A girl not much older than me tittered from behind the cover of her fan. "What can you expect? New merchant money *and* no mother."

"—had to buy their land and title! Can you imagine?" Her companion answered.

I balled my fists and focused on Hansel's back to avoid separation again. In our village, such words would have invited a thrashing from their parents, but it seemed that nobles didn't teach their children manners.

". . . dreadful for her father. But have you seen the brother?" Another young woman on the hunt. Her cheeks bloomed pink as she batted her eyelashes in Hansel's direction.

Another girl grinned. "Of course he's handsome. He's the Witchkiller, after all."

"Smart, too. My cousin told me he's the one responsible for their wealth. Convinced their father to invest in . . ."

I shuddered as Hansel's admirers moved out of earshot. Despite the girls' mean comments, I would not wish either of the men in my family on anyone.

If only I could scream that my impropriety was all Ansel's doing. If only I could find some way to flee. Escape this night. Escape this life.

But no one was coming to rescue me. All I could do was follow my father and brother with a plastered smile on my face, pretending I was none the wiser to the insults that wafted through the halls and bore our names.

My smile faltered as we reached the dance floor, and I suddenly found myself wishing that I could stay by my brother's side. When the first suitor to gather the courage offered his liver-spotted hand, Hansel did nothing to spare me from my fate. Father pushed me off into the man's repulsive clutches.

I pantomimed my way through dance after dance with strange men. Everywhere I turned, I met the unwelcome eyes of the other guests. Girls my age branded me with disdainful glares; some were marked with jealousy of my full dance card, others were those lucky few who partnered only with themselves. Perhaps the latter judged me for acquiescing to the marriage market that my father was determined I should feature in. Could they not guess I had no choice?

"—shame you couldn't do away with it entirely."

The acrid voice pulled me from my own thoughts and back into the present. I'd all but grown numb to the presence of my partner, so easy he was to mistake for another. But now I was all too aware of the man before me, whose eyes roved over my exposed chest with no pretense of gentlemanly discretion.

My heart thumping against my ribs, I forced myself to make it through the rest of the dance so I could withdraw without causing a scene. At last, the song ended. I excused myself, stomach churning, and made my way to the edge of the room, taking deep breaths all the while.

I found a shadowy corner that offered privacy, but not so much seclusion that I had to worry my former dance partner—or one of the many others—might accost me. These men were bold enough in public view.

I rubbed my temples and took deep breaths, in through my nose and out through my mouth. I angled my body so one side of it pressed against the cool pane of the nearest floor-to-ceiling stained glass doors. My eyes fluttered closed. It was a unique kind of taxing, the onslaught of all these new people, new rules, new places.

After several moments, I opened my eyes again, steeling myself to enter back into the fray before my father had a chance to notice my absence from the center of everyone's attention. But as I pushed off the glass, movement outside caught my eye.

At the edge of the woods bordering the palace, a young woman crept through the trees. Her bright red hair hung loose, catching the glint of the moon. She did not appear dressed for the ball, with a large shawl wrapped around what seemed to be a simple woven dress, the kind I wore in my previous life. A bright, russet fox who shared her coloring trotted alongside her.

How was someone able to come so close to the palace without

alerting the guards? Curious, I checked over my shoulder to be sure that no one was watching, then slipped quietly through the door and out into the night.

I took in a breath of fresh air. Removed from the newfound scrutiny of the nobility and the withering gaze of my own family, my chest loosened, despite my absurdly tight corset laces. I couldn't linger on the sensation, however, if I wanted to investigate where the girl in the woods was going.

I wheeled around and made for the staircase that went down from the balcony.

Then found myself staring at the sternum of a very tall young man.

His hands clasped my shoulders, steadying me, before we sprang apart. We were not dancing; it was inappropriate for him to touch me. Yet if he hadn't, I would have smashed my face into his ribs.

I gazed up into my barrier's face and a soft gasp escaped me. This was not just *any* very tall young man.

It was the face I'd seen dozens of painted variations on only hours ago. He was all the more captivating in person. Prince Wilfried had his mother's warm, honey-blond coloring and his father's angular features. He looked like a marriage between the sun and the moon, and I had never witnessed a lovelier union.

How is he not yet betrothed?

We stared at each other for a moment, neither of us blinking or breathing. His hands were still held aloft to prevent me from running into him, as if wary I might try for a second round.

"Your Highness." I dropped into a curtsy, remembering myself.

He held a finger to his lips. "Shh, shh, not too loud." His bright ochre eyes were wide with entreaty.

As if I would disobey him.

I lowered my voice and my gaze. "I apologize, Your Highness, I did not intend to disturb you. I needed some fresh air."

He placed a finger beneath my chin. Another inappropriate touch. My heart turned over as I reflexively steeled myself for a blow. When he lifted my face, however, the corners of his eyes were crinkled with mirth. "Would you believe me if I said I sought the same?"

How curious, to wish to avoid his own birthday party. All the boys and men of my acquaintance would never waste an opportunity to be celebrated.

"Do you dislike crowds, Your Highness?"

He smiled and I smiled back at him. This marriage mart business would have been much easier if he were the one asking me to dance.

"Please, call me Wilfried. Lady . . . ?"

"Gretel. You may call me just Gretel."

He tilted his head. "I am not convinced there is anything 'just' about you. Nevertheless, I shall be amenable to your wishes."

I nodded, too stunned to speak. No one ever gave much thought to my wishes.

"Now, Just Gretel, might I entreat you to venture away from the windows? I am not eager to be seen by anyone—present company excluded, of course." He moved toward the balcony's railing before I could reply.

I followed without hesitation, enraptured. We leaned against the cold stone and I welcomed the cooling it provided. I did not dare stand close enough to touch him, but I looked. Away from the torchlight that filtered through from the ballroom, the contrast in his features was thrown into even greater relief. His pale skin was almost silver beneath the moon, but his eyes and hair were all burnt honey and late summer.

He broke the silence. "To answer your question: Yes, I dislike crowds. I find it difficult to be myself around strangers, much to the chagrin of my mother's advisers."

"Perhaps your sense of reserve is a trait gifted from the queen?" I offered. After all, his mother was also once a commoner, the daughter of a baker, and surely had also found the court overwhelming when she first arrived at the palace.

His grin widened. "I suppose it is, though she forgot to also gift me with her charm, for use on nights like these."

"I do not think she did, sir," I blurted. Heat flooded my cheeks. "My apologies, Your Hi—"

He raised a brow.

"I mean, Your Wilfri—that is, just . . . I apologize. Sir." I stared at my shoes.

"Worry not, I am not so easily offended." He bent at the waist and brought his mouth close to the shell of my ear, careful not to touch me. "Though perhaps I will endeavor to feign irritation, if it continues to make you blush so prettily."

This close, he smelled of fresh sugared almonds, just like at Yuletide.

Emboldened by his flattery, I rolled my shoulders back and raised my gaze to meet his. "Well, as I am a stranger, am I to assume this version of you is only a performance?"

"I suppose you must learn me better and discover for yourself." One eyebrow and the side of his mouth rose in joint merriment.

I matched his smirk. "I would not wish to cause you discomfort."

"Would you believe me if I claimed not to remember the last time I felt this at ease," he murmured, drawing the rest of his body nearer.

My heart flopped and stretched and panicked. Any wit I'd scrounged together fled the scene. I opened my mouth and hoped for words to come, when—

"Gretel!" My brother's harsh voice broke through the silence. I jumped back from where I was standing, sure it was too close to the prince for anyone to bear witness. Wilfried took a small step forward, but reading the panic on my face, he retreated into the shadow cast by the palace wall instead, as if lying in wait.

Hansel grabbed my arm at the elbow with such force, my

joint popped as he whirled me around to face him. "Where have you been?"

"I was merely taking in some fresh air. I grew overheated." I fixed my gaze on Hansel. Though I was certain the girl from the woods must have disappeared by now, I didn't want to take any chances on what this new version of my brother might do if he saw a young girl wandering the edge of the woods alone. What was more, I feared what Wilfried might think of me if he saw the breadth of my brother's anger on display.

"For several dances? I don't believe you." He narrowed his eyes and gripped my elbow tighter.

"Ahem." Wilfried cleared his throat and stepped partially into the light.

Hansel sneered at him, barely glancing up. "We're having a private conversation."

"Is that how you address a prince, Lord . . . ?" Wilfried's voice was cold, the complete opposite of how he'd spoken to me. He stepped fully into view and all the color drained from my brother's face.

Hansel sketched a bow, his expression a frozen mask of worry. "I apologize, Your Highness, I didn't recogni—"

Wilfried held up a hand, silencing Hansel. "No matter, I do not recognize you, either." He looked at me, though he spoke to my brother.

Hansel's jaw popped in my peripheral vision.

"Shall we all return inside together?" Wilfried suggested.

Perhaps it was only my imagination, but it seemed he asked for my benefit.

I dropped another curtsy. "Of course, Your Highness." I addressed him formally once more. This time, he did not object. He must have agreed it was important that we not seem too familiar or provide speculation fodder upon which my brother—or any gossipmonger—could pounce. Princes might be free to flout social mores as they liked, but not young ladies.

As we made our way back inside, Wilfried extended his hand to me and seemed on the precipice of asking me a question. Before he could utter a word, however, his mother appeared. Like her son, she was even more striking in person than her portrait suggested. It was no wonder that Richmond Varnhagen—Wilfried's father, the deceased king—had fallen in love with her.

Growing up, the story of their meeting had been the stuff of many a common girl's fairy-tale dreams: On the return from a hunt, the young king had spied Galen Hevanna selling her family's baked goods at the market. Upon his arrival at the palace, he ordered the kitchens to only buy flour from the Hevanna family going forward. Naturally, Galen helped with the deliveries and Richmond made a point of being nearby as she arrived. Over time, they developed a friendship that blossomed into something more.

I may not have spent as much of my girlhood dedicated to the idea of marrying a noble as some of my friends, but I couldn't deny the appeal of a love story like the king and queen's—I certainly wouldn't have been opposed to finding myself in a similar tale.

I blushed at the thought of how much closer I was to such a possible story now. Not close enough, I knew. If the gossip I'd heard in the entry hall earlier was any indication, Wilfried would marry a princess or the daughter of a dignitary. Someone who would bolster our kingdom's security. Still, it was nice to daydream.

Hansel bowed and I curtsied before we greeted the queen as one. "Your Majesty."

The queen was staring at me, her mouth slightly open.

But no sooner had I noticed than she blinked away any feelings she had and donned a neutral expression. "New friends, my son?"

Her gaze passed over me, and once again, something almost like recognition flickered over her. It was quickly extinguished.

"Perhaps," Wilfried said, eyes only for me. My brother's plastered smile tightened. He could do nothing in front of the queen and the prince, however, and a slight shiver of pleasure rippled through me at that realization. The part of me that had acquiesced to the changes in my brother thrilled at seeing him in a position of disadvantage.

"Then I regret that I must tear you away, but the dignitaries from Mainz wish to speak with us regarding your goat relocation program. I know you're eager to see that move forward."

A piece of my hope withered. The delegation from Mainz had

many eligible young ladies in their party. I continued smiling and pushed my feelings down.

"Of course, Mother. I'll join you in your office momentarily."

The queen squeezed her son's shoulder and wove back through the crowd as it parted around her. My heart ached at such a tender, familiar touch between family members.

"I regret that I cannot ask you for a dance," Wilfried said to me, taking my hand in his as he bowed over it. "I hope to see you again."

"As you wish, Your Highness." I curtsied again and then he was gone, without so much as a glance at Hansel. I braced myself for the payback I would certainly receive for the blow to my brother's ego.

But Hansel was silent, his face an impenetrable sheet of marble save for the steely look in his ice-cold eyes. We stood for several moments at an impasse. At last, I resigned myself to the fact that my best option for taking leave of him was to throw myself back into the chaos of the dance floor.

No sooner had the idea entered my mind, however, than Hansel took my hand in a vise grip. "It is time for us to go home."

His tone brooked no argument. I followed him along the edge of the crowd, knowing better than to assert that I could do so without him dragging me along. My hand grew numb clenched in his.

"Aha, there's our Witchkiller now!" Ansel announced as we drew near to the corner of the ballroom where he'd spent the night carousing with other businessmen.

Our father was well enough into his cups that it took almost no effort for Hansel to steer him away from the circle of men he was bragging to about Hansel's bravery. Back in the carriage, I waited for Hansel to reveal that I'd shirked my responsibilities and spent a good portion of the evening with Prince Wilfried—a man so far beyond my station, surely even my father was not foolish enough to think him an actual marriage prospect for me. Removed from the warm cocoon of Wilfried's kindness, I was not so naive as to hope for such things.

But my father took no notice of my brother, choosing instead to prattle on about how well he'd finessed my standing in the pool of eligible young ladies who my would-be suitors had also danced with that evening.

"Yes, yes, I think we made a very good first impression for the season, thanks to my cleverness. And Gretel managed not to botch anything. All in all, a good showing. Don't you agree, Hansel?"

"Hm." Hansel shrugged, looking resolutely out the dark window.

"Quite right, quite right," Ansel said. Moments later, he was snoring.

Hansel and I did not speak for the rest of the ride home.

As we walked toward our castle doors, Hansel held me back, letting Mrs. Chambers take the lead with a teetering Ansel.

"My silence comes at a price, Gretel."

CHAPTER THREE

The next weeks passed in a whirl of ball after ball, suitor after suitor, recounting after recounting of Hansel's heroism and bravery in defeating the Wood Witch. Our new neighbors and acquaintances were more than happy to add to the ever-growing tapestry of his story: Anecdotes of the Wood Witch terrorizing the peasants on their estates. Cautionary tales of stolen livestock and strange illnesses.

I was the only one who remembered the Witch as a solitary creature. She was alone when we crossed paths, that much I could recall. It was one of the reasons I was so confounded by not knowing what had led Hansel and me to her cottage in the first place. Our father had hated witches for most of my life, ever since they were unable to cure my mother of the fever that killed her when I was still a toddler. So I could not conceive of what would have compelled either of us to seek one out. And Hansel never would explain that piece of the story.

For the most part, neither my father nor brother seemed concerned with the state of my mind, so long as I went along with whatever story they decided to tell.

Though I still resented much of this new life—in particular the effects it had wrought on my once-sweet brother—I couldn't deny that one of the blessings of our sudden wealth was that I found myself with long stretches of time on my hands. Entire afternoons and several evenings when, instead of doing the chores required by our former life, I could keep to myself and remain unbothered by Hansel or Ansel. Though I still treasured the small collection of books left behind by our mother, I took advantage of the castle's stocked library, embracing the first time in years that I'd had new stories to discover. When I could not bear being cooped up inside any longer, I roamed the estate, both on foot and horseback. The woods at the edge of our castle grounds became my favorite refuge. There, I could pour out my thoughts and worries to the trees and moon and stars.

What's more, some of the little creatures that made their homes near ours had become friends of sorts, always waiting for me to bring them crumbs of food in exchange for their companionship and listening ears. I didn't have to worry that they would divulge my concerns and fears around the troubling mess of my memories, or that one of them would betray the truth about my family and our past to any busybody who cared to know.

Removed from the refuge of the woods, I still had to contend with the realities of my new life. And perhaps no event made that more apparent than Hansel's birthday party. The guest list included only the most boring and obnoxious nobles in the district—people so devoid of their own stories, opinions, or personalities that they never seemed to tire of hearing Hansel recount the story of "his" battle with the Witch over and over again. They delighted in each new version, especially when they recognized a fresh detail as one they'd previously supplied.

My brother's first performance was already well underway by the time we all adjourned to dinner. As we meandered into the Great Hall, Ansel abruptly fell back from the group and pulled me aside.

"Gretel, I have been more than generous." He said the words with a smile, all his teeth on display. Anyone passing by would have assumed this conversation was a positive exchange between father and daughter, the tending-to of a well-planned surprise for the birthday boy, perhaps.

I blinked away the spittle that flew from his mouth. I would not give him the satisfaction of saying I did not know to what he was referring.

"Of course you have, Father." I matched his manufactured grin.

"Many fathers would not let their daughter have any input in the matter at all. I pride myself on being a charitable, modern-minded man. But even my generosity has limits."

I nodded.

"If you have not chosen a suitor by the end of Hansel's birthday celebrations, I will choose one for you. I do not think you wish to see my hand forced in this."

Oh, of course it was about marriage. His only concern for me.

"You are right, Father." I sketched a curtsy, if only for the excuse to hide my face, my quivering lip.

I removed myself at once and prepared for an evening of pretending to celebrate my brother while trying to assess which of the pompous men at our table would make the least objectionable husband. I usually found myself at odds with the way the dark hours dragged this time of year; the longer the night, the more time for my brother to prattle on. For once, I appreciated the extended time for delaying my decision.

Just when I thought I might fall asleep atop my place setting, a lapse of detail in Hansel's accounting caught my attention.

"Gretel had fainted and the Witch held a weapon above her, ready to plunge it into her gut. So I—"

"Remind me, brother, what was the weapon?" My heart beat furiously against my ribs, as though wishing to escape its alliance with my body. I was playing with fire.

Hansel stuttered, his cheeks growing red. In all the times I'd watched him tell his story, not a single person had dared interrupt him or question what he said. A sheen of sweat broke out across his forehead.

Then he remembered he had the upper hand and tossed aside his discomfort with the careless practice of throwing off morning bedcovers. His smile was dangerous in its false conviviality. He was confident I would not risk social ruination by revealing myself.

"As I said, *sister*, you were unconscious. I fail to see why the weapon should be of any import or interest to you." For one moment, tension stretched between us, the eyes of our guests volleying back and forth. Then he laughed, and everyone joined him.

I stayed my risky course.

"Of course, *dearest* Hansel," I said, my smile honey sweet, not a hint of bite to my words.

He took this as an assent and adjusted his posture, ready to leap into the story once more. "As I was saying: The Witch—"

"—but that is why I must look to you, for how else shall I know the details of my rescue?" I wiped the corners of my mouth with my linen, the perfect lady, the portrait of decorum and deference.

A thin vein popped at the center of Hansel's forehead. Would this be the transgression that led him to shove all pretense aside and attack me in front of everyone? A disturbed part of me welcomed it.

The wide entry doors to the hall flung open.

Prince Wilfried entered, flanked by members of his personal guard and his mother's Council. The room hushed, held its breath in a momentary standstill. Though they'd been sufficiently attentive prior to the interruption, the prince inspired a fresh sense of jubilee amongst the party, if their overwrought expressions of frozen glee were any indication. Everyone appeared thrilled to see Wilfried.

I certainly was.

Everyone except Hansel.

"Forgive my late arrival; we've only just returned from Hesse and I came here straightaway." Wilfried looked around at the other guests with sheepish contrition. He did not spare Hansel a moment of attention.

So he can hold a grudge.

I bit back a giggle. This slight imperfection of his character intrigued me.

Hansel stood from his seat and bowed to Wilfried. "We are honored by your presence at any hour, my prince." He gestured to the seat at his right hand. "Please, join us."

"We'll content ourselves with open seats and save your servants and other guests the trouble of rearranging the room." Before Hansel could protest, Wilfried sauntered through the room and took the seat near the foot of the table, opposite mine.

When I turned to assess my brother's reaction, he was glaring right at me. Wilfried had reined in Hansel's displeasure for now, but it would reappear soon enough. I smiled at the prince and pushed all fears to the back of my mind to be dealt with later.

Once the final course of the meal was over, we made our way to the ballroom.

A fragile hope that Wilfried might ask me to dance curled up my spine. As if hearing my thoughts, he materialized by my side the instant we'd crossed the threshold of the Hall.

"I believe I owe you a dance, Miss Henoth." His smile was just as gentle as I remembered. There was no hint of the wolfish possession that I'd seen reflecting back at me from the eyes of the many lecherous men I'd been forced to partner with these past weeks.

My father's warning sat in my stomach like a stone, but I would not let it pin me down. By midnight, I would be promised to someone else. But for now, my night was my own. I would give my dreams leave to partner with my feet and pretend that a different path—one that wound its way to the palace—lay before me.

Prince Wilfried was a steady partner, his steps light and sure. All I had to do was follow. One dance flowed into three until, sensing the glares of others who spun and hopped around us with their own subpar matches, I stilled Wilfried in the pause between songs.

"I believe some of the young ladies are feeling neglected." I tipped my chin toward one of the small huddles of sullen girls across the room.

Wilfried shrugged. "Then they are sensible, for I am neglecting them."

I blushed; I couldn't help it. I didn't blame the other girls, considering the less-than-ideal alternatives that surrounded us. I would, in fact, soon be among their ranks. After all, Wilfried likely had as little choice in a spouse as any of us did—perhaps less—and I would have bet all my father's wealth that a former peasant was no option for a prince's bride. Still, it was nice that while he had an illusion of control over his time, he chose to spend it with me.

I didn't have long to relish in that knowledge; the girls weren't the only glum ones in the room. As the music began again and Wilfried took me back into his arms, my father glared at me over the prince's shoulder. Ansel gestured toward the large clock on the wall with a frown. Little more than an hour left. My head began to spin, and not from the series of turns Wilfried was leading me through. I broke away from him mid-step, ripping myself out of my waking dreams. I was too flustered to keep pretending.

"I'm sorry, I need to go," I forced myself to say before bolting from the dance floor.

Behind me, a stampede of eager replacement partners rushed to accost Wilfried in my absence.

I was thankful for them, for the head start that they gave me to make my escape. I needed to reach the freedom of the outdoors. To go someplace I could be alone. Somewhere I could pretend that I hadn't just embarrassed myself in front of the only genuine person I'd encountered since stepping into this dreadful society.

I tore through the halls and did not stop until I was outside in the southern courtyard, the one that abutted the woods. I braced my hands on my knees to catch my breath and gulped in the crisp, cleansing air.

The moon shone high and full overhead, casting the grounds in a romantic glow. For a moment, I was soothed by the soft hoots of owls and other creatures of the night.

A twig snapped nearby and I froze.

I hadn't been out in these woods by myself *this* late at night.

Steeling myself against what I might see, I raised my head and peered into the trees.

There!

The flash of something white, followed by two streaks of red.

I squinted. It was the red-haired girl and her fox! The same pair that was wandering the edge of the palace grounds on the night I met Wilfried.

I dashed across the courtyard, and onto the grounds. I would not lose sight of her this time.

But when I reached the trees, she was nowhere to be found. I paused, hoping for another broken branch or rustle of a bush to reveal her whereabouts. After several moments of silence, I turned around, defeated and shivering, ready to go home.

Instead, I immediately collided with Wilfried. The image of running into my brother the morning of my first ball took over my vision as bile rose in my throat, choking out every other thought.

I screamed on instinct, then grew truly afraid when he clapped his hand over my mouth and grabbed me by the upper arm to prevent me from moving.

Hot dread and despair coursed through me; he'd followed me from the castle.

And now he was going to trap me here.

He was just like the others, after all.

Not caring that he was a prince and I barely part of the titled class, I brought my knee up to his groin with enough strength to startle him into letting go of me.

Tears of frustration blurred my vision, but I didn't care where the woods might lead me or what I might find along the way. Anything was better than here, where even the sweet could become bitter in a single breath.

I did what I should have done the first time the spirit of our father looked out at me through Hansel's eyes and proved to me that no man was truly trustworthy.

I ran.

CHAPTER FOUR

"Gretel, wait!" Wilfried didn't even sound winded as he crashed through the brush behind me.

I blundered on, briars and branches scraping at my hands and face.

"Gretel, STOP." The tone of authority in his voice was so thick that I did as he bade me. The fog of my breath floated out around me, further obscuring my vision with each exhale. I was so utterly alone out here.

No one would hear me scream.

If they did, would they care?

If they found us, would they stop him? He was our prince.

My blood ran cold as this fact sank in. I'd grown too comfortable. He was the prince and I had defied him. I braced myself for punishment.

His hand clasped my shoulder as soon as he reached me and I couldn't help it: I flinched. Tears stung my eyes. To think that all those girls had been jealous of me for capturing his attention. To think I'd been a little smug over their glares and whispers. I waited for him to force me to face him.

Instead, he removed his hand. Silence unfurled between us, thick and sobering.

In time, I turned.

"I did not mean to frighten you," he whispered, eyes downcast.

I lowered my gaze in deference. "I should not have run."

"But you were frightened."

"My deepest apologies, Your Highness." My voice was wooden, detached. My body knew what to do, even when my brain did not. My body had not forgotten the years of Ansel's temper. "I assure you, sir, that my father will find no fault with nor broker any objection to whatever punishment you deem appropriate for my behavior."

His hand rose halfway toward me and I braced. He dropped his arm, clasping his hands behind his back. "Gretel, look at me, please. For I dare not touch you."

Once again, I obeyed him.

"What purpose do you fear I have in these woods tonight, Gretel?"

I was still capable of blushing, the warmth a mix of shame and anger. "It is not fit for me to say, Your Highness."

Anger stole over his expression, matching the terror that roiled through my stomach. "What horrors you must have faced."

"Another inappropriate conversation for a lady."

"And one with which I will not push you to engage further.

But I meant no harm in my pursuit of you tonight. Please know that."

By which you mean that you expected my compliance.

It was an uncharitable thought, but I did not regret it. I was beginning to see him like any other man of my acquaintance.

I nodded. "Of course, Your Highness."

"It is only that these woods are not safe for a young woman alone. Though I suspect you know that."

"Because of the witches, you mean?"

He cocked his head to the side, brow furrowing in confusion to add to his frustration. "The witches are no harm to anyone. They are not the monsters I fear forcing their acquaintance upon you."

The bite in his words was jarring. Men never acknowledged that other men were dangerous. And no one *defended* the witches. Regret pushed out some of my fear. Had I misjudged him?

I shivered.

"You're cold," Wilfried said, concern replacing the frustration in his eyes.

My resistance melted. "Perhaps we should return to the castle?"

I would take him at his word that he meant me no harm. After all, what choice did I have, save for running farther into the woods, wholly unequipped for survival?

We made our way back along the path we'd come. This time, however, I had the benefit of Wilfried going before me, holding branches back and pointing out briars in time for me to avoid them.

He waited to speak until we'd emerged from the woods and crossed back onto the manicured grounds. "I am sorry."

"Your Highness?"

"Sorry not only for the misunderstanding in the woods, but also that I overwhelmed you with my company and gave you cause to flee the ballroom in the first place."

A small laugh escaped my lips, bitter and surprised. "Oh, believe me, dancing with you was hardly the worst option for me this evening."

"I see, I am merely the least offensive choice."

The defeat that weighed down his words took me aback.

I studied his shadowed features, the chagrin etched all over his pale face.

A different breed of shame clawed at me. He really had just been worried for my safety.

"No," I said, my tone gentle. "I mean only that you were not the cause of my distress."

I dared to touch him, to place my hand along his jaw and coax him to look at me. "You were a brief respite from it."

"I suppose that should bring me relief, but I confess I find none at knowing you were otherwise distressed."

My lungs forgot their single purpose. Every time I found a kernel of boldness within me, he produced a field of it.

I snatched my hand back. It was foolish to indulge in the

strange audacity his very presence awakened within me. "Please, do not trouble yourself."

He crossed his arms, frowning. "Oh dear, I'm afraid I cannot promise that." The corners of his mouth twitched, taunting me.

"Your Highness?"

"It's true. You see, once I've identified something troubling, I find that I am unable to set it to rest until I have solved the issue."

I couldn't help it. I played along.

"Well, I cannot bear being the cause of such concern to the Crown."

"On the contrary, I have found almost nothing else so worthy *of* my concern since first you accosted me in my own courtyard."

My mouth dropped open. "Accosted?! I did no such thing." Heat bloomed across my face and neck. He hadn't forgotten my clumsiness. Another hope dashed.

"Do tell me what troubles you, Gretel," he beckoned, all joking cast aside. He stepped closer and took one of my hands. "Allow me to help, if it is within my power."

My heart squeezed: He was earnestness in every inch.

I permitted myself a flash of the indulgent dream I'd had while we were dancing. An engagement. A wedding. A future. Safety.

I hugged myself so tight it hurt. I wasn't in a dream, after all.

I needed to steer him away from this topic altogether and accept my fate. I stepped back, away from the reach of his helpful hands. "Not even you have the power to alter this course, sir."

"Then at least I might share in the burden of it. As your friend."

I sighed. He was as relentless as anyone I'd ever met, including myself. I could see no other way of stalling or putting him off.

"I am to marry," I admitted.

I took off walking again, but not fast enough to miss the way his encouraging smile drooped in the wake of my misfortune's reveal.

Neither of us spoke another word as he joined me.

I paused at the threshold of the back courtyard. Distant sounds of merriment floated out from the ballroom. A funeral dirge for the life I was about to leave behind. Suppose I escaped once more, disappeared into the woods forever, and let the wilds have me? They could not be more vicious than the wolves indoors, who disguised themselves in kin's clothing.

Wilfried stopped next to me, preventing me from progressing toward my prison with a hand on my elbow. "Are you betrothed already?"

"No, not yet."

A deep sigh emanated from his lips and cascaded through his entire body, his shoulders relaxing as his smile returned. "Oh, that is wonderful news."

"But I will be before the night ends."

He blinked at me.

"My father has been parading me before suitors for weeks. I am to name my 'choice' before the midnight chimes conclude tonight or he will choose for me."

"Name me," he blurted, taking hold of my hand once more.

I could not convince myself to pull away, though I was sure I'd misheard him. I stood still, anchored by shock, my world narrowed to the point where his fingers met mine. His hand was warm and dry, calloused in places that spoke of a life filled with horseback riding and sword training. I wanted to linger.

"I'm afraid I don't understand."

He searched my face and seemed to read distaste for him in it. "It need not be binding."

"That is not my understanding of marriages, Your High—"

"*Please*, call me Wilfried."

"*Wilfried*, then."

"Thank you."

I nodded, curt at last and free from misguided fancy. "I may not always understand my father's aims, but I am quite certain he means for this decision to be a permanent one."

"Then we shall play it as permanent, just long enough to help both our plights." His eyes were bright with triumph, as if he had stumbled upon the long-searched-for answer to an equation.

I tucked my disappointment away—it was clear he did not wish to marry me for *affection*—and focused on my need for facts. "I do not understand, sir."

"I know more of your ordeal than you might imagine." He led me over to sit upon one of the low stone walls nearby. "Though I will grant that I have the benefit of a parent who seeks to minimize my suffering rather than amplify it."

It was my turn to blink at him.

"Miss Henoth, surely you must be aware that, by burden of my position, I, too, am required to wed."

Of course I knew. Had I not pitied him for that very fact on the night I first entered his palace weeks ago? I nodded, an encouragement to continue as much as a confirmation of my understanding.

"When my father was still alive—"

"'God look after his soul.'" Some rules born in my old life had carried over to this one and the benediction fell from my lips without thought.

What would my former friends and neighbors—with whom I'd exchanged this particular call and response innumerable times—think, to see me speaking such words to the prince himself? About his own father, no less? I could see Sophie Klein now, looking on in awe, slack-jawed as a startled doe.

"Erm, yes. 'Through this age and all the others hereafter.'" Wilfried sped through the response, jolting me back to the present as I endeavored to tuck my uncharitable thoughts tight away in the shadowy corners of my mind.

"Well. During his life, my father and my mother were eager for me to take my time in finding a spouse. They eschewed the typical games of marrying for political advantage."

"How generous of them."

"Quite." He took a step nearer, bending until our foreheads almost touched. "Having experienced the benefits of a love match themselves, they longed for me to one day find the same. And in recent times, my mother has been none too eager to place additional responsibility upon me. She already thinks my position too much a burden."

I only hoped he could not hear my heart's skipping, eager beat. That organ was reckless, but my brain was firmly rooted to reality, sturdy as my feet on the ground. I held no delusions that a fairy tale waited at the end of this explanation.

At best, this was the preamble of a business contract.

"Now that several months have passed since the end of our mourning period, however," he continued, "the Council grows restless."

"They wish you to take a wife quickly?" I ventured.

"Yes. They fear that a long period of rule by my mother makes us appear weak to our would-be enemies."

I held in a snort. No doubt every seat on that Council was filled by a man.

"They wish to see me betrothed within the year, that I might marry at first light upon my eighteenth birthday and ascend the throne that very night."

"I am sorry for your dilemma." I cut my gaze to the ground in an attempt to hide my gathering jealous tears from him. He had nearly an entire *year* to forge his future; sans a miracle, I would be attending to one of the revolting creatures currently swanning about my father's ballroom within a fortnight.

Wilfried placed the tip of his finger beneath my chin and lifted it until our eyes met. "Don't you see? We could *fake* a betrothal!

Then you won't have to marry one of your father's friends, and I won't have to indulge the politically motivated options my Council will press upon me. We'll both have time to find someone we love."

I looked and looked and looked at him. Discovering nothing but sincere hope, I found myself with no choice but to consider his proposal.

He was correct; such an arrangement would buy us time. But, being a man, I supposed there was no way for him to know that it would only delay the inevitable for me. For once we were betrothed, I would no longer have the same opportunities to gad about and find a different boy to fall in love with. Outside my family, I would no longer be allowed in the company of single men without a close chaperone, likely my fiancé on most occasions.

Of course, he knew all the rules. But also, of *course* he hadn't given much thought to what their repercussions would be for me.

Nevertheless, a year was a year. Some freedom was better than none.

Wasn't it?

And yet . . . would it not be even more difficult to let him go after knowing him at close range for an entire year?

Already, his presence drove my spirit to fantasy, my heart to fancy, my mind to storybooks. Twelve months hence, how would I muster the resolve to let him leave me to a sorrier fate?

Still . . . did I not deserve a crumb of happiness in this bleak existence? Would I not have this year to cherish and mull over for decades to come, to hold close on harsher days that awaited me?

He was patient while I considered. Quiet as I worked through the consequences both pleasant and contrary. All things weighed, it was clear: Only a fool would not accept his offer.

"Yes," I said at last.

"Yes?"

"Yes, I will . . . pretend to be engaged to you."

"Yes!"

On the heels of his quiet cheer, Wilfried scooped me into his arms and spun me around. And for this moment, this sliver of time when both my internal and external worlds seemed to desire my happiness, I gave myself up to it. I tipped my head back and laughed, caught up in the sparkle of the story, quite willing to don my role and play a part in this unfolding charade dreamed up by the prince who held me in his arms.

CHAPTER FIVE

When we reentered the party, it remained much the same as before, with a half hour or so of added age upon it. Many of the attendees were still dancing. Refreshments sweated upon long tables on either side of the ballroom. Many of the men had chosen one of the makeshift courts presided over by either my brother or father. The unpartnered ladies stood in cliquish clumps, gossiping with one another's mothers. It did not seem we were missed.

I had spent so much of the last several months feeling torn between this life and my old one, neither quite right, but one more familiar than the other. In the next few moments, Wilfried's announcement would pull me into another chapter entirely, one Polly had not anticipated preparing me for.

Wilfried strode into the center of the festivities, free of any self-consciousness or doubt. Was this just a mask he'd acquired to perform his role as the crown prince? Or was the performance that of the gentle boy I was getting to know in private? Was he always merely curating for an audience? Had his advisers and tutors trained him so well that the transition was seamless?

But he had nothing to gain from being kind to me that he did not already possess in spades. Plenty of other royal heirs chose cruelty as their legacy and he could just as easily have done the same. It was the gift of being a son instead of a daughter; his ability to obtain what he desired did not hinge upon his being kind or well-liked.

Everyone traced his progress across the floor with watchful eyes and whispers hidden behind gloved hands, but the room quieted when he lifted his arms in a gesture for silence. The music halted. The whispers died mid-syllable.

Imagine having that kind of power.

My brother's voice echoed in the sudden stillness. He alone had not noticed Wilfried. "—well, she was so tall, you see—and better with a sword than . . ." He trailed off, scowling at the prince before scanning the room to find and bestow his glowering upon me. I avoided making eye contact, focusing instead on Wilfried as I rolled my shoulders back and prepared for my life to change once again.

"My friends," Wilfried began, turning his attention to each clustering group for a moment before continuing. A few of the boldest girls dared to bat their eyelashes at him and I wondered if one of them would eventually be the girl he settled on. The one with whom he'd ultimately wish to share his life rather than me, a wounded animal he'd merely shelter for a time.

I told myself I didn't know him well enough to be truly sad—it wasn't as if I had developed deeper affection for him, specifically.

It was only that I was jealous of his life, his freedom, his choices. I was jealous of the woman he would someday love because, assuming his character proved to be true to his word, she would have a life of joy and meaningful companionship and intimacy. She would marry someone who both loved and liked her.

Meanwhile, I would someday become the dirt beneath another man's shoe, scraped from my father's boots and picked up from the ground by the underside of my husband's.

Wilfried saved his last look for me. I gave him a nod and he continued.

"I apologize for the interruption and for removing any attention from Lord Henoth and his heroic tale. However, as this is a matter with time most sensitive, and one which regards his most beloved sister, I am hopeful that Lord Hansel can forgive me." His smile was wide and easy, sure of pardon for any offense.

I endeavored to match it with my own, for everyone was now splitting their attention between our prince and me. My father glared at me from across the room, his gaze heavy and singular even amongst a hundred onlookers. Ansel did not like to be left outside of any plan. He wished to be the sole orchestrator of my life.

Wilfried beckoned me to join him. "Miss Henoth?"

The instant I was within reach, he held out his hand and, when I took it, tucked me gently into his side. Murmurs caught flame and traveled about the room. I raised my chin and tried to imitate the ladies I'd grown up watching at the market, the ones who were my mother's age. Or the age she would have been if she were still here. The ones whose unwitting guidance I relied upon in her absence.

With Wilfried standing beside me, who would possibly protest my presence and risk his displeasure? I tried to channel his confidence as well, tried to pretend that my place in this world had always been assured. He squeezed my hand once before speaking again; the warmth of his palm against mine gave me courage.

"The news of my betrothal has been long expected and longer awaited," Wilfried said.

The eyes of our audience grew rounder, if it was possible.

"For years, I despaired of the task that lay before me. Those who knew my parents well will understand that I held little hope of finding a love that held a candle to theirs."

"God look after King Richmond's soul," the crowd chorused on cue.

"In this age and all the ones hereafter," Wilfried and I said as one. Another hand squeeze.

That was when a few jaws genuinely fell loose among the guests. It was one thing for Wilfried to hold my hand, for him to stand before everyone with me by his side. Princes were free to have dalliances, after all. But the benediction was sacred business. Only the royal family and those expected to join it were allowed to speak the response if one of the royals was present.

Still across the room, Ansel himself was a study in contradictions. As he began to piece together what was unfolding before him, the purple face of his anger at being bested gave way to eyes that danced with greed and the delight of standing upon a perceived precipice of power. This was the only engagement I could have made without his knowledge while escaping his wrath. Wilfried was the sole man in the realm who required no prior permission.

The prince cleared his throat, requesting a renewed hush in the now buzzing room. "Several weeks ago, however, on the night of my own birthday, fate smiled upon me and I met Miss Henoth. On that night, my heart began to hope."

The audience tittered and sighed in a wave that passed through the room. Their jealousy could not overrule their romanticism.

Wilfried looked down upon me with fondness before continuing. "And on *this* night, I have been given cause to rejoice. For it is with the greatest pleasure that I share with you our happy news: We are engaged to be married."

Every possible emotion was on display across the ballroom, but I had hardly a moment to process it. For no sooner were the official words out of his mouth than eager social climbers rushed us to be the first to offer their congratulations.

My brother and father were the only ones who hung back. Ansel allowed those who wished to curry favor to come to him. Meanwhile, Hansel sulked and stewed in his displeasure, furious and unable to say so—a prince is a prince, even on one's own birthday. In my peripheral vision, I couldn't help but notice that his cup never ran dry throughout the following hour.

The rest of the evening was a mingling of baptism by fire and celebration. Where once the other ladies my age had viewed me as competition, now they turned their sights on a different future, one where I would soon be a princess. And someday, a queen. At both stages, a royal in need of friends, coconspirators, and ladies-in-waiting. I did not fault them for any of it. The stakes were so high for all of us in this world, I couldn't take for granted that I would have kept my morals tucked tight about me if circumstances were the slightest bit different. As it was, my own comfort would expire at an as-yet-unknown date that would no doubt arrive on feet too swift for my liking.

So I did not begrudge any of the girls or hold them at a distance in some misguided demonstration of power. Nor did I open myself right up. I could not afford to grow close with anyone who might turn me out like a serving dish of so many scraps unto a hog's trough after Wilfried found his *true* love and left me behind.

But I laughed and danced. I quipped. I dodged probing questions. I met my prince's eyes many times throughout the evening and thrilled at every glance, a reminder that we shared a delicious secret, one that I would allow myself to savor as reality for at least this one night.

When the sky was at its darkest, the last remaining guests departed and Wilfried escorted me upstairs, showing no sign of leaving my side until he'd seen me safely deposited into the company of my maids.

"I will send word for you tomorrow. You must meet my mother properly very soon." Then he kissed my hand, eyes glittering with mischief as he peered up at me through his lashes, and disappeared.

I was immeasurably safer in this house now than I had been mere hours earlier, but I was nevertheless grateful to have seen Ansel and Hansel stumbling off to their beds, barely upright, as Wilfried and I had exited the ballroom. Ensconced in my room alone with Annika and Frida at last, we all looked at one another and burst into giggles.

"You must tell us everything, Miss Gretel!" Frida squealed.

They were the closest things I had to friends in this house and I found myself more grateful than ever for them. But our giggles soon turned to yawns we could not stifle. It was late.

"Once we've had some rest," I promised, my words fuzzed by the fatigue slipping over me. "Bring my breakfast here tomorrow, and I'll tell you everything."

Yawning in turn, the girls nodded jointly and busied themselves readying both myself and the room for sleep. Once I was appropriately dressed, the covers turned down, and all the candles blown out save three—one for each of us—I bade them good night and they puttered off to their own beds.

Faint streaks of moonlight fell across the floor. I walked over to the window nearest my bed, intent upon pulling the linens tight for a chance at some real sleep. Though I was so tired I could hardly keep my eyes open, I knew that the moment full dawn was allowed into the room, my body would refuse to allow me to drift off, the product of nearly two decades of life spent rising at sunrise for chores. So I forced myself to attend to the curtains.

Even the most straggling of the stars could be seen peering at me through the tall panes. Had they, too, heard the gossip? Had their more punctual brethren—who'd stood sentinel over the courtyard and eavesdropped upon Wilfried and me plotting—already informed them of our planned deception?

I would always wonder what my life might have looked like if I'd taken my chances and simply crawled right into bed. I would never know. For I saw her as soon as I reached the window.

It was the Girl of the Woods, as I'd begun to think of her. Standing at the edge of the trees that bordered our back courtyard once more. And though she was hundreds of feet away, I could have sworn that she was looking right up at my room.

At me.

Ice replaced the blood in my veins. I was as awake as if I'd received a full night's sleep and drunk not a drop of spiced wine. My heart hammered in my chest. What cause could she have for returning if she did not mean to be noticed? Unless she'd heard the party earlier and assumed that we would all only just now be turning to our beds. Did she think to find the castle all asleep, including the guards?

My fatigue evaporated. I did not care that I might be jeopardizing my safety; I had to know who this girl was and why she continued to appear over and over again. I told myself that perhaps she brought good things and happy tidings. In any case, I resolved that I would don a coat and shoes and steal back out of doors, into the darkest hours of the night, and confront her.

In the end, my deliberations cut my almost-adventure short.

I dallied.

I blinked.

She was gone.

My plans thwarted, I left the curtains alone and climbed into my bed. I was too awake to sleep, light or no light. Instead, I waited for morning, watching the changing shadows along the walls and floor of my bedroom that shifted with the moon and clouds. I held my breath at intervals, listening. The cavernous dark of my too-large room swallowed me up bit by bit, the lone candle on my nightstand a poor fight against the gloom.

I felt his presence before I heard him, that sibling string between us pulled taut. My brother was in the room. I knew it though I could not see him. I sensed it though he did not announce himself. Slowly, Hansel materialized from the darkness, stepping just enough into the light that I could see the beginnings of bruises forming below his eye and along his cheekbone. The evidence of some altercation with Ansel. With the distortion of the shadows cast by the moon, he was all the more frightening.

I fluttered my eyes closed until only a slit of my vision remained, feigning sleep.

He was at my side in an instant, faster than should be possible for a human. As if space itself bent beneath his will.

Once again too quick, his hand was over my mouth.

My eyes flew open at the sensation of a sudden heat that boded danger.

He held my candle between us, freed from its holder. Hot wax dripped between the crevices of his fingers and bothered him not.

Every ingrained response to danger that I'd learned as a member of this household fled my mind as fear and fight rose up within me. I began to thrash about, certain that Hansel was about to set me ablaze in my own bed. I prayed that Frida, Annika, or Polly would hear. They were, after all, the only ones in this castle who cared enough to save me.

He held both my legs down with the weight of one of his own, his too-long limbs trapping my arms at my sides.

The flame of the candle tilted, too close, a pool of wax forming in the divot at its center. It threatened to spill as he crushed me in silence, watching my panic mount as I waited for the wax to spill onto my face. I could not convince myself to close my eyes. I wondered for a moment if death might be better than whatever torture he had planned.

"No doubt you think this is for only today, but this is not merely for your selfishness at my party. You have always considered your own happiness more important than mine."

I whimpered in response.

What could I have done? I argued with myself. How could he think me capable of harm?

Were not you able to kill a witch? a meaner part of me fought back.

"My memory is longer than yours, Gretel. I have not forgotten any of the times you abandoned me. Nor every attempt you've made to place yourself above me."

I did not understand. His words no longer went together. I had certainly allowed him to stand between Ansel and me many times. Too many, perhaps. But I could not think of a single occasion when I had tried to best my brother, certainly not in a race for our father's esteem. My entire life had been one of bending and scraping, of trying to disappear, of fleeing out of sight toward private occupations and interests whenever the opportunity presented itself.

Perhaps he alluded to the moments in our battle against the Wood Witch for which I had no recollection. Had I been so different then? Was I cruel? Heartless?

I could not remember. So how could I atone?

I pleaded with my eyes for him to comprehend how deeply he'd misjudged me, but I might as well have been looking into the face of Ansel for all the understanding I received in return.

At last, the wax fell.

But my brother was fast. Faster than the wax itself. Faster than my own whimper, which I could not keep from escaping as he turned his hand over. Pressing the back side of his hand against my mouth, he created a cup for the wax with his palm. He did not so much as blink as it pooled over his skin.

I was too stunned to speak, though he no longer restrained me. I was too terrified to move as he lowered his mouth to my ear.

"You will regret ever crossing me, Gretel."

He blew out the candle and disappeared.

CHAPTER SIX

I could not possibly sleep.

I did not wait for my eyes to adjust to the darkness. As soon as Hansel was gone, I fled the castle, pausing only to swipe a pair of gardening boots from the back door.

It was so cold. Even the moon looked like it wanted to shiver.

I ran across the frostbitten grounds, my loose nightdress fluttering. My feet were numb before I reached the edge of the courtyard, so I could not feel my thin sleep stockings growing wet as I ventured farther. Beneath my feet, blades of half-frozen grass scratched me as they fell, their shattered casings scraping like hundreds of little needles.

Only when I reached the forest's edge, where I was confident Hansel would not venture, did I stop and force my freezing feet into the worn leather of the boots I'd clutched to my chest all the way there.

Tucked inside the alcove of trees I'd claimed as my own, a refuge from the horror of the place I now called home, I finally allowed myself to cry. I could not go back inside. The only explanations for Hansel holding himself back tonight were that he didn't wish to risk our father's wrath and that he knew drawing out his cruelty would only increase my suffering. He'd learned that technique directly from our father, how to spool out terror in just the right doses until that fear was permanent. It was a cycle we were caught in: Hansel forever looking over his shoulder for Ansel, me looking over mine for both of them.

How could I go on living like this? I could not depend on my maids or Polly to protect me forever. Wilfried, for all his chivalry, was little more than a stranger, and pity was not likely to entice him to actually marry me. Our charade of an engagement was the only protection I had in this world, but I could already see the holes in my new armor. Once he broke things off, I wouldn't need to worry about Ansel marrying me off to someone twice my age; I would need to prepare myself for Hansel to make that altogether unnecessary.

Whoever had replaced the loyal brother I once called my best friend was a young man who would sooner kill me now for his own gain than sacrifice his safety for mine, the way he had as we grew up.

A small part of me longed to hold out for the hope that my relationship with Wilfried might grow into something beyond a business arrangement or friendship. But I knew this world and its penchant for shattering my dreams too well to cling to such a silly thought.

Curled against the trunk of the oldest of the trees, my tears gradually subsided. Soon, I no longer shivered. After a time, my eyes opened slower and slower with each blink. Eventually, I slid closer to the ground, until only my head was propped against the tree. Perhaps I would give in to the elements and allow the woods to claim me before any man could.

"It is a nice place to fall away."

I was so cold and so tired, my teeth couldn't chatter. The clouds above me began to overtake my vision, slate-gray mist creeping in from the edges of my line of sight.

Suddenly, a blur of orange.

It shook the perimeter of my consciousness, like an innervating slap across the face after being pulled from deep water. I blinked and found two amber eyes staring at me.

It was the fox! The one who'd stood beside the Girl of the Woods, its coat a twin to her bright, coppery hair.

I jolted fully awake. Even now, I did not wish to be eaten. To fall asleep and not wake up was one thing; I was not so close to death that I could lie there and accept becoming prey. I tucked myself back farther against the tree, waited for the fox to pounce. But he stayed in one spot. Watching me.

Looking. *Looking* at me. Foxes do not "watch."

But this one did. I stood and chanced a few steps forward, holding out my hand as if he were a dog. Still no movement.

"Are you here for me?"

It was an absurd question to ask of an animal, especially an undomesticated one.

The fox lifted his snout in the direction of the castle.

"I am all alone," I promised.

However preposterous, it must have been the kind of reassurance the fox was waiting for. For at my words, he turned and began to walk back into the forest, pausing after several steps to look back over his shoulder. He was waiting for me.

It was a foolish proposition to consider. There could have been any number of horrors waiting for me in those woods, but if I was at the point of considering allowing myself to freeze to death . . .

"What lies before me cannot be worse than what lies behind me."

So into the woods we went.

The trees grew thicker and thicker with every passing minute. In full summer, this area would be all but impassable by humans. Moonlight crisscrossed through the branches. Even still, I could hardly see. Soon, the fox was no more than a flash of orange. At one point, I almost lost him, until he doubled back and started walking just before me, his bushy tail swishing against my shins as a sensory guide. I resisted the urge to try to pet him.

Just when I thought I could walk no farther and considered the possibility that the fox was a hallucination brought on by the cold—or that the forest itself had called me in to have my death on its terms—we reached a breaking in the trees.

And there she was, bathed in the light of the icy moon, humming to herself as she placed penny bun mushrooms and black walnuts in small baskets hanging on each of her hips.

The Girl of the Woods.

The girl I'd seen with a fox—*this* fox, presumably—only hours ago from my bedroom window. And before that, at the edge of the palace grounds. Her unmistakable hair still hung loose down her back, squashing any possible doubt that she was someone different.

I'd reached her. At last.

The fox bowed. To me, or to her, or perhaps to the moon itself. I could not be sure. Before I could ask anything more of him, he scampered back into the trees and out of sight.

CHAPTER SEVEN

I was amazed at the silence as I followed the girl through the woods. The ground appeared to have taken my side, for I didn't break a single twig or inspire the croak of one frog. She led me, unbeknownst to her, all the way to a row of trees that had grown up into one another, until their tops formed a woven tunnel. The tree arch reminded me of when Hansel and I were small, when we were a united front against our father and you could hardly tell where one of us ended and the other began.

The girl paused at the entrance. I hid behind the trunk of a stout and towering oak several yards back, then mimicked her stillness.

A strong scent of cloying sweetness and decay emanated from the tunnel. Unsettling echoes of old laughter skipped forward from the branches and passed over me. I thought I heard the shadow of my own voice, but surely it was the woods playing tricks on my mind. Or perhaps it was the girl herself, producing some conjured imitation. Was she only pretending to not know that I was trailing her?

She entered the tunnel, where the darkness swallowed her up.

Pushing my own misgivings aside, I continued my pursuit.

Goose bumps popped to life everywhere my skin was exposed. All manner of disquieting elements flourished in the tunnel. Snakes coiled around the bases of young trees and slithered through the thick branches of their elders. Spiders great and small skittered across the ground before me. Leaves in shocking hues of black and purple still clung to the trees overhead. It all existed in defiance of the cold weather that should have spelled death or hibernation.

This must be the work of witches.

Fear crept over me as I pondered what might lie at the end of the tunnel if this was only the precursor to whatever terrible things lay in wait. Would I find myself in another battle to the death? Whose would it be this time? My own, or another witch's?

But I could not convince myself to turn back.

Everything that frightened me pulled me forward.

As we neared the end of the tunnel, it grew darker and darker, until the branches overhead were so thick, I could no longer see the moon. Suddenly, the girl disappeared, as if she were being swallowed by whatever awaited on the other side of the trees. I pressed forward, into the darkness. My steps grew tinier and tinier. I did not dare to put my hands out before me, for fear of what might grab them.

Once again, laughter wove through the branches, joined by murmuring voices swept up in conversation. I thought I even caught snatches of songs.

Without warning, I emerged from the darkness and into a world I would have thought unimaginable only moments before. I wasted no time in hiding myself behind a large boulder that stood just to the right of the tunnel's end.

And then I watched, enraptured by all that unfolded before me.

It was a village of sorts. Cottages were scattered around the forest floor—usual enough—but there were also dwellings tucked into the tallest trees. In every direction that I looked, an intricate arrangement of dense forest and strategic walls of rock protected the area. Behind me, the pitch-black maw of the tunnel waited, like a snare.

Witches of all ages, shapes, and sizes milled about, each absorbed in their own work or play. Some gathered herbs and other supplies. Others prepared them. Some were providing medical care to visitors on the porches of various buildings. They served both common villagers and nobles alike. The latter were easy to spot by their expensive cloaks with hoods pulled low over their faces to prevent being recognized. I did not yet know the individual members of the nobility well enough to guess who they were beneath their disguises.

In the yard before one of the less-busy cabins, a row of younger witches sat one behind the other, braiding one another's hair into intricate plaits.

Throughout it all, hovering lanterns bobbed over the little groups, perfectly placed to best light their charges. Here and there, too, were candles that did not melt from use and clear jars that held thriving fireflies, despite the late autumn season.

I could not look away. Everything about this place was so different from the terror I associated with the Wood Witch I had been forced to kill and all the stories I'd been told. For a moment, I wondered if perhaps I was mistaken and these were not witches at all. But who else would have floating lanterns? To whom would such varied clientele otherwise pay their visits while taking great pains to remain anonymous?

What's more, it was well after midnight and yet the village teemed with activity as though it were midday. I could not think of any people besides the witches who would feel so secure at such hours, who would work and play with such confidence during the most dangerous stretch of time.

And yet, here you stand, as upright in the dark hours as any of them.

I pushed the thought away. I was different. I had been seeking refuge. I was not at home here.

You sought safety and you found them.

I watched them in silence, waiting for the sinister natures of the witches to reveal themselves at last. I was confident that their benevolence and cheer must have been a ruse. A plot to lure these unsuspecting people in need of aid into their lair. After all, hadn't Ansel always said they did the same to my mother? Offered her a cure when she was desperate and then snuffed out her life with one of their concoctions? According to Hansel, the Wood Witch had enticed us to her cottage in a similar predatory fashion. Each time he told his version of the story, it was one of the few details that rang true and remained consistent.

They'd reveal their true selves in due time.

Not so.

Instead, the longer I waited, the more inviting the village became. The kind of care and compassion and happiness that seemed unimaginable in the confines of my home appeared abundant among the witches.

It almost seemed familiar, like I was reaching back through time to grasp at the wisp of a memory. But every time my fingers brushed against it, that whisper was choked out by every warning I'd ever received about the witches over the years.

"Witches use human ingredients to enrich their potions and powders."

"Witches want to bring down our society."

"Witches are the reason you don't have a mother."

And on and on. In spite of the warnings clanging in my mind, I was no longer content to merely watch them. I wanted to know more. I wanted to see their work and community up close. I wanted to know where they were hiding their true natures and how it was they'd managed to display only positive qualities while I'd been watching them. I wanted to take a risk.

So I came out from my hiding place and walked down into the village, taking the well-worn path that I'd seen the red-haired witch use when we emerged from the tunnel.

This is dangerous behavior.

I hushed the voice inside my head a final time, rolled my shoulders back, and steeled myself for suspicion at best—outright hostility or kidnapping at worst.

Once again, the witches surprised me.

It was the little girls who saw me first. One looked in my direction at just the right moment, and before the others had a chance to see what prompted her, she dropped hold of her pinafore—spilling the midnight marigolds she'd gathered onto the ground—and took off running toward me.

"She's here! It's her! She found us!"

Any hope I had for a stealth entrance was shattered as her high voice echoed through the clearing. Her companions followed her without question, chattering one over the other so I could hardly make out what they were saying. Curious faces peered out from several of the windows. None of them seemed as unabashedly energized about my presence as the little girl. I still wasn't altogether certain if her outcry was in celebration or warning. I could have turned back and sprinted for the tunnel that would take me into the woods and point me toward the familiar frying pan of the castle instead of this unknown fire, but I was rooted to the spot.

The gaggle of girls reached me in a flurry, tugging on my clothes and clamoring for attention. Question after question was lobbed my way in unison. The leader must have realized I couldn't understand any of them over the din of the others, for she quickly took charge.

"Aw, she can't hear us! Hush!"

The girls quieted, but they needed to get their jabs in. "Cora, you sound like Sena," one of the shorter ones with red hair and dirt smeared across her cheeks accused the leader.

"I'm trying to, so what of it?" said Cora, the leader, hands on hips.

The redhead stuck out her tongue but said nothing else.

A fervent tug on my night shift nearly pulled me over. I looked down to meet brown eyes the size of saucers. "How did you find us?"

"Prince Wilfried sent her, Miffy." A new voice belonging to a young witch with close-cropped brown hair piped up. She seemed to be the same age as the others, but stood a head taller than all of them.

"I love him, then," Miffy whispered to herself, eyes even wider, if possible.

A round of giggles rippled through them at the mention of Wilfried's name. I did not understand how this was such a clear, positive fact to them, when I would have bet all the wealth in my father's coffers that none of them had ever met Wilfried. Perhaps the mere mention of a prince was enough to set them off. They'd surely read and heard just as many fairy tales as I had at their age.

The redhead couldn't resist an opportunity to cast her oar in.

"Just because she's marrying him doesn't mean he told her where to find us."

"What do you know, Mebby? How else would she have got here?" The leader again.

"Shoo now, what if she's needing our help and you're just hassling her there." A witch around my age, maybe a few years older, was marching toward us with a toddler on her hip. Her blond hair hung loose and long.

"Sorry, Aster," several of the younger girls mumbled to the blond.

Miffy with her saucer eyes tugged my cloak again. "Do you need our help?"

Leader Cora began patting me down. "Nothing seems broken."

The toddler wriggled down from Aster's arms. "You tummy hurt?" She poked my stomach for emphasis.

Aster swooped the little one back up again. "Clove, we don't touch people without asking. 'Specially strangers."

"Sawwie." Clove popped her thumb in her mouth. Perhaps to keep herself from getting into any more mischief.

I could see another pair of teen witches coming down the path. They were a bit younger than Aster, but older than the first group of girls. Twins, from the look of them. With their matching faded brown hair and gray eyes, Cora could have been their miniature triplet.

Aster bounced Clove on her hip. "No one's with you?"

"No."

"Are you hurt at all?" the twin with her hair in two braids asked. It seemed that served for a greeting around here.

"Or sick?" Aster inquired on her heels.

"No. I don't think so."

The older girls all exchanged a look.

Aster turned to the young ones. "I'm serious, go find some way to make yourself useful."

This time, the group acquiesced, as if they recognized the particular firm look in the older girl's eyes and knew there would be no argument. The girls began to dutifully scatter, looking over their shoulders all the while.

"Revel, wait," Aster called.

The tallest of the younger witches, the one with a short haircut, turned back. "Take Clove with you."

She handed the toddler off. Once they were all out of earshot, she turned back to me.

"Miss—

"Oh, you can call me Gretel."

"Very well." She leaned in closer, lowering her voice. "Do you need the herbs, Miss Gretel? My ma can make you some."

"What kind of herbs do you mean?"

"We would never judge, miss," the twin who hadn't spoken yet assured me.

"Just Gretel. Please."

Aster nodded. "You're safe telling us. You'd hardly be the first. Everyone here is good at secret keeping."

"I'm sorry, I don't under—"

But I was distracted and didn't finish my question. Because the girl I'd followed through the woods was making her way across the open area toward us. Her face was stern, guarded. An older witch kept pace with her. Her arm was in a sling, but she walked tall, her chin up and shoulders back. They looked like near copies of each other; the only differences between them were the streaks of gray that ran through the older's hair and the light lines that crisscrossed out from the corners of her eyes. The older one also seemed less wary and more curious.

The older witch took my hands as soon as she reached us. "Gretel, we are pleased to receive you here, a most pleasant surprise. My name is Orlantha. This is my daughter Katharina."

"You know my name?"

"Yes." Orlantha smiled but offered no further explanation.

"Hello," I said to Katharina, to cover the awkwardness.

Does she know she's the one who led me here?

She narrowed her eyes. "You are alone, yes?"

"She is a guest." Orlantha gave her daughter an admonishing look.

Katharina shrugged.

The older witch extended her uninjured arm. "You are very welcome here in Galwin, Gretel."

"Thank you for having me."

I said thank you because I didn't know what else to say. I'd imagined different directions that all this could take, but none of them had included hospitality.

Still bewildered by meeting Orlantha and Katharina, I was suddenly surrounded by more strangers as the entire village poured out from their homes to greet me. The little girls returned, parents and older siblings and more friends in tow. Orlantha's seeming approval must have been enough assurance for the others to introduce themselves. There was no alternate accounting for any of it. No other way to make sense of the waves of introductions and invitations they all competed with one another to provide.

Come join us for a meal.

Come bake bread with us.

Come gather flowers.

Come sample a medicinal salve.

Come.

Come.

Come.

It felt like safety and it felt like slipping.

I did what I had always done when unsure and unmoored: I shoved down all my competing feelings and took the hands of those with more ardent agendas than my own.

Hours passed like breaths.

The sky was two shades lighter when I finally noticed that time had not stood still during my visit. I extracted myself from the impromptu welcome gathering and made my way back to the tunnel at the edge of the village.

"Wait." Katharina's voice landed on my shoulders and stopped me instantly, as if she'd placed her hands there.

I turned back to see her standing next to the rock where I'd hid, holding up a round of rye.

"My mother wants you to have this."

I took the bread. "Thank yo—"

But she started walking away before I could get the words out. I hugged the loaf to my chest.

The fox materialized at my side once more. He nudged me as if to say that it was time for me to depart. Maybe if I stayed too long, I would be stuck there forever, like a faerie story.

But where was I meant to go?

I had no ability to survive in the woods, that much was certain. When I'd first fled to my alcove of trees earlier that night, I couldn't see a reason to keep going until tomorrow. But fresh curiosity brewed within me and I wanted to learn more about the witches, about Katharina, about Galwin, the strange little village that flew in the face of all my expectations.

So I would return to the castle and hope for survival there. I would consign myself to going home, in exchange for the chance to come back.

Knowing that it was entirely possible the fox would not always appear to guide me to the witches, I paid extra attention to the way as I followed him. All along the unmarked path, along the tunnel to the clearing where I'd seen Katharina gathering mushrooms, then through the dense thicket of trees that took us back to my father's grounds. Every few steps, I pulled off pieces of Orlantha's bread and left the crumbs behind me.

Once out of the forest, I stared up at the outline of the looming castle, backlit by the moon, and whispered a prayer to the sky.

"Please let me make it through the night."

Chapter Eight

"We should wake her, Annika."

"Shh. It isn't late enough. It's not our place."

"Then why are you waiting here with her tray already?"

Frida and Annika were sniping at each other, their voices muffled as though they were far away. Sleep still held me in its arms, the warmth of my bed lulling me back toward dreams. They could let themselves in.

Something outside clattered to the ground. I jolted awake.

They *couldn't* let themselves in. I had locked the door the night before. My one protection against Hansel.

"Frida," Annika hissed.

"I'm sorry, I'm sorry!"

"Girls." The voice of Mrs. Chambers broke through.

I catapulted out of bed and dashed across the room. I wouldn't have my maids getting into trouble on my account.

"What are you two doing—"

I wrenched the door open. "My mistake, Mrs. Chambers. I must have locked the door without realizing it last night. Frida and Annika were endeavoring to solve the issue."

Our stern housekeeper eyed the girls. "Is that true?"

Please, this once, let Annika content herself with a small lie.

Annika dipped her chin in deference. "Yes, ma'am."

Frida was quick to echo her. "We should have been quieter, ma'am." She turned to me. "Our apologies, miss."

"Our apologies," they repeated together.

I swallowed a yawn and forced a smile. "All is well. Please, come in. Let us prepare for the day."

Frida and Annika scampered around me and began to arrange the contents of my breakfast tray on the small table near the fire. I was not far behind them.

"Good morning, Mrs. Chambers." I resisted the urge to curtsy to her. We were in a sort of tug-of-war of power because I did not exert my station over her the way my father and brother did. She was of an older mindset and did not approve of my familiar rapport with either my maids or her daughter, though Polly's position as my governess provided a slight margin for familiarity.

So we existed in a strange limbo, never quite at ease nor fully formal.

We stood there, challenging each other in silence.

This time, I won out. Surprise flickered in her gaze when she realized it; where was the shy girl who used to bow beneath the weight of anyone else's whim, I was sure she asked herself.

In truth, that version of me still stood at the back of my mind, peeking out from behind a distant door, watching to see if this emerging variation of us might bring about a punishment. To an outside observer, it would not seem such a triumph that I was learning to hold my own against a housekeeper, but I recognized this small victory. I held it dear.

Mrs. Chambers cleared her throat.

"Begging your pardon, Miss Gretel. I only came to deliver the news that Lords Ansel and Hansel have gone away on business. They will not return for three days' time." Mrs. Chambers's smile was tight, revealing nothing more than professional neutrality.

My stomach flip-flopped in tandem with my speeding heart.

They were gone. For three whole days.

I waited for the snare to trip and yank me off my feet, for Mrs. Chambers to reveal some dreadful strictures left behind by Ansel to bring me suffering in his absence. It was their first overnight trip since I'd entered into society.

Mrs. Chambers eyed the maids over my shoulder. "However, it seems you were already informed."

A chill slid down my spine as her words sank in and I understood my misstep; I only ever ate meals alone in my room when Ansel and Hansel were away. Had she overheard me last night telling Frida and Annika to bring my breakfast to me this morning so we could discuss the events of the ball?

A pinch of smug satisfaction turned up the corner of her thin mouth.

I needed to regain control.

"No, not at all, Mrs. Chambers."

Her smirk melted back into its place, a chastised soldier falling into line.

"I have simply learned that I am more fatigued the morning after a ball. Given the *unique* events of last night's festivities, I anticipated that I would require some additional privacy and informed the maids as much during my bedtime preparations."

"I see."

"Now that I am aware of my father and brother's absence, I will likely keep to myself for the rest of the day."

A vision danced across my mind, of me galloping across the floor and launching myself back into my bed, rolling beneath the covers and keeping company only with a book from the neglected stack upon my bedside table. No mutinous brother, no cruel and overbearing father. Just the muffled sounds of the birds and the wind whistling gently through the odd pucker in the casing of my windows. Every now and then, a handful of words from one servant calling to another. A day of true peace.

"As you wish, Miss Gretel." Mrs. Chambers dipped her head. "Girls? Are you finished?"

I looked back at Frida and Annika, promising with my eyes that we would find our time to gossip soon. Perhaps I would call for a bath at midday. My mind tripped on this thought, for this was the kind of behavior I had considered the stuff of only fairy tales not six months prior.

Eyes downcast, the pair dutifully returned to Mrs. Chambers's side in the hall.

"Thank you." I moved to close the door.

Suddenly, Polly came bounding up the stairs, two at a time. Extremely unladylike for her. I pulled the door open once more.

"Polly Chambers!" Mrs. Chambers's tone conveyed enough astonishment for the both of us.

"My apologies, Mother. A most important letter has arrived."

Mrs. Chambers snatched the extended envelope out of her daughter's hand. Her eyes widened as she flipped it over and surveyed the seal.

Frida, risking life and limb, craned her neck over the housekeeper's shoulder for a better look. She gasped. "It's a letter!"

Mrs. Chambers pressed the letter against her chest. "How observant of you, Frida."

But her mocking tone did nothing to dampen Frida's excitement. She turned to me with bright eyes. "It's a letter from the queen! For you!"

Only the propriety that Polly had spent months instilling in me stopped me from ripping the letter out of Mrs. Chambers's grasp.

Breathing deep, I held out my palm. A request she had to grant.

The seal broke easily.

I scanned over the handful of lines. Every emotion I could name swooped through me.

"It is an invitation. The queen requests that I join her for tea this afternoon."

I was going to meet Queen Galen.

Alone.

CHAPTER NINE

I made use of my carriage ride to the palace and reflected upon my night with the witches. It was almost like a dream. I could not reconcile their kindness and warmth—the beauty of their homes and community—with the scraps of brutality I remembered of my encounter with the Wood Witch, nor the narrative that Ansel had instilled in me of their responsibility for my mother's death.

Maybe it was just that the village witches were much different. Strong and resourceful, and lacking any proclivities for violence, from what I could tell.

They were generous to me; meanwhile, I lived off the stolen riches of their slain kindred. No matter if they were different from her, they were witches all the same. Would the tenor of their welcome have shifted if they knew I was the one responsible for killing the Witch, not my brother? Or would they have continued to show me the same hospitality that they showed everyone I witnessed cross their borders?

A question loomed: Would I go back? It was dangerous to venture into the woods on my own. In the aftermath of Hansel's attack, it had seemed worth the risk. In the light of day, however, I wondered at my recklessness. And yet, my heart thrummed at the prospect of returning. The forest all but called me to shrug off the endless list of rules that dictated so much and left me so little in the way of choices.

I yearned to embrace the unknown, even if it meant courting danger.

Of course, I was en route to another kind of unknown entirely. What would Queen Galen think of me? Yes, she was once common herself, but that offered no guarantee she would approve of her son marrying someone lowborn. All my previous brushes with her were positive, but distant: Extra stores of food sent from the palace to the poorer villages in the winter; distribution of the tonic to cure stoneground fever at no cost to the recipients. The Crown had implemented the dispensation program the winter after my mother died from the fever. A year too late to save her, but in time to spare scores of people across the kingdom. Due to the rumors that the cure was first developed by witches, many parents would still not admit to dosing themselves or their children, but cases of illness plummeted all the same.

Elders in our village had often spoken of the shift toward peace and stability that King Richmond and Queen Galen's rule brought—a welcome turn from the chaos and want of war—but I had nothing to measure them against. Were they truly good rulers? Or were their predecessors simply so inept, they seemed miraculous by comparison?

And what of the conditions of my engagement to Wilfried? Her invitation to tea bore no indication that she was any the wiser to it being a ruse. If she *did* accept me, how would I contend with the guilt of lying to her?

The carriage slowed to a stop in front of the palace and I stepped out, tilting my head back to take in the view. Without the cloak of night, it was more grand than I remembered.

I took a deep breath and followed the queen's attendant up the grand staircase. I was determined to make a good impression upon Her Majesty. No matter what.

The day-to-day palace was a different animal than the one I experienced at the ball. While it was by no means empty, the comfortable bustle was accompanied by the low hum of the staff and permanent residents accustomed to its splendor. It was the exact opposite of the bombast and jostling for favor that had marked the evening of the prince's birthday.

The attendant ushered me into a small parlor.

"Please make yourself comfortable, Miss Henoth. Her Majesty will see you shortly." He bowed, leaving me to my own devices.

I had no sooner arranged myself in the center of a brocaded settee than the attendant reappeared.

"Her Majesty the Queen."

I leapt to my feet and curtsied low as the queen entered. When I raised my eyes to meet hers, a brief flash of recognition stirred across her features, similar to the night we first met. Once again, however, the look disappeared before I could study it.

"Please be seated, Miss Henoth."

"Thank you, Your Majesty."

The queen and I settled across from each other.

"It is a pleasure to welcome you to Cannick Palace, Miss Henoth." Her expression was open and warm. I believed her.

I resisted the urge to bow my head. "Thank you, Your Majesty. I am honored."

"I regret that we were unable to become better acquainted at my son's birthday celebration. Of course, I was unaware of his intentions regarding you at the time."

I did not know how to respond. Would she find it suspect if I claimed to share her unawareness?

I did not want to lie to her more than was necessary. "In truth, Your Majesty, so was I."

The ghost of a chuckle sounded in her throat.

I had made the right choice. One obstacle cleared.

"You are newly out in society, are you not?"

"Yes, ma'am. Prince Wilfried's ball was my first official event."

"I remember my first. It was shortly after my own betrothal." The corners of her eyes crinkled at the memory. "My husband and I had a longer courtship than you and my son, but our situation was slightly different."

She looked past my shoulder, into a distant time that neither of us could reach. Her eyes softened as she walked through a memory, even as her mouth tightened to steel against the inevitable pain. I recognized the expression from my patchy recollections of Ansel in the early months after my mother died.

"I am sorry for your loss, Your Majesty," I said, averting my eyes for her privacy.

She sniffed. "Yes, you know some of my backstory. Well, I should like to hear of yours."

My stomach backed up into my ribs. I breathed as deeply as I could without risking her taking notice of my nerves. I'd memorized this story well. I only needed to summon the courage to tell it, to lie to my sovereign.

"My family made our living off a small farm near Birnover until several months ago. For my entire childhood, my father raised us on his own and set aside whatever coppers he was able. Late last year, he was provided with the opportunity to invest in a small merchant company that has grown quickly. We are blessed."

The queen smiled. "It is good, I think, for our highborn families to grow accustomed to stories of industry such as your father's."

"Yes, Your Majesty."

The lies curdled in my gut.

But Polly had trained me well and I said nothing further. I was only ever to answer the question asked, to assume silence when I reached the boundaries of the scripts I was provided.

"Have you given any thought to how you will endeavor to shape our country in your position as queen consort?"

This was not a question my governess had anticipated. In fairness, she'd tutored me only with the aspirations that I might marry a similarly ranked merchant's son.

"I have not, ma'am."

The corners of her mouth turned down for a blink of a moment before she recovered herself. "I suppose everything has been rather sudden. You have time."

I could not abide her frown. The craving for her approval scraped at my core, desperate for appeasement. For a moment, I disregarded the rules I was told to play by, and offered her a vulnerable piece of myself in response to a question she had not asked.

"Forgive me, Your Majesty."

She indicated for me to continue.

"I *have* thought, however, about the way that your and the king's generosity touched my life as a child. I do not know what it was like in our realm before this long-standing peace." I lifted my chin, more confident with every word, now fully meeting her piercing eyes. "But I have felt the warmth of a monarchy that considers its poor, and I can only hope to water the goodwill your family has sowed among your subjects."

Approval and triumph glittered in the queen's eyes. She opened her mouth to respond, but we were interrupted by the scurry of patent shoes on the spotless marble floor.

"His Royal Highness Prince Wilfried, Your Majesty," the doorman panted.

Wilfried strode into the room at a clip, still wearing his riding boots. His dark blond hair was windswept, his cheeks pink with the early autumn chill. "Mother, I was unaware we were entertaining my fiancée today."

At his reference, I hastened to stand and curtsy, mumbling an address in the pause before his mother responded.

"We were merely becoming acquainted, darling." The queen angled herself back toward me. "Is that not so, Miss Henoth?"

"Yes, ma'am."

"See? Nothing to fret over." She exchanged a teasing look with her son.

What was it like to be so loved, so at ease despite the most regimented of environments?

"I hope my mother has not needled you into wishing yourself out of our engagement."

"Not at all—"

The queen glided to my side of the sitting area and slid her arm through mine. "Nonsense, Wilfried. Before you blew in like so much hot air, I was going to invite Miss Henoth to join us for tea again tomorrow."

Several seconds passed as they both gazed at me with expectancy. Wilfried himself leaned forward on the balls of his feet. For a moment, I held the power of the room.

"I would be delighted, Your Majesty."

She gave my arm a squeeze and released it with a pat. "Splendid. You must share all your favorite treats and preferences with one of my cook's assistants before you leave. She'll see that our kitchen prepares them."

Golden warmth sloshed through me.

I had passed the first test.

CHAPTER TEN

In the end, I could not resist the allure of the witches and their world.

That night, I counted down the minutes until the castle was still and I could sneak back to Galwin. The fox was waiting for me at the edge of the forest, his coat bright against the dark shadows of the trees.

The inviting scent of warming cinnamon greeted me when I emerged from the tunnel of decay. Excited voices mingled on the wind with the smells of fresh baking, pulling me toward the village.

Below, every cabin and cottage door in the main clearing was thrown open to make way for those bustling in and out. Older witches set out trays of bread to cool on windowsills. Girls a bit older than me carried piles of baking stones to and fro. The dozen boys and men who lived in the village were gathered around giant washing tubs, scrubbing and rinsing and drying in various assembly lines, voices lifted together in working songs.

I followed the yeasty, sweet aroma down into the hubbub.

Through one doorway, I spied the twins from my first visit,

Sena and Ama. They were lined up around a counter with other girls our age, pulling string through logs of dough to form buns they then dusted with beet sugar.

Little Cora and her merry band scampered across my path, too absorbed in their caper to notice me. Each of them held piles of various seeds in their cupped hands, outstretched before them as they trotted along.

But it was the center cabin I sought. Orlantha and Katharina's.

Forever watchful, the older witch looked up as soon as I crossed the threshold.

"Gretel, you've returned!"

My insides squeezed. "Is that okay?"

Katharina glanced up but said nothing, still focused on the thin sheets of dough she was pressing out on the floured counter before her.

"Of course." Orlantha brushed a fallen section of hair from her face, leaving a smear of batter behind. "This is a wonderful day for a visit. We're preparing for Erntvin, one of our harvest rituals."

"Can I help?"

I did not have many baking skills. I'd honed the basics of cooking the meat and vegetables that fed us throughout my childhood, but beyond simple bread loaves, the ingredients for baked goods were not often available. Nevertheless, I was learning that the easiest path into the community of Galwin was finding a way to be of service.

"Please! 'Rina, give Gretel something to wear. She can't return home with her night shift covered in flour and nutmeg." Orlantha winked at me.

Her daughter sized me up, expression neutral. "Something of Aster's should fit her."

I wondered at her assessment of me. After a lifetime spent living with a father who hung his every emotion out on his face for all the world to see, Katharina's unflappability was like an intricate lock. I was determined to find the right tool to pick it.

"Run along to the Mulworths', then, and be quick about it!" Orlantha shooed her out the door.

I fell quiet during her absence. To Orlantha's credit, she didn't push a conversation. Simply continued about her business, the quiet hum of a tune she sang to herself keeping the room from falling into total silence.

Katharina returned in short order and thrust a bundle into my arms. She tipped her chin in the direction of the steep staircase at the back of the kitchen. "You can change in my room."

Like her mother, she punctuated her directions with a wink.

My throat turned warm and I tucked the ball of clothing under my chin to hide my flushing, but there was no need: Also like her mother, Katharina was already fully absorbed, once again, in her baking.

I shuffled past them and took the rickety stairs two at a time.

They ended in a small, open room with a sloped ceiling. I took a tentative step forward and a lantern floated up from the floor to hover just ahead of me, a single flame dancing in its center.

"Thank you," I whispered.

Now I could see the small bed that was pushed against the far wall, the simple end table by its side. I itched to read the titles on the spines of the small stack of books that rested there.

I laid out the clothes on the edge of Katharina's bed. They were similar to those from my old life, a simple homemade blue dress paired with a cream pinafore apron. When I slipped them on, the well-worn fabric smelled of cloves; the brush of cotton on my skin was like a homecoming.

"Gretel? Everything all right?" Orlantha called.

I was needed downstairs.

"One moment!"

I bounded back to the kitchen, intent upon making myself useful.

But the flow of Katharina and Orlantha's work stopped me in my tracks. They moved with the purpose of an ant colony and the grace of migrating birds.

I have no place here.

I was petrified by the sudden, heavy fear of being useless; while my body remained rooted to the ground, my mind galloped back through other moments when I didn't know what to do or how to act.

Suddenly, I am four again, waking up to the sound of Ansel crashing into the cottage well after midnight and yanking Hansel from his pallet, dragging my brother outside despite his protests.

I am ten and stumbling over my words in front of the entire class. Their laughter bounces off the tight walls of our one-room schoolhouse.

I am freshly seventeen and waking up in the castle for the first time six months ago, unsure of my place in our new, stolen life.

Orlantha placed a light hand on my elbow, startling me back to life.

She'd noticed my bewilderment.

I bowed my head to hide my burning cheeks.

"Gretel?"

I forced myself to meet her eyes.

"You can make tea, yes?"

The cool water of relief ran over my bones.

I nodded. I was excellent with tea.

"Run yourself down to the Mulworth cottage two over to the left. Tell Ms. Birdie I've sent you as an extra set of hands."

Orlantha smiled, like I wasn't making a fool of myself, like helping with tea was an important task. I fought back the cruel thought that jostled to overrule the kind ones: that her smile was the sort you pull out for distracting a toddler who's more hindrance than help. I could practically see Hansel making the observation and sneering.

Over her shoulder, Katharina had paused spreading the thin layers of dough with apple butter before she stacked them together. She was watching me. Witnessing my uselessness.

Solving the puzzle of her be damned, I couldn't stay in that kitchen one moment longer.

"I will," I mumbled before fleeing.

The Mulworth home was filled with a delicious fog that smelled of ginger, pumpkin, apples, sage, and rosemary. Underneath, the air was rich with the faint earthiness of black tea. It hit me all at once. This was several orders beyond the chipped clay teapot and everyday breakfast leaves with which I was familiar. Every surface I could make out was covered in a hodgepodge of bubbling pans, whistling kettles, and steaming teapots.

Ms. Birdie puttered through the maze of it all, humming so soft beneath her breath that I could more sense it than hear it. She paused at each station. Stoked the miniature fires. Stirred those that required it. Tasted others.

I cleared my throat. "Ms. Birdie?" My voice cut through the mist, disturbing its delicate alchemy.

She did not speak until we were standing close enough that I could finally see her clearly. A perfect copy of Aster, give or take seven decades, her blue eyes shone through all the wrinkles with a clarity that matched the sky on the first day of spring.

"You must be Gretel."

"Yes, ma'am." Deference pushed at my back, compelled me to curtsy.

Ms. Birdie patted my arm. "Ah now, none of that."

"Orlantha sent me to help you."

"Mm." She fixed me with her piercing stare. "I've heard tell of you, Miss Henoth. No mention of a prowess with stuff that's meant for sipping, however. What do you know of tea and cider?"

Faced with the brusqueness of her questioning, any confidence I'd mustered on the matter in front of Orlantha walked right out on me.

"Very little in comparison to you, I am sure," I admitted.

Her tongue clicked against her teeth. She was disappointed.

And I was tired of coming up short.

What was I, if not adept at rising to the occasion? Had I not ingratiated myself into an entirely new world in less than a year? Was I not gifted in suiting myself to my environment? Had I not risked everything to be here?

I would not shrivel at the task before me. I would not shrink until there was nowhere else to send me but back to the castle with no invitation to return.

I lengthened my spine and lifted my chin. "But I am quite strong. And more than quick of study. I can carry whatever you need."

A gap-riddled smile replaced her scrutiny. "I like strong girls." She squeezed my arm. "Come, come."

I followed her deeper into her beverage menagerie. Soon, I was weighted down with a tray of teapots and mismatched cups and saucers.

"Aster and her friends are six cabins down, making sweet rolls. Off you go."

After conquering the rickety stairs off the porch of Ms. Birdie's home, I took double-long steps toward the cabin at the end of the lane, where I'd seen the girls my age earlier.

"Is that fresh tea?" A young woman with raven-dark hair leaned over her railing and called down to me. She couldn't have been more than a year or two older than me. She was standing on the fenced porch of a tree house overhead. The tiniest baby I'd ever seen was swaddled against her chest. She shifted back and forth on her feet, bouncing the babe in a soothing rocking motion. Dark circles ringed her eyes.

"It is."

"From Ms. Birdie?"

I nodded.

"Oh, can you spare a bit?"

I hesitated. I'd only just begun to work my way into Ms. Birdie's good graces and she'd provided specific instructions. But as I took in the fatigued eyes and sagging shoulders of the new mother, I could not imagine refusing her.

"Of course."

I set the tray on the nearest porch, tucked my skirt into my waistband, and climbed up the ladder built into the side of the tree trunk.

She did not stop bouncing the baby as I handed her the cup of tea and she breathed in its scent. "Thank you. I've been up through three sunrises with this little one." She brushed the tip of her nose over the infant's thatch of dark hair.

"I hope you're both able to rest."

I turned to make my way back down the ladder. I didn't want to leave the tray exposed to bugs or any curious animals for too long.

"I'm Millie."

I paused, my foot on the first rung. "I'm Gretel."

"She's Millie, too." A nod at the bundle. "I call her Mills."

"You named her after yourself?"

"No one else in her life worth borrowing a name from."

"Oh." She was alone.

"Orlantha offered me a home in Galwin when my papa turned me out. But it's just been us up here. My hands've been too full to do much mingling."

"No one's looked in on you?" I fought to keep my face neutral, but this was a vein of neglect I had not yet witnessed in the witches. Was this a sign of their true nature, poking through their performance of hospitality at last?

"They leave food and things at the door. I just can't bring myself to open it." She turned away. "It's hard to accept help."

Shame lanced through me. I'd been quick to judge the witches and it wasn't at all their fault Millie was struggling. Pride had held a firm grip over our old village, too. Maybe someone would have intervened with Ansel's treatment of us if it hadn't.

I placed my hand on her shoulder. "I try to think of it as friendship."

I wasn't sure where the words came from, but I realized them to be true as soon as I spoke them. Wilfried and I had agreed to help each other. Annika, Frida, and Polly helped me navigate my new world and, in turn, I tried to give them a place of reprieve from my father and brother. I was still torn between ingrained skepticism of the witches and the tentative friendship that bloomed between us. But I hoped that, given time, I would come to trust in the latter.

"That's not a bad idea," she said.

Little Millie began to stir.

"Someone's hungry," her mother cooed, eyes fixed upon the bundle. "Thank you for the tea."

"It was nice to meet you." I meant it.

She disappeared into the small house and I made my way back to the ground.

The next few hours were a blur. I quickly memorized the groups and their corresponding cabins, learned which of the witches wanted something different from her fellow workers. Ms. Birdie and I found a rhythm all our own. The night chugged on until eventually I found myself back in Orlantha's doorway with the fresh pot of black tea she'd requested.

I lingered at the threshold, watching as she and Katharina moved around each other with soft jokes and often wordless communication. Not wishing to disturb their harmony, I set the pot softly on the nearest shelf and raced back to the Mulworth cabin.

Before exhaustion could get the best of me, I volunteered to take jugs of mulled pumpkin juice to the cabin of littles. The girls sat in small, joyful circles, making misshapen bird biscuits out of seeds and walnut butter while their minders looked on. Cora and Clove pulled me toward their group the moment my hands were free.

I watched the sky shift from black to deep blue through the window. The work would soon be over. "Very well. I can take a short break."

The girls cheered and smacked their sticky hands together.

They then folded me into their work without hesitation.

Before long, little yawns took over the room. One by one, parents and older siblings picked up the girls to take them back to their homes.

Fighting the contagious fatigue, I dragged myself back to Orlantha's cabin to change. The kitchen was empty, all the cakes she and Katharina had made wrapped and lining the counters.

"Hello?" My voice echoed through the cabin with no answer.

Taking that as evidence they weren't home, I made quick work of changing back into my night shift and boots, leaving the borrowed dress and apron on Katharina's bed.

The village was quiet as I made my way across the main clearing. Only a few stragglers remained, and they were all bound for home and bed.

At the mouth of the tunnel, I stopped and peered back over the village, dimly lit by the early dawn light filtering through the trees. The night had begun with difficulty, but ended with the sweet welcome of the little girls. A circle where the stakes were low and the time precious. In between, increasing ease. The longer I'd committed myself to focusing on the work, the more I was myself without trying, without working to sand off my edges.

"You figured it out. A place for yourself." Katharina emerged from behind the rock where I'd first watched them all from afar.

My head whipped around. I took in that she was alone, watching me with her typical cool, surveying gaze. "It was that or give up."

"Most would have done the latter."

"I'm not most."

We maintained eye contact as she circled me, drew close enough that I could smell the cinnamon on her breath. "Perhaps not."

Then she was gone, leaving behind nothing but her scent.

And me, as unsteadied by her as ever.

CHAPTER ELEVEN

The next morning, I was thankful that my impending second visit to the palace gave me an excuse to sleep in. No one wanted a princess who looked underslept. Indeed, the exhaustion from staying up all night and sneaking back in beneath the pale pink dawn was the only thing quelling my nervousness. I mumbled a good morning to Annika and Frida when they entered my room with breakfast and drifted back into a dreamless sleep against the backdrop of them scuffling about with their chores.

I did not wake until noon, at which point Annika insisted they begin readying me at once.

True to the queen's word the day before—and the formal invitation that had purportedly arrived that morning for good measure—a carriage arrived promptly at two o'clock. I raced to the stairs as soon as I heard the horses, nearly knocking Frida over in my haste. She flew after me, fussing over the last stray pieces of my hair. Annika scurried behind the both of us, carrying my coat and gloves.

My smile crumpled as the front doors opened. My brother and father crossed the threshold, cruelty cascading in behind them like a wave of manure. Over their shoulders, I could see a carriage from the palace fast approaching as well.

"It is only the afternoon," I blurted.

Hansel snorted. "Well spotted, Gretel. I see engagement has only made you smarter. How lucky the prince will be to have you weigh in on matters of the kingdom."

They weren't supposed to be back until late that night. I'd hoped and planned to go to the palace and return without interference.

Ansel took in my appearance. "Just where do you think you're gallivanting off to, Gretel?"

"Prince Wilfried has requested that I take tea with him this afternoon. He and the queen invited me yesterday." I left out the detail that they invited me in person.

I willed my chin not to quiver as I prepared for Ansel to protest.

My father did not prohibit my plans. He did something worse.

"Very well. Hansel and I will join you, of course."

"But, Father—" my brother sputtered.

"Hush, Hansel. I'll not have you jeopardizing one of our most promising endeavors yet."

My brother's mouth snapped shut. The muscles of his jaw pulled taut as he ground his teeth and submitted to Ansel in silence.

"Mrs. Chambers?" Ansel called. The housekeeper appeared immediately, almost as if she'd materialized.

"Yes, sir?"

"Hansel and I will be joining Miss Gretel. Please have Rothin put away our carriage and instruct Lev to tend to the luggage."

"Yes, sir." She bobbed a curtsy and it was just the three of us once more. Plus Annika and Frida, hovering in the background.

He turned to my maids. "You are no longer needed. After you hand over Gretel's coat and gloves, you may turn to your regular duties."

My two friends looked at me, but there was no fighting with him. I, too, relented to my fate and followed Ansel and Hansel to the carriage. I only wished that I could warn Wilfried.

The ride to the palace was blessedly uneventful.

To my surprise, Wilfried and the queen were waiting outside in the courtyard when we arrived, instead of an attendant. The knot between my shoulders unfurled the tiniest bit as I caught a glimpse of Wilfried's kind, welcoming face through the carriage curtains.

Breaking what I was sure were at least a handful of decorum protocols, the prince skipped across the pathway and opened the carriage door himself. He was already half leaning inside, his hand extended for mine, when he realized that I was not alone. He recovered his composure with the conditioned quickness of a royal.

"Lord Henoth and Lord Henoth," he said, stepping back with a curt nod, his face now the impervious mask of someone who'd been trained to shield his feelings from the world for his entire life.

"Miss Henoth?" He offered me his hand and I took it as quickly as propriety would allow.

Without a second's hesitation, he steered me toward his mother.

"I apologize," I whispered fervently. "They were expected to be away on business until later tonight. I know you were not expecting extra guests."

"You owe me no apologies, Gretel. I intend to pay them little mind. I hope you will be able to do the same."

There wasn't time for us to say anything else. Ansel's and Hansel's steps echoed off the walkway from close behind us, and before I had time to process any of it, I was standing before the queen.

CHAPTER TWELVE

The queen did everything in her power to make the best of the situation. I tried to make my body as small as possible while sandwiched between my brother and father on a couch facing the chairs where the queen and Wilfried were seated. I did not want either of them to associate me with my family. An impossible desire, but I held to it.

"We anticipate that the public will be thrilled to celebrate Wilfried and Miss Henoth's nuptials. Due to the war, everything was so small and rushed when the king and I married." The queen smiled at me before taking a sip of her tea.

King Richmond and Queen Galen were wed during wartime. It was only a couple of years before the prince was born that the king had been able to reach a treaty leading to the peace that our realm had enjoyed for nearly two decades.

Despite her own nontraditional marriage, it struck me how gracious she was being about all this. She might have hoped to leverage her son's marriage in favor of diplomacy. Even kings did not often choose their own wives. Certainly not without consulting anyone. With the combination of protocol and

Wilfried's mild nature, it was no doubt a shock to her when Wilfried arrived home from Hansel's birthday ball and announced that he was betrothed.

Yet she didn't seem to have any doubts about my suitability as a partner for her son. Had he informed her of the details surrounding our arrangement? I still hadn't asked him. There was so much we had never discussed. I had originally hoped for an opportunity to speak privately following the tea service, but Hansel and Ansel would make it impossible.

"Yes, I'm sure the citizenry will be more concerned with a wedding than the stability of their country." Hansel mimicked the queen's tea sipping, an overt jab.

Ansel was quick to cover for my brother. "What he means to say, Your Majesty, is that you needn't trouble yourself any more than necessary. Gretel will be happy with whatever choices you make for the wedding service. She's an agreeable girl."

"Miss Henoth and my son will plan their wedding together, of course." She smiled without a trace of disdain, but a message undergirded her words: This was common knowledge in the palace. So should it have been amongst us Henoths.

My face burned with shame. Despite the queen's kindness, it still seemed like I was a head of livestock for sale and not a person. After months in this new life, I still balked at the notion. At least when we lived in our village, I was seen as human, if not beloved.

The queen broke the silence. "What is a royal wedding if not a sign of strength for the royal line?" She smiled at Ansel, ever the diplomat.

Hansel smirked. "Are you so sure that the rest of the country will celebrate the prince marrying a girl from a new-money family?"

Hansel was very near to provoking Ansel to strike him.

"Well," my father said, clearing his throat. "It seems my son has forgotten your own inspiring origins, Your Majesty."

"Our family has long celebrated the unusual." The queen seemed determined to continue steering the conversation back to a place of normalcy. An outsider would never have guessed she was not born into this life.

"You must forgive the lad; he has not experienced the power of love himself."

I fought the urge to roll my eyes at my father's put-upon mannerisms and puffed-up language. I couldn't dismiss the idea that love meant something to him, though, much as I wanted to. Years ago, when I told Hansel I was starting to forget Mama and I was afraid to lose her a second time, he would tell me stories about what she and Ansel used to be like.

How Ansel would wake up before dawn on cold mornings to make Mama "tea," though some years we were so poor, it was only hot water. Or the way that the two of them would sit up late before the fire, weaving dreams together while Ansel peppered in jokes that made her shoulders shake. Hansel once said he could still hear her giggling in his dreams sometimes.

But grief had calcified Ansel's heart into a lump of cruelty, and every day I found it harder and harder to picture the man my mother fell in love with.

An awkward silence filled the space between us once more. I searched my mind for something, anything, appropriate to say. The smallest handful of words to convince the queen that she was right to trust Wilfried to choose his partner.

Once again, it was the queen who spoke first. "All the late king and I wished for Wilfried was that he would find happiness. With your daughter, it seems he has."

It stretched the bounds of credulousness to describe anything about the present situation as "happy," but unlike my brother, I was certainly not about to correct her.

"A true wonder, for I have never known Gretel to bring about anything but a headache." Hansel drained the dregs of his tea and poured himself another cup.

I'm going to pummel him. I bit the inside of my cheek to stop myself from asking him if it was a headache for him when I saved his life.

"Perhaps Gretel, like many, simply flourishes under the right circumstances and with the right company." It was the closest Queen Galen had come to insulting my brother.

Ansel's face turned puce.

I bit back a smile as the queen caught my eye.

I finally found my voice. "You are kind, Your Majesty."

"I am merely observant."

The conversation was blissfully interrupted for several minutes then, as an efficient succession of advisers and staff stepped in with matters for the queen and Wilfried to attend to.

She and the prince stepped away.

Hansel took the liberty of leaving the seating area to gaze out the floor-to-ceiling windows that looked over the grounds, sipping his tea at calculated intervals. The shadows cast over him by the casement made him look like he was standing in a temporary prison created by the sun.

Next to me, Ansel sat perfectly still. Likely the only way to keep himself from exploding. I turned my attention to Wilfried and his mother, watched the seamless way they negotiated with each other and their advisers. My heart ached for the closeness they shared. If my own mother were still alive, she could have helped me navigate this precarious world and its rules.

The palace had proven to be the opposite of our quiet, ill-tempered castle in nearly every way. Throughout the tea service, servants, advisers, and other staff had slipped in and out of the sitting room in a hitchless rhythm. We disjointed Henoths were a breach in their hive of efficiency.

Too swiftly for my liking, the important matters were attended to and the queen and Wilfried made their way back to us.

"Now, where were we?" The queen tapped her hands together. "Ah, yes, the goals of a parent: namely, the happiness of their children."

Hansel turned to face us from his place at the window. "I

thought we were speaking of strengthening the realm?" His voice carried through the room with seemingly no effort.

Ansel forced a chuckle. "Apologies, Your Majesty. Hansel has taken an interest in politics of late."

"Well, as we all know: For this family, that is one and the same. Perhaps your son will soon find a place for his . . . intrepid disposition."

"That he will, Your Majesty. In business, however, rather than the political. For that is what we are, men of business."

"Oh yes, yes we are. Shrewd ones, too." Hansel came to stand at my father's side, towering over all of us. "We examine every purchase carefully. Especially mares. I am sure Prince Wilfried will do the same."

I looked to Wilfried, expecting him to say something now that Hansel had invoked his name directly. But he said nothing, and wouldn't meet my eyes.

The queen ignored Hansel, speaking to my father instead. "I can assure you that my son is scrupulous and dignified in all his dealings, Lord Henoth."

She did not look at her son, either. Was she disappointed in his silence in the face of my brother implying such crass things about me? Then again, the prince and I hardly knew each other. Perhaps his silence signaled that he was beginning to believe the things my brother was suggesting—or stating outright, in some cases.

As it sank in that Wilfried hadn't said a single word in my

defense during this entire time, I began to worry that there was less hope than ever that I might find a happy ending in all of this.

It was clear that there was a lot riding on this engagement for my father, and I began to fear how he would react once the engagement was eventually dissolved. Would he think back on this tea and blame me for not speaking up more, for not doing a better job at giving my brother less space to make a mockery of me?

In the periphery of my focus, I noticed that Wilfried was uncharacteristically drawing further and further into himself. His arms were crossed tight over his chest, his jaw so tense a muscle popped there every few minutes. But no one did anything to draw him out. Including me.

Instead, as the conversation between our parents droned on, I, too, withdrew into my mind, disengaging from the discussion entirely.

At last, one of the queen's men came in to advise her that she needed to prepare for a function she was attending later that evening and the whole horrid affair came to a blessed close.

As I followed my brother and father out of the sitting room, I noticed Wilfried finally trying to catch my eye. I mustered a brief glance and half-hearted smile before following Ansel and Hansel. I wondered if I only imagined the sagging of Wilfried's shoulders that I caught just before turning the corner out of the room.

He must have shrugged off the sense of defeat quickly.

Moments later, the prince intercepted our leaving.

"Lord Henoth."

All three of us stopped and turned back. Wilfried stood in the center of the hallway, his vest askew in a betrayal of his typical regal appearance.

Ansel inclined his head. "Your Highness?"

"May I have a word with Miss Henoth before you go? In private."

"Of course, Your Highness. Come along, Hansel. Gretel, we'll await you in the carriage."

"Yes, Father."

I noted the edge of a self-satisfied smile on my father's face as he turned to leave.

"You wished to speak with me, Your Highness?" I directed my gaze to the floor, the embarrassment of my family washing over me anew.

Wilfried closed the distance between us and caught my hand in both of his to pull me to him.

My breath hitched between my ribs. It was not appropriate for us to stand this close outside of dancing.

"You are not like them, I know it."

"Your Highness?"

His eyes burned with a righteous fervor. Not one of passion, but justice. "I could not bear for you to leave with any fears that their vile behavior might color my opinion of you or jeopardize our future."

Our *future*.

The words cast a fog over my mind, drowning out every other important thing. Surely he meant each of our futures. Individually. Or our near futures. But I could not be certain, and it was in that gap of surety that I chose to linger.

"Y-you are kind, sir." A clumsy compliment for such a moment. Who could fault me, with his perfect face so near mine? His warm hands so solid around my own?

"If I were less kind, less proper, I would thwart all expectations and find a way to take you away from there immediately. Bring you somewhere safe."

He did not say somewhere safe *with him*, and I could not afford to entertain the possibility that he aimed to imply anything more than a concern for my safety. Already, I was too much in danger of liking him more than was wise.

I stepped back, desperate for even a single extra inch of space to break the spell between us. "Do not worry for me, Your Highness. It is enough to know that I have not lost your favor."

"Nor could you."

We gazed into each other's eyes for several moments, neither of us breathing. What might have happened, if we were somewhere else? He the son of a farmer and I still the daughter of a woodsman? Just two people with light expectations from the world, no barrier of modesty to stand between us.

As if some unseen force was eager to remind us how impossible such a dream was, the rhythmic footsteps and muffled chatter of two maids turning the corner startled us from our reverie. We sprang apart.

"They are waiting for me," I blurted.

"Yes, of course. I do not wish to keep you."

"If only you could." I bobbed a curtsy and turned fast on my heel so that he would not see my blush.

But as I made haste for the door, I tucked away a secret: I had seen his.

The carriage air was thick with the unspewed ire of my father; coated with the transgressions of my brother. None of us spoke. For once, Hansel did not litter his own emotions across his face. His features were as unreadable as our father's and all the more terrifying for it. For now, the openness of thc roads home—where anyone might pass by or look out from their windows at any inopportune moment—protected us. But I dreaded what Ansel might unleash within the privacy of the castle.

I entered the foyer first. Eager to create distance between myself and Ansel's line of fire, I doubled the length of my stride as soon as I descended from the carriage.

A hush hung over the castle. Almost as if, like mice, the staff had sensed the approaching threat of my father and scurried for corners he would not deign to touch. Would they hear the roar of my father and return on cue, or leave Hansel and me to fend for ourselves alone? As we faced an impending battle, I could not help but think of Hansel and me still as comrades-in-arms.

All the exits from the foyer were dark, the rooms beyond lit only by the beams of light that snuck through the few windows that weren't covered by closed curtains. The castle itself seemed to mold around whatever purpose it was needed for in the current moment to place the action in the most dramatic light. Like the shifting scenery of a traveling play that had once visited our village back when Hansel and I were small and our father's grief over Mama's death had not yet transformed to rage.

I did not have long to ponder that history, for Ansel exploded as soon as the door slammed closed behind him. Rounding on Hansel, he unleashed all his pent-up ire at last.

"Impudent, ungrateful, stupid boy! Do you wish to wreck everything I have built?"

"I think it was I who built you this life, Father, was it not?" Hansel brushed past me, creating a charged tunnel of space between him and our father.

Everything in me bristled. I hated watching Hansel take credit for what I had done. Yes, it was a horrible thing. I'd killed someone, after all. But it was in defense. Still, our wealth was stolen. And I had provided my family the opportunity to seize it. I wrestled back and forth with myself as their fight unfolded before me.

"First sign you were a know-nothing. A real man would have kept the gold and jewels for himself. But you was too stupid to know what to do with it." Anger sliced through Ansel's mannered façade, revealing his rough-spun roots.

"Too stupid? Or too loyal?" Hansel drawled.

Hurt lurked in Hansel's eyes, despite the arrogance in his tone. Unfortunately, our father saw it, too, and pounced upon his weakness. In two strides, he swallowed up the distance between them and grabbed Hansel by the breast of his coat. Heavy brass buttons landed on the floor. The resulting ringing echoed through the room as he pulled Hansel so close, my brother was forced to his tiptoes to maintain eye contact.

"Loyalty is worthless in this world. Worthless! Your mind is as much a sieve as your sister's, grasping nothing, retaining nothing."

"You need not continue pretending you're so learned, Father. Nobody is here to watch."

Ansel snapped then. His fist cut across Hansel's jowl, just missing his nose.

I shrank into the shadows as they went round and round, tearing at the fabric of each other's selves and clothes alike.

I'd anticipated that this moment would arrive eventually. It was part of the cycle. He rarely exploded like this, but that was strategic in itself. For when he did, he was unleashed, with no care for the devastation that might ensue.

For years, Hansel had maneuvered himself to somehow keep me out of harm's way. Always making sure he was one step ahead, forever contorting and shifting himself into the line of attack that I might be spared.

Did I owe him a similar defense, despite his changed nature?

Though he had turned on me, was I still responsible for him in some way? He was my brother, even in this.

I wondered if all our life, Hansel had been standing between our father and me, desperately hoping—like I had with Wilfried this afternoon—that I would cut in and stand up for him. But as I watched their fight move from the entryway and into some private, more hidden part of the castle, I could not bring myself to make a sound. When my brother's scorching blue eyes locked with my own just before our father drove him beyond my sight or hearing, I met his gaze and said nothing.

CHAPTER THIRTEEN

That night, I was eager to get to Galwin as soon as possible.

At long last, the castle fell quiet and the only people not abed were the guards. I had taken the trouble to learn their patrolling schedules, so I could move with confidence that I would be able to slip by without notice.

Dodging the squeakiest of the floorboards, I tiptoed through the castle, collecting a candle, shawl, and shoes along the way.

Outside, fear slipped from my shoulders. I was going to a place where I was wanted. Or at least where I was not reviled. A place that surpassed all others as a refuge, for among the witches, it seemed that everyone was free to be fully themselves. Even if I did not yet know how to live in such a way, I was curious to see if I could learn.

That curiosity soon betrayed me.

"Going somewhere?"

Hansel's oily voice slithered out from the shadows and froze me in my place.

Inch by inch, I turned as he drew nearer. Facing him was almost more frightening, for I could see the predatory vexation carved into his frame.

"I could not sleep."

He was too quick.

His fingers made prisoners of my wrists before I could take another breath.

He pushed me back against the stone wall that bordered the courtyard, plunging us both into darkness, so the guards would not see, were they to happen past.

"Do you think me so dull, Gretel?"

I was not fool enough to answer.

"I know that you are lying," he growled. "Tell me why you are out of bed."

My mouth was dry. I swallowed hard, begging my body for enough saliva to give me back my voice. "I would not repeat myself and further risk your displeasure, brother."

He shifted his grip to pin both my hands with one of his own; with the other, he produced a knife. Thin and sharp for precision work.

Mere nights before, I had cowered beneath the heat of dripping wax, shown deference in the face of a raised hand, sought to soothe his menacing temper.

But I had known nothing of freedom then. This time, faced with his wrath, something of the forest rose inside me to answer his threat.

"If you kill me, the entire kingdom shall be aware of your

crime. You'll become the murderer of a promised princess, rather than the hero who killed a reviled witch. Worse, Father will know it was you who forever ruined his chances at power."

Confusion, rather than fear, wound across the shadowed outlines of his features. He had not expected me to fight back, let alone to weaponize Ansel against him. I pushed away the thread of loyalty that fought to dissuade me. Yes, my threats were low, previously uncharted territory in our sibling disputes, but he had called for desperate actions.

Still, that did not cow him completely. His grip tightened.

"Why should I be concerned?"

"Because you still care for him, Hansel. I fear you always shall."

I'd pressed a nerve.

On a snarl, he drew his hand back, preparing to bear the knife down upon me. Something instinctual took over, cast aside any lingering bond I had with him. Without further thought, I rammed my knee into his groin. Taking advantage of his surprise, I broke free from his grip and made to dodge around him.

But I was not fast enough.

The tip of his blade caught near my elbow, split the thin cotton of my shift with ease, and traced a line down my forearm as I squirmed and pulled. Blood splattered across my chest and into my mouth. Bits of hair ripped from my scalp when he pulled at my braid.

I did not spy Katharina until Hansel was crumpling to the stones before me.

Her arms were still held aloft from striking him. In between them, a stone the size of two clenched fists.

"Is he dead?" I gasped.

"No. Unfortunately."

"What are you doing here?"

"My mother sent me to look out for you, of course." She grabbed the hand of my uninjured arm and dropped the stone. "We have to go."

She unbuckled the belt at her waist and cinched it around my arm, just above my elbow. "That will stop the blood, for now."

Then we were off, scampering across the grounds as quickly as we could. Several times, the earth rose up to meet me, but she caught me by my hand and prevented my fall over and over. Each time her fingers grazed mine, I had to remind myself to keep breathing.

Once we crossed from my father's land into the forest, Katharina stopped and removed the flannel shawl she wore beneath her coat.

"What are you doing?"

She wrapped the fabric over my wound. "You don't want to snag that on any branches."

I nodded, understanding. She was right, of course, but the extra weight on the cut made the pain more noticeable. Not wanting to appear ungrateful, I swallowed the scream that begged to unleash itself from me and jogged to catch up to where she was already tearing down the path.

It was a quiet night in Galwin when we arrived. Hardly anyone was outside. I was grateful for the absence of a welcoming committee.

Orlantha was also alone in the medical cabin when Katharina threw the door open.

I leaned against the doorframe as she explained. "Her brother attacked her. She needs sewing up."

Orlantha shifted into action without hesitation. "Fetch my suturing kit."

"Thank you, Kat." The familiar version of her name slipped from my mouth before I could stop it. The heat in my cheeks burned hotter than any gash.

She nodded once, eyes wide, then disappeared into the other room as Orlantha steered me over to a nearby chair and removed the bloody flannel. She was methodical and gentle, but I still winced as she peeled back the cloth from places where the blood had dried and caused the fabric to attach to my skin.

"We must teach you how to protect yourself in this world of men, Gretel."

CHAPTER FOURTEEN

As soon as she'd finished stitching me up, Orlantha had launched into teaching me about herbs, tinctures, poisons, and antidotes.

"The essentials for surviving as a young woman," she'd claimed.

I'd barely made it back to the castle before the servants woke, and by the time I was eating breakfast, an invitation to another ball at the palace had arrived. My first as the prince's betrothed. This past week had been a cycle of days preparing to be introduced to society as the would-be princess, and nights studying alongside Orlantha and Katharina.

I swallowed a yawn and tried to blink myself into alertness, to pull myself into the present. "We'll have to go out there at some point."

Wilfried exhaled from just behind me where we stood watching the crowd of dancers from a private alcove that overlooked the ballroom. His cool breath misted over the back of my neck. I shivered and hoped he did not see. Or would pretend to not notice.

"You are right, of course." He flopped down on the settee in the corner. One of the many privileges in which I could not share due to the obstruction of my voluminous skirts. Not that I would trade them. If there was anything in this new life I would not relinquish for my old one, it was the clothing. With the exception of being forced to tightlace my corsets, of course.

This was the first time I'd seen Wilfried since the unfortunate tea with our families. He'd left to visit a neighboring dignitary the next morning. So I'd heard.

When we'd arrived at the ball, Wilfried's butler had met Ansel, Hansel, and me at the front door and requested that I follow him—alone, for the prince wished to see me before greeting his other guests. I'd hoped that meant all was well, but Wilfried's hesitancy to venture into the ballroom suggested otherwise.

"Do you not wish to be seen with me?"

Wilfried sat up. "Whatever do you mean?"

"I would understand if, after reflecting, you decided that my father and brother's poor behavior before the queen changed your opinion of me."

He was on his feet at once. I tipped my chin to the ceiling to stem the tears welling up in my eyes. It was foolish of me to be upset. This was a business arrangement—a deal of friendship, at best. We'd seen each other only a handful of times. But that had not prevented me from hoping he might have some deeper affection for me. Especially since he promised that Ansel and Hansel had not cost me his favor. *Especially* since I'd made him blush so soon after.

"Gretel, look at me."

When I did not immediately obey, he tucked a knuckle against my chin and tilted it until our eyes met.

"*You* do me an honor by acquiescing to be seen in my presence." He brushed a thumb over the blush that heated my cheeks. "Let us remain clear about that."

"Any lady in that ballroom would delight at being your partner."

His gaze moved over me. "Then should my preference for you not speak all the louder?"

My lips parted in the tiniest gasp. I moved away, eager for the cool air that stepping outside would provide. I settled for hovering near the paned glass door that stood between the room and a small balcony. I could not desert him entirely. But neither could I stand the confusion he stirred in me.

When we formed our arrangement, he'd presented it only as a way to help us both. An opportunity to forestall the inevitable. We were alone now, and he did not seem one to toy with another's emotions, so why would he say such things? When no one was watching and we were free to be plain?

"Have I offended you?" He drew near again, his natural warmth canceling out the chill from the windows.

I dodged his question. "Do you not fear that you will hobble your future prospects by displaying such a public fondness for me?"

A huff of dry laughter escaped him. "Gretel, you are my fiancée."

Apparently, I was not the only one adept at dodging.

"I suppose I did not consider what a royal engagement would entail."

All humor drained from his face as he searched mine with a fervent gaze. "Do you regret saying yes?"

I hesitated. Did I regret the time our deal had purchased for me? No. Did I regret being able to see the kindness of my prince up close? Certainly not. But I mourned already the bruise this would place upon my heart when it was time to say goodbye, when no longer being in this battle with myself to not develop feelings for him meant that I was no longer engaged in a delicate dance with him at all. I could not say that, however, so I said what was easy, though it didn't tell the complete truth.

"No." I took his hand. "I could never regret your friendship."

Something lurked in his eyes, pulled the corners tight even as he smiled and squeezed my hand in return.

"Of course. Friendship."

I searched his face for more clues, eager to understand him. With a single breath, however, he assumed the expected placidity of a prince. He was neutrality personified once more. I did my best to match him.

"Shall we?" he asked.

I nodded. It was time to face the guests.

It was so much worse than when Wilfried announced our engagement at Hansel's birthday.

The entire room held its breath when we walked in,

mid-dance. Music, conversation, social jostling—time itself stopped for the prince of Tairen. Everyone bowed as we passed them, an undulating wave of deference. I caught my brother's glower as he bent before us. A girl my age simpered next to him. Beneath my carefully arranged sleeve, the week-old stitches in my arm stung in response, a plea for distance from Hansel that I wished I could heed.

Whispers sprouted up in our wake. Every cluster of merrymakers we greeted was quick to have my name on their lips the moment we parted their company. Always in admiration or disparagement. Always extremes. Those who revered me spun stories of my cunning, of the "vaunting ambition" and "beguiling audacity" that had won me the prize of the prince many had sought to claim. My detractors tarred me with language not fit to be repeated.

None of them considered that I was just a girl, like so many of their own children. No one gave me the benefit of imagining that, perhaps, I was only trying to survive in the vicious world they helped create. Not a single person seemed to recognize that I would be drowning in a forced marriage were it not for the lifeline of this betrothal that Wilfried had tossed my way.

So I did as Polly taught me: I smiled. Lingered with those who wished me well, offered nothing more than a glance of passing regard to those who yearned for my downfall. Clung to Wilfried's arm so tight, the pulse of his wrist beat against my fingers. His face remained impassive, though, his mask of benign gentility never breaking.

By the time we took our place at the center of the room so the dancing could resume, I felt like bread baked in a too-hot oven: charred to a crisp on the outside, unfinished goo in the center.

Wilfried nodded to the musicians and they began to play. With a flourish, he swept me into his arms. I followed the steps with ease. My body remembered, though my mind was scattered.

"What troubles you?" Wilfried whispered.

I forced myself to speak my mind. "Does it not bother you? That so many do not approve of me? Of . . . us?"

"I try not to think of anyone else when I am with you." Something akin to fondness warmed his eyes, pulled up one half of his mouth. "It is light work, truth be told."

Heat rushed from my chest, over my collarbone, and up my throat. I dipped my head to hide my feelings. It unsettled me, how he always found just the right words to unravel my resolve to hold him at arm's length. Despite my best efforts, I could not form an immunity to his words, or the many implications that might or might not have been hiding beneath them.

He pressed his hand against the small of my back, pulled me close enough to murmur in my ear. "Do not look at them. Look at me. You'll see I have eyes only for you."

Indeed, a brief glance confirmed it. "But—"

"If their objections are such that they would question their prince—"

He spun me out in time with the music, head held high and

proud. Placed me on display before the crowd. An unspoken declaration.

He twirled me back into his arms, close as propriety would allow. "Then they can make their grievance plain and speak it to me directly, instead of cowering behind the veil of ballroom gossip."

His thumb traced the middle of my spine. The guards in my brain lit torches signaling danger; the optimistic washerwomen in my heart doused them with buckets of water.

"Who would dare to question you?" I breathed. There was so little space between us, I had to crane my neck to meet his eyes.

His smile was wide and easy. "Exactly."

A man of his word, Wilfried had a gift for making everyone else disappear. He remained by my side for the rest of the evening, taking advantage of any opportunity to flatter me or cast me in a favorable light while speaking to his guests.

By the time he escorted me outside, I was almost free of worry or concern. We stood in companionable silence at the top of the steps in front of the palace, waiting for my household's carriage. Ansel and Hansel were already at the bottom of the staircase. Would they have noticed if they'd left without me? Sometimes, it was as though my father already considered me the Crown's burden, rather than his own.

"You were splendid tonight," Wilfried murmured.

"I owe it to you."

"We really do make a good team, Gretel."

"Shame it's only temporary," I quipped.

Before he could respond, the carriage pulled round. In a surprise move, Ansel and Hansel both looked over their shoulders for me.

I curtsied to Wilfried. "Good night, Your Highness."

He caught my hand and kissed it. A formality. Brushed his thumb over the underside of my wrist, just past the edge of manners—and just within the margins of my still-healing wound.

I winced at the tenderness, then quickly rearranged my features into the semblance of a smile. But I was not quick enough.

For when I bobbed my head in respect and once more tried to take my leave, he did not release me.

Brow furrowed, Wilfried turned my hand over, palm facing up. I pleaded with my eyes for him to look at me, but he was intent upon my forearm. With the utmost care, he pushed up the sleeve of my dress and gasped. I watched, frozen, as he studied Orlantha's sutures.

"Gretel, what—"

"Gretel!" Hansel's sharp voice cut through the tension between us.

"I have to go," I said, half yelp and half whisper.

Before he could object, I yanked my arm from his grasp, fixed my sleeve, and scampered down the stairs.

When I pulled back the carriage's window curtain as we drove away, he was already gone.

CHAPTER FIFTEEN

I woke to the sound of arguing voices. Opening my eyes was like pushing up through a pool of sludge. I was so exhausted when we returned home the night before, I'd barely allowed Annika and Frida to help me out of my ball gown.

Early morning sunlight filtered through the crack between curtains I didn't remember closing. I lay still and tried to catch up on the argument unfolding on the other side of my bedroom door.

"—it's very unusual, Your Highness, you understand. She's still a young woman. Her father's entrusted her to my care. I have a responsibility and—" Mrs. Chambers. She was clearly irritated, which wasn't unlike her. But who in the castle would she address as—

No.

Surely Mrs. Chambers couldn't be having a dispute with—

"Mrs. Chambers, I am not engaging in an argument. Need I remind you that your duty to the Crown surpasses all others?"

I sat up immediately.

There was no question: That was Wilfried's voice! Whatever reason could he have for calling so early? And unannounced?

"But, sir, what will Lord Ansel think—" I could practically see her wringing her hands.

What would Ansel think, indeed. I'd grown accustomed to Wilfried having the ability to flout many of the rules that the rest of society lived and died by, but this was a bit much, even for him. He could only be visiting for a serious matter.

In a rush, our last moments together came barreling into my mind.

What if he no longer needed to worry about propriety because he was going to call off our arrangement? He'd seen the sutures—*I'd* seen his reaction. What if that was the stone that tipped the balance? The difficulty that made him realize he didn't want to deal with all the family turmoil that came attached to me? What kind of princess ran about with such injuries? I was too much of a hassle. Too much of a liability.

Mrs. Chambers's voice pulled me out of my spiraling thoughts. "—how can I tell them that I let you—"

"You may tell them that you were following instructions from your prince. I'll not make polite requests any longer. Stand aside."

A few raps at the door.

"Miss Henoth?" Wilfried called. "Miss Henoth, if you can hear me, please make yourself decent so that I might speak with you. Alone."

"Oh, Your Highness!" Mrs. Chambers admonished.

I threw my bedcovers aside. "One moment!"

"Your services are no longer required here, Mrs. Chambers. Miss Henoth will see you after I speak with her. I expect there to be no disturbances."

"When Lord Ansel and Lord Hansel return, it'll be them you can expect to deal with . . . Your Highness." Her tone was thick with disdain. Apparently, Hansel wasn't the only one of our household unafraid to cause strife with the royals.

Wilfried maintained a level voice, ever the gentleman. "*If* they return before I depart, I will proceed accordingly. Good morning, Mrs. Chambers."

I wasted no time after that in following his instructions.

It was too early. As I surveyed my dressing options, it was clear how dependent I had become on Frida and Annika. I didn't know where to find all my clothes anymore. I would have to choose between a housecoat and my slippers or the extremely plain dress I'd worn to wander the grounds yesterday. I was stuck between indecency and underwhelm.

I went for the dress. He was the prince; he could afford to breach rules of modesty that I could not.

I was still tying the ribbon in my bodice as I went to open the door.

His eyes were bloodshot, as if he slept even more poorly than I had.

"Gretel!"

I curtsied. "Your Highness."

"I have been a fool. I am so sorry—"

"—I understand why you're here—wait. Why would *you* apologize?"

He closed the door behind him as he stepped in, then took both my hands and led me over to the small table tucked into the corner of the room. Away from the window and any prying eyes below.

"I'm ashamed of how I've sat back and allowed you to be treated so abominably in this household. I should have taken the way your father and brother behaved at tea more seriously. But I never dreamed . . ." He gestured toward my injured arm.

I blinked at the remorse etched across his face. This was not at all what I had expected.

"N-not to speak ill of your family!" He seemed to take my silence as offense.

I could not keep from smiling, just a little. What a relief to witness someone else criticizing them. "You may speak ill of them."

Relief washed over his features, replaced quickly by fire once more. "I should like to speak much worse of them."

He fell into one of the nearby chairs. "Oh, Gretel. I feel that I have failed you. You are my betrothed and I should have been protecting you."

"Well, we aren't really betrothed."

He snapped his head up. "Whatever do you mean?"

I wasn't used to seeing him this flustered.

I sat across from him. "Only that I am not holding you to the standard I would if this were a more traditional arrangement."

"Quite right." A grim look settled over his face. "Yes, you're right. Of course." He stood and paced away from me, then abruptly turned back. "But they do not know that. And they needn't. I promised you that doing me this favor would benefit your circumstances as well, and so far I have done a poor job of upholding my end."

Now it was my turn to be embarrassed. "I understand if it's too much to deal with."

He held my face with both hands. "Gretel, you've done nothing wrong. Please do not apologize."

I leaned back. "I just want you to know that I do not blame you if you wish to break things off."

"Break things off . . . Gretel, what are you talking about? I have no intentions of the sort." He moved his arms in quick succession from his hips, to crossing them over his chest, to running one hand through his hair. He was nervous.

I made the prince of Tairen nervous.

And he made me confused. "You don't?"

"On the contrary." Wilfried resumed his pacing. "I came here to offer you my apology and, provided you did not despise the sight of me afterward, to tell you that I intend to visit you here every day this week. If you must remain here, I can at least try to minimize the time you are not protected."

"Oh." It was all I could think to say. All I was *capable* of saying. My lungs were suddenly starved for air.

How could I tell him that the times when he would leave would be the most dangerous for me? How could I explain that the only reason I was not in danger for the whole of most nights was due to the refuge I'd found in Galwin?

He cleared his throat. "If you approve, of course. I do not wish to impose upon you."

He always took my silences as apprehension toward *him*.

"Of course I approve. Of course I do! Thank you." I couldn't speak the words soon enough, couldn't close the space between us fast enough.

"I only wish that I could take you away from here, but I fear that might be beyond even my authority." He smiled, though it did not reach his eyes. "I must display *some* sense of decorum."

The truth of our situation hit me again. Once he eventually broke off our engagement, it would open both of us up to too much criticism if I were to stay at the palace for too long.

I reached for him, then stopped short. "It is enough that you will come here. More than enough. For more reasons than you realize."

"As much as my responsibilities allow, I will be by your side." He closed the distance between us and I willed myself not to enjoy it too much.

It's not real. It's not real. It's not real.

I squeezed his hand. "You're very generous, Your Highness."

That was it. That was what was real. He was kind. This didn't mean anything else.

"How many times must I insist you call me by my name? I wish us to be great friends, Gretel, if nothing else."

If nothing else.

"I would like that . . ."

I hesitated and he raised his eyebrows.

"Wilfried." He smiled and I could not resist matching him. "I cannot thank you enough for the kindness you have shown me. I hope I can one day repay it in kind."

"You will accept my apology, then?"

"Yes, of course. You had no reason to assume the worst before last night. I cannot harbor any hard feelings toward you for not being perfect." I took a step back. Smoothing my hands down the front of my dress, I gave my best impression of haughty detachment.

He pressed a hand to his heart. "Ha! And you say *I* am generous."

The sound of hoofbeats against the cobblestone drive saved me from a response. I went to the window. Hansel and Ansel were galloping up the way, neither looking too pleased.

"Oh, it seems my brother and father are returning home. I cannot think for what business they were called away so early that would have also concluded so soon." Across the room, Wilfried began studying his nails.

"Hmm, yes. Whatever *can* it have been?" He cast his gaze to the rafters and hummed.

"Why do you look like you're hiding something?"

"I am the portrait of innocence, Miss Henoth. This is providential timing, however, as I wish to make sure they both understand that I will be returning tomorrow morning with the intention to spend the day here."

I narrowed my eyes. "Providential indeed. Some might go so far as to call it orchestrated."

"Some might."

I could not hold back an eye roll. "I'll walk you to the door."

"Then onward we go." He extended his arm and I took it.

Ansel's disgruntled appearance disappeared as soon as he laid his beady eyes upon the prince. "Your Highness! We did not expect to have the pleasure of hosting you."

Hansel hung back, his twisted features made all the more gruesome by the extreme shadows cast through the open front door.

"Especially considering we've just returned from answering your summons to the palace, only to be told that you were not at home," my brother drawled.

"How strange." Wilfried's too-innocent tone confirmed my suspicions. I bit the inside of my cheek to keep from laughing.

So he was *behind their absence.*

Wilfried frowned as he continued. "I told my men expressly to send word of my impending arrival here. Well, I'm disappointed to have missed you, gentlemen, but I've addressed my business with Miss Henoth and I'm afraid I must make my way back to the palace."

"We are equally sorry for the confusion, Your Highness." Ansel's eye twitched beneath the strain of his feigned congenial expression.

"Fret not, you'll see more of me soon. I intend to return tomorrow and every morning this week to spend more time with Miss Henoth. I'm sure I'll find her in good health and spirits." Wilfried's face was open, his tone light, but I could see the glint of nerve behind his eyes as he fixed my father with a level stare.

He turned his attention to Hansel. "Whole and hale in both body and mind."

Ansel stretched his smile to the very bounds of his face. "Of course, Your Highness. We're always honored to have you."

"Excellent. Miss Henoth, I shall see you in the morning." He kissed my hand.

"Your Highness," I said, curtsying.

Wilfried turned to Ansel and Hansel.

"Lord Henoth." He tipped his head to my father, observing niceties only for my sake, I privately wagered.

Ansel bowed. "Your Highness."

He turned to Hansel. "Lord Henoth."

Hansel, however, had no one he wished to impress. He took his time, waiting several seconds before offering a begrudging farewell only once he realized that the prince had no intentions of surrender. "... Your Highness." His voice dripped with disdain.

Wilfried locked eyes with me one last time. "Until tomorrow."

"Tomorrow," I breathed.

A thrill of hope dislodged a sliver of the ever-present fear in my heart.

CHAPTER SIXTEEN

I carried the same hope with me to Galwin later that night. The gaggle of little girls was up to their usual gallivanting and I was swarmed the instant one spotted me and alerted the others. But Katharina was too quick for them.

She slid between me and the group, her arms filled with supplies. "All of you give Miss Gretel room to breathe."

Once we were freed from the clutches of the littles, she turned to me with a serious face. "Here. You'll need this basket as well as the dress and apron today."

I took the dress and slipped behind a tree. "Why?" The sound of the girls' chatter receded as they moved on to their next source of interest.

"Still no sense of trust?" Katharina called.

"A perpetual sense of curiosity."

I emerged from my changing spot and took the offered basket.

"We are going on a bit of an adventure today."

Her gaze traced over me as I finished tying the apron.

I raised a brow. Did she find something lacking in my appearance?

Our eyes met.

She cleared her throat. "We're going to be foraging."

I couldn't contain my excitement. "Really? Your mother thinks I'm ready?"

"Ready to watch and carry what I pick? Sure."

I followed her into the woods.

"When did you start learning how to do this?"

"Before I can remember." Katharina stopped near a small bush and knelt in search of its bounty beneath the tight-woven branches. "Mama thinks foraging is one of the most important skills a forest witch can have." She dropped a handful of small, puffy mushrooms into the basket.

"Why so?"

"Knowing how to spot the differences between mushrooms can save your life and those around you."

"Do you like it?"

She emerged from beneath the bush once more and wiped the sweat from her forehead. "Yes. It's nice to be alone with nothing but the sounds of the woods for company."

She dumped one last handful of mushrooms into my basket and I helped her up from the ground.

"I'm sorry you've been saddled with me, then."

She wiped her hands on her apron. "I can make exceptions."

My cheeks must have been the color of red currants.

"I guess having people around you all the time can be just as overwhelming as not having any," I said.

We began walking again, which was good. Better for concealing any further blushing.

"Are you so very alone in your castle?" she asked eventually.

"I try to be."

"You like the solitude, too."

"I like the security it gives me. I like feeling safe," I hedged.

"We have wards around the village to protect ourselves, though we take additional precautions, as well. The tunnel is one of them. It feeds the rumors about us and keeps unwanted visitors away. But safety also comes from our community, in taking care of one another."

"I do feel safe when I'm there. I like it."

She fixed me with one of her unsettling stares. "Because your family isn't safe."

It was a statement, not a question. Was she hinting at the violence she'd witnessed from Hansel? Of course, growing up in Galwin, I was sure an unsafe family would once have been unimaginable to her, based on the harmonious way the witches lived.

"Even before you knew everything was not well in my home, did you not wonder at the fact I risked spending my nights with a village of witches, despite everything you know most of us are told about you?" My words came out sharper than I intended.

If she took any offense, she hid it well.

"Some of the older women sensed you weeks before you followed me here that one night. I've always felt like you were meant to find us. Mama has, too. She's the one who sent me to the castle to watch for you." Katharina shrugged. "She trusted you would seek us out eventually."

"You knew I followed you?"

"Do you not recognize where I've led us?"

I turned in a full circle. After we'd emerged from the tunnel that protected Galwin, I hadn't paid as much attention to the path we took as I'd thought. But now I noticed the intermittent bread crumbs. The few that hadn't been scavenged by the non-human inhabitants of the forest still remained on the ground from where I'd dropped them on my way back to the castle after my first night in the village.

"Well, you're right. I was running from something."

"And you found us."

"I found *you*."

She raised an eyebrow.

I cleared my throat. "Erm, all of you, I mean."

She tested the weight of a tree limb before swinging herself up onto it. "Are you glad about it?" she called down.

"I haven't altogether decided. But most of the time, I would say yes."

"You still believe some of the lies."

I averted my eyes, embarrassed.

Katharina jumped easily to the ground, three frost apples in her hand. "I understand. It's hard to uproot the things you've been taught all your life. I don't think I could simply forget the foraging knowledge I have, for example."

"But that kind of knowledge *helps* people. I think the beliefs I've been taught are harmful. Many of them, anyway."

"Well then, Mama would say, 'It sounds like you've begun weeding out what you no longer wish to tend in the garden of your mind.'"

Have I?

"Maybe so."

Our talk shifted largely to her providing information on the various nuts and plants we were gathering, but I kept turning her words over in my mind. Despite the fatigue and the fear that still ran beneath me like the current of a river, there was that sliver of hope now, too. I was changing as I grew closer to the witches. I liked it. I liked how peaceful their ways were. I admired how they'd insulated themselves so well from the threat of violence that permeated my own world, the one ruled by mundane men.

How could I resist the safety of their community? Especially when, day by day, I grew more and more intrigued by the witch next to me.

CHAPTER SEVENTEEN

Wilfried was true to his word. For the rest of the week, he arrived on horseback each morning as I finished dressing. Sometimes, he had unavoidable paperwork to work through. We passed those days comfortably seated across from each other in the library; he worked, and I read. When he didn't have other matters to attend to, we packed up provisions and spent hours upon hours out of doors, wandering the grounds and talking as it suited us.

I told him all about my life growing up in the village, taking care to leave Hansel out whenever possible. I didn't yet know how to explain to him that we were once close, that in spite of his cruelty, a small part of me believed he could transform again, and become the Hansel I once loved.

Wilfried, in turn, told me about his parents, what it was like to grow up as both an only child and the first royal born from a formerly common mother. The expectation of the Crown was a heavy weight to bear, but a challenge he was eager to step up to. The more I got to know him, the more we talked or just spent time together without speaking, the more I liked him. And, against my own will, I found myself imagining what it might be like to continue on in this fashion for years to come.

It took a small amount of effort on my part, but I was able to avoid both my brother and my father almost entirely for that blessed week. I spent my days with the safety provided by Wilfried's presence. In the evenings, I took my meals privately in my room and pretended to retire early.

As soon as the castle was still, I'd sneak back out and make my way to the edge of the woods. Every night, I'd follow the fox to Galwin. Every dawn, my heart would sink when he appeared to escort me back to the castle that was more like a cage and less like a home with each passing day.

I hardly slept all that week. The sky was always turning orange when I climbed back into my bed, sometimes too tired to change fully out of my clothes. But I was happy, buoyed by the warmth of my blossoming friendships with both the witches and Wilfried.

Our long walks about the estate grounds became a highlight of my days. The movement made learning how to talk to each other easier.

Wilfried lightly spun his walking stick through the air, tossing and catching it in between steps. He was buoyant today, more than usual.

"I feel better out of doors, don't you?" The question was so in line with my own thoughts, I wondered for a moment if I had said them out loud. This happened sometimes, where we seemed more in sync than two new friends had a right to be.

"Yes, I always have."

"I don't mind being inside usually, but there's something strange about the castle. I hope you don't mind me saying."

"Not at all. It's comforting to know I'm not the only one. I've been telling myself I just wasn't used to living somewhere so large."

Wilfried frowned. "But I am, and it's still unsettling to me."

"Did the palace feel very large when you were small?"

He settled onto a large boulder and I joined him. "I don't know. I think by the time I had anything to compare it to, it already felt like home." He handed me an apple from the knapsack his housekeeper had sent him with that morning. "What was your home like? The one you lived in before you moved into the castle."

"It was small. You could have fit it in my room now and still had room to squeeze around the edges. But it was cozy."

"Do you miss it?"

I wasn't as quick to answer. I had to think about how to word the complicated feelings I harbored toward my past life. "I don't miss not having any privacy. But I do miss feeling like I knew where everything was at once. It was a small kind of comfort to see my entire world in one glance. Or at least, most of my world."

"It was safe."

Images of Ansel throwing the front door open in the middle

of the night and thrashing Hansel awake passed through my mind.

"In some ways. In others, no." I considered the wing that separated my rooms from my father's. "I guess there are some things about this new life that I like."

"Hopefully one thing, at least." He glanced up at me through his lashes and his expression was so open, so hopeful. It unnerved me far more than his teasing.

"Can I ask you something?" I deflected.

"No, I despise questions." He attempted to look cold and unfeeling, but couldn't manage it for more than a second.

We both laughed.

He nudged his shoulder against mine. "Yes, go on."

"What made you suggest we pretend to be engaged?" I busied myself with unraveling and replaiting the end of my braid.

He paused and the air shifted between us, thick with something I could not name. My question was meant to steer us into surface waters, but I'd miscalculated.

"Do you want the honest answer or the selfless one?"

I spoke around the swift-forming lump in my throat. "Both."

"You seemed trapped, and I thought I might be able to help free you."

"At least for a time." My retort was laced with a tinge of bitterness, unbidden and instantly regretted. I could not afford to risk his displeasure.

He knocked his knee against mine. "A long time, I hope."

"And the other answer?" I could scarcely breathe.

"I wanted to know you better. Ever since you ran into me on the balcony."

Finally, something ripe for jokes: my own embarrassment. "So you could suss out the best way to torture me for the crime of causing near-injury to the Crown?"

He gasped. "However did you guess?!"

"Or, no, I have a better one: I was the first person to talk to you like you were a regular person and not just a prince." I abandoned the rock and fake swooned into the grass.

Wilfried joined me before answering. "Do you think me such a cliché as the princes you might read of in a story?"

"You're the first prince I've met outside of one," I said, turning on my side to face him.

"I wished to know you because when you came barreling out of that ballroom, you were so intent on whatever you were seeking, the rest of the world disappeared for you."

He caught the braid I'd abandoned, plucked its ribbon from my hand, and secured the end. He held my gaze all the while.

"I wondered how it might feel to be a worthy recipient of your focus," he confessed.

I blinked at him. He was so capable of speaking his thoughts and feelings exactly as they unfolded. I wished to possess his talent for openness, his confidence that vulnerability would always be well-received. Beneath my envy, I yearned to take him at his word, to believe that maybe he did find me as fascinating as he implied.

But I could not afford such indulgences.

I cleared my throat. "And now you have the benefit of my meticulous focus on the task of helping you find a suitable wife."

Hurt guttered out the brief flicker of hope in his eyes.

For a moment, neither of us spoke, suspended in between his openness and my deflection.

He cobbled an expression of amusement together. "Yes. That is the primary reason for my interest, of course."

"Well, tell me what you're looking for."

"She should be kind."

I nodded sagely. "Ah, so you're selective."

"Not afraid to say yes to unusual adventures."

"Naturally. Someone sheltered, but not *so* sheltered that she isn't allowed into society."

"She pays *attention* to the subjects she cares about."

"Of course. You don't want to marry someone who can't keep matters of state ordered in her mind."

He stared at me for several seconds without saying anything. His eyes darkened. My throat went dry.

Finally, he broke the silence. "Is that enough to begin your search?"

"I believe so," I rasped. "I shall report back when I require more specifics."

"I appreciate your diligence. Now it is my turn to ask you something more personal."

"Oh dear, I can only entertain quandaries with the highest

degree of universalism." I rolled away, creating space between us to break the spell.

Wilfried sat up, braced his arms against his knees. "Has your brother always been violent toward you?"

A stone settled in my stomach as all the air whooshed from my lungs. I forced myself to a sitting position, facing Wilfried.

I was compelled to take up for Hansel. "He wasn't always this way. He used to be incredibly kind. Thoughtful. He looked out for me when we were younger."

"What happened?"

I couldn't tell him. Not the parts that were a mystery even to me, or the ones I held tight to my chest, a secret from everyone except Hansel himself.

"Well . . . I . . ."

"Do not trouble yourself. I should not have pried." He squeezed my shoulder before standing and helping me up.

We turned to lighter topics then and I was grateful for it. Every time I wanted to tell him the details about the bleaker realities of my life with Ansel and Hansel, about the refuge that both his and the witches' company provided me, I refrained. I skirted around any piece of myself that was truly vulnerable and peppered my speech with light quips and jokes. Anything to keep from him seeing me too clearly. At least, I tried.

What I did not want to acknowledge even to myself at that point, however, was a sharper truth: I resented him, in some ways. Yes, for now he provided safety and shelter from the rage and wrath of my kin, but one day he would take it all away. One day, he would leave our arrangement behind in favor of true love and I would be left in a worse position than ever before.

"We should make our way back," I suggested, looking up at the darkening sky.

Wilfried followed suit. "Ah, yes. I didn't realize how much time had passed."

"I think it's another strange feature of the estate. It gets darker faster here."

In the time it took us to brush the bits of grass and dust from our clothes, the sun slid so quickly behind the horizon, we could only make out the edge.

"Indeed," Wilfried said, frowning. "It feels like the sun itself is eager to rush us into the night and on to the next day."

CHAPTER EIGHTEEN

I was truly alone in Galwin for the first time since I'd crossed the threshold of the village nearly two months prior. This cottage, held for teaching and examinations, was reserved for my private use through the rest of the night. After weeks of shadowing Orlantha during her work and lessons whenever she could spare the time, it was time to put my training to the test.

Before me lay a table of ingredients and tools. Bundles of hawthorn, thyme, lavender, and mint. Braids of garlic. Nubs of ginger. Bowls of licorice root, valerian, and chamomile buds. Mortar and pestle sets. Several knives. An assortment of spoons. Vessels both for mixing and pouring. A vial of wild blueberry juice, precious in late autumn. All arranged around a heaping pile of foxglove leaves, carefully harvested and wrapped in beeswax cloth to prevent unintentional skin contact.

When combined with various forms of the foxglove, the other ingredients would create four brews that were essential to the witches: a tonic for treating stoneground fever, a sleeping draught, a tincture for concluding a pregnancy, and an antidote for poison. Four of the most common reasons someone visited the witches for aid.

In Galwin, children were taught to give foxglove a wide berth from the moment they could crawl. Certainly, those of us outside the witch village were given similar warnings by our own caregivers. A matter of safety. But as the young witches grew older, many of them had no wish to work with such a dangerous plant. Over time, the number of foxglove specialists had dwindled.

If I wanted to be of service, Orlantha was adamant that I needed to not only learn how to brew these four concoctions but be able to make them with ease and identify them without hesitation. A skill that could spell the difference between life and death. Tonight would be the test of all that I had learned so far.

Before sunrise, I would successfully produce the treatments and gain an invitation to work more closely with Orlantha and Katharina in the medical cabin—or I would fail and return to tea duty and carrying baskets for foragers until six months hence, when I'd have another chance to prove myself.

But it was bigger than all that. The more I learned about the powerful medicines the witches could create, the less I believed Ansel's conviction that the tonic was responsible for my mother's death. At the same time, I couldn't understand why it hadn't been enough to heal her. My uncertainty only fueled my determination. I'd witnessed lives saved and families spared by these remedies; if I could learn how to help, I could prevent countless women and children from experiencing the pain and suffering I'd endured.

Light work and low stakes, to be sure.

To begin, I lit several of the large pillar candles placed around the room. One of the dutiful charmed lanterns followed me in my business, keeping me bathed in a circle of light even as its kindred cast shadows upon the walls near their own hovering places around the cabin. My last stop before tending the primary fire was to hang the kettle on a hook above the small nook fire that had been built into the wall for such a purpose.

I tended to the fire and filled the large cauldron near to the brim with water. Scattered rosemary before the hearth. Said a prayer for all those lost to stoneground fever before the tonic was created.

The kettle whistled for my attention. I stirred in the appropriate tea leaves for blessing this venture and reviewed the handwritten instructions for each brew.

Too quickly, the tea was drunk and I could put off starting no longer.

Back at my station, I began by extracting the *méerco* from the foxglove. The leaves went into large bowls of *kwish* water to soak; I set them aside and turned my attention to chopping and pulverizing the other ingredients.

Time slipped away.

The work quieted my mind and absorbed me like nothing else. Each step was both meticulous and artful, the precision of needlework and the possibility of music. All the fear and self-consciousness that so often plagued me during times when I was under similar pressure evaporated amidst the steam undulating from the simmering cauldron.

Every so often, a thought would pierce my consciousness, remind me that all of this was temporary. But the work before me was too fulfilling to allow that thought purchase. I pushed it away each time, replaced it with renewed marveling at the concoctions taking shape beneath my hands. Tonight they were mere test samples; if I completed them correctly, on some distant night, they might save a life or alleviate someone's suffering.

Through the darkest hours, I labored. Until finally, I reached the last step.

Holding my breath all the while, I poured a thimbleful of the blueberry juice into the waiting vial of the almost-complete stoneground fever tonic. Only when the liquid transformed into a shade of pale pink did I exhale. My vision blurred with tears of relief and pride.

From the doorway, someone cleared their throat.

I held back a gasp. The earliest rays of sun were poking into the cottage, silhouetting Katharina against the dawn light. A basket filled with foraged walnuts rested at her feet.

"Well, well. It appears someone will soon be relieved of tea duty." She stepped into the room—smirking, but with an air of approval.

For once, I had no retort. For once, I did not feel lacking in her presence.

I'd made something beautiful—something important—with my own hands and mind.

No one could take that away.

CHAPTER NINETEEN

Since my betrothal to the prince, my father finally had begun giving me the wide berth I'd craved most of my life. I supposed he did not see how expending any energy or time upon me could prove any more useful. Moreover, as our place in society rose, his business grew in tandem.

A business I still knew little of. Any attempts at wheedling information from him were met with firm resistance. Eventually, I tired of prying, but my curiosity was not to be sated. I resolved to investigate the next time he and Hansel took one of their longer trips. It would require breaking one of the first rules Ansel had set for me when we moved into the castle: Under no circumstances was I to visit the east wing.

That side of the castle was entirely his and Hansel's domain. Of all the staff, only the pair of valets my father had hired were allowed regular access. But they always accompanied my father on any business travel, so the wing would be empty.

Two days after I'd successfully completed my test, I woke up and could sense that Ansel and Hansel were away.

I checked the stables to confirm. Their horses were not in

their stalls, though the carriage remained. It was a short trip, then. I didn't have much time.

I rushed back inside.

I wandered through the back corridor that connected the two sides of the castle. Suddenly, a strong draft blew through the hall. It pulled me deep, deeper along until I was standing in front of the entry to the forbidden wing. The door was both unlocked and open.

I wandered over the threshold into another long hallway. All the doors were locked. Except one, at the end. I turned the handle. It was my father's study.

I stepped inside. If there was any place where I would find more information about Ansel's business dealings, this was it.

I rifled through drawer after drawer until I found the key to what I was looking for: the copy of a letter from Ansel, explaining our history. It was addressed to the leader of a group of men with particular skills.

I had spent many hours ruminating over what might have led Hansel and me to the Witch's cottage, but none of my ideas were as frightful as the story that unfolded via my father's records of correspondence.

According to the letter, during the spring prior, Hansel had grown fed up with being a poor woodsman. Seeking an opportunity to partner with our father, he'd gone to Ansel and told him a tale of a witch in the woods who was said to possess a great fortune, though she lived humbly. The two conspired to attack her and steal her riches.

I could only conjecture that I must have grown suspicious of their intentions and followed them to the cottage, for there was no mention of me joining in their plot or even having awareness of it. The rest of the story matched Hansel's version of the battle with the Witch: He'd killed her at the last minute and taken everything she had of value.

Their success in defeating the Witch and stealing her wealth had provided them with the confidence that the larger community of witches who lived deeper in the forest was vulnerable to attack and extortion.

A series of letters and documents revealed my father and brother's intent to begin staging attacks in the coming months on local villagers and those in the surrounding area. They would also start organizing harm to befall members of the nobility. It would all be pinned on the witches.

This was the primary reason for Ansel's endeavors to ingratiate us into higher society. Though he used the guise of marrying me off as a veil for his true purposes, he'd never intended to pursue it as ardently as he'd claimed.

Instead, the movement into the social circles we newly occupied had been coordinated with the purpose of figuring out the weaknesses and desires of our various acquaintances.

My engagement to Wilfried had been a mere stroke of luck, an opportunity to further cement our social status while standing to gain ever more power and influence through my position once the wedding occurred.

Through the rest of the document, I discovered that all of their "business travel" had centered around forming agreements with men who would do their dirty work for them, in exchange for money. Once upon a time, they'd planned to engage solely in low-stakes opportunities, so as to not raise alarm.

But, poised to hold a position of favor in the royal court, my father now possessed greater ambitions. He planned not only to increase the discrimination against the witches in our community; he sought to see them wiped from the realm, all possible traces of the village erased and any wealth or power the witches once held taken, greedily shoved into Henoth coffers.

I stepped back from the desk with shaking hands, my mind reeling.

Now I knew why Hansel and I had ended up in battle with the Wood Witch.

Now I knew my brother and our sire were capable of more monstrosity than I had been willing to imagine.

Surely I would always have objected to this level of organized cruelty. Though I still had no memory of following Hansel to the cottage, I must have hoped to stop his plan, to prevent him from committing such atrocities, even against those we were raised to see as enemies. For even when I thought the witches evil, I still recognized them as human. But now I'd borne witness to their kindness firsthand. I'd experienced their compassion and, dare I say it, their friendship.

Yet what could I do? I had no power in this manner. Any sway I would one day hold would only move the Crown if my desires aligned with the queen's and Wilfried's own purposes.

Down the hall, a door slammed. Voices carried into the office.

They were back early.

I shoved the letters back where I'd found them and raced from the room, not stopping until I was safe on the other side of a closed door in my own chambers.

I wished I had never looked. I did not know how I would bear the horrific knowledge I now carried.

CHAPTER TWENTY

The next morning, I forced myself awake and dressed to meet Wilfried. I'd spent half the night staring at my ceiling, the other half falling asleep only to wake moments later, petrified by lingering nightmares of Galwin on fire.

As I walked down the main stairs, Hansel stepped into view, placing his foot on the bottom step and blocking my path.

"You look tired, sister."

I kept my tone level, betraying nothing. "I am very busy these days, *brother*."

"Oh yes, how exhausting it must be, preparing to be a princess."

My control splintered and gave way to anger. "And one day your future queen, to whom you will pay respect."

I climbed one step back, so we were almost the same height. A shimmer of delight stole over Hansel's eyes.

"Is that a challenge, Gretel?" Malice lurked at the edge of his words, venom gathering in the fangs of a snake poised to strike.

My shoulders slumped and my eyes slid closed. I said an internal prayer for patience. "I have no interest in arguing today,

Hansel. The prince will be here shortly. Please allow me to pass."

As if on cue, Wilfried swept dramatically into the entry, arms held aloft in a comically tragic pose. "'Call me and I will answer!'"

I shouldered my way past Hansel and turned my attention to the prince, feigning light applause for his antics. *"A Midsummer Night's Dream*. Act four, scene one."

"You finished reading it?"

"Yesterday. It was a good recommendation."

"I am delighted to hear that."

"I cannot say the same, being forced to listen to your prattle," Hansel mumbled.

Wilfried turned his attention to my brother as if he'd only just noticed him. "How convenient that we have no need of you, Lord Henoth. You are free to go in search of pursuits that you would find more amusing."

Hansel's scowl deepened, but he bowed his head to Wilfried all the same. "As you wish, Your Highness."

Wilfried motioned me to draw closer. "Now then," he said in a hushed tone. "I come bearing exciting news. That is, I hope you will find it exciting."

"I might, once you tell me of it."

"My mother would like you to come stay at the palace for a couple of days, to shadow her and have a glimpse of what your life will one day be like."

That was a serious invitation. My heart swelled at the prospect, but I could no longer avoid asking him the question to which I'd longed to know the answer ever since having tea with her. "Does your mother know the truth of our arrangement?"

"N-no. No, she doesn't." Some of the wind went out of his sails. "She needn't, for the time being." Certain of his opinion, he puffed his energy back up again. "But, Gretel, don't you see? This means you will have a perfectly valid excuse to leave this place for two days."

The truth of his words sank in and my own grin grew to match his. "Your Highness, I must confess: I find your news *most* exciting."

We left right after breakfast, as soon as Frida and Annika had packed for me. Wilfried had requested that a carriage from the palace follow him to the castle that morning, leaving us no reason to linger. There was no opportunity for me to warn the witches that I would not be visiting them for a night or two, but I hoped that they would assume I simply had other responsibilities to attend to. I did not want them to worry for me. I was also worried for them; I still hadn't found a way to warn them about Ansel and Hansel's plans. I hoped that my time at the palace would provide an opportunity for me to ascertain whether I could count on help from Wilfried when it was time to take a stand against my father and brother.

Moreover, I yearned to sleep somewhere far from my brother's reach. On the rare occasions that I made it home with several hours to spare before I needed to be back up and about again, I was never able to doze for long. I woke every few minutes, it seemed, certain I'd heard the creak of Hansel's feet on the floor or the strike of a match lit to set fire to my bed with me inside it.

A visit at the palace would be a welcome reprieve, I was sure of it.

The rest of that first day went well. I was taken on a full, proper tour of the royal estate. The sheer scale of the buildings was overwhelming. Yet I could imagine myself feeling at home there.

I attended several meetings with both the queen and Wilfried, together and apart. Buoyed by all the information I found myself learning and remembering with ease, I took quickly to my temporary routine. Far removed from the gloom of my father's castle—which muddied and distorted all but my simplest thoughts—the bustle of the palace cleared my mind and brightened my spirits.

The final stop on my itinerary was an initial dress fitting for the wedding.

Queen Galen and the royal clothier were waiting for me in Her Majesty's parlor when I was ushered in by Elke, the servant who was attending to me during my stay.

I curtsied to the queen. "Your Majesty."

"Miss Henoth. Allow me to introduce you to one of my most trusted and important advisers: Madame Violette Sartre."

The woman beside her wore a severe black dress with a high collar and sleeves that gathered tight at her wrists. Her appearance suggested someone who despised fashion rather than made her living by it. I would have to trust the queen's judgment.

"Madame Sartre will design and oversee the creation of your wedding gown and, eventually, your entire wardrobe."

"Bonjour, madame." It was the only French I knew.

The older woman raised one thin eyebrow. "Vous parlez français?"

I shook my head. "I've only overheard a few words at the market."

"She does not speak French *yet*," the queen clarified. "Your educational opportunities will expand once you are married, Miss Henoth."

"I am eager to learn, Your Majesty."

Madame Sartre clapped her hands together, just once. "Come, come. I am here for furthering your appearance, not bettering your mind."

She waved me over to a small stool and motioned for me to sit.

Madame clapped her hands again, twice this time.

The queen arranged herself on a small sofa nearby and nodded at the servant hovering near the parlor entrance. "Now, Elke."

Elke bobbed a curtsy and opened the door. A trio of assistants dressed in sharp black frocks identical to their mistress's fluttered in, each carrying a stack of fabric samples. There were more shades of blue, pink, and silver in their arms than I'd known existed.

The next few hours were a blur of sitting very still as two of Madame Sartre's assistants held up swatch after swatch to my face and the other diligently transcribed the whispered notes Madame Sartre dictated in response to each option.

Despite the tediousness, I loved it. The colors. The fabrics. The possibility of what it all might become.

I envisaged myself enjoying this kind of life.

I was afraid to want it.

As the sun slipped behind the trees, my lids grew heavy. Periwinkle- and poppy-colored spots hovered at the edge of my vision every time I blinked.

The clothier clapped her hands once more.

I startled into sitting up straight and swallowed a yawn. "Are we finished?"

"Oui. For today."

I rolled feeling back into my shoulders and ankles as I slid from the stool. "Thank you, Madame Sartre."

"Well, madame?" the queen asked, rising from her seat.

"She has amenable coloring. We will make her shine."

The corners of Queen Galen's mouth twitched. "I have no doubt."

Madame Sartre and her staff curtsied as one, then swept out of the room.

The queen laid her hand on my shoulder. "Thank you for your

patience, Miss Henoth. It is a quality that will serve you well here."

"You are kind, Your Majesty."

"Miss Henoth, His Royal Highness is waiting for you," Elke announced from the door.

I looked to the queen.

"You may go. I will see you in the morning."

One final curtsy, then I was free. It took all my willpower not to sprint out of the room.

Wilfried was watching the door with such rapt attention when I emerged, a delighted giggle skipped out of my mouth before I could catch it.

"Miss Henoth."

We bowed and curtsied in turn.

Our grins mirrored each other, wide and eager, the picture of two schoolmates who had been given leave to play.

He offered me his arm. "May I interest you in a stroll about the gardens?"

I nodded as I tucked my hand into the crook of his elbow. I didn't trust myself to speak.

The gardens were a sight to behold, filled with plants and shrubbery both familiar and brand-new to me. Despite the late season, they were a riot of color and greenery.

"It's so lovely here," I sighed. "Your gardeners planned the spaces well."

He steered us to a bench beneath a towering weeping willow. "They have my mother to thank, actually."

“Oh?”

“Horticulture is a special passion of hers. This land was my father’s wedding gift to her, to oversee and use as she pleased.”

“What a comfort this space must be to her in his absence.”

He nodded, then changed the subject. “We’re meant to be choosing flowers for decorating the chapel on our wedding day, but I want to show you my favorite spot in the gardens instead.”

“You have a favorite spot?”

“Can you keep a secret?” Mischief glimmered in his eyes.

“That depends. Who will I be keeping the secret from?”

“Well,” he said, lowering his voice, “everyone.”

Before I could respond, he grabbed my hand and hurried us through a maze of hedges, moving quick enough that I would not have been able to find the way out by myself.

We stopped before an iron door that only reached his shoulder. Surrounded by interlacing brambles and vines of ivy, it was a place that did not wish to be discovered. Elaborate cobwebs were spun across the greenery, a gossamer tapestry that implied a longtime lack of disturbances.

“My mother does not know that I am aware this spot exists. She’s kept it hidden from the entire palace.”

Mist curled at our ankles in spite of the clear evening.

The hedge maze was dark—a warning or a shroud. Perhaps both.

"Is this safe?"

Wilfried's smile was rogue, impish in a way I didn't associate with him, even when he was bold. "The Thicket has always welcomed me."

Sliding his long fingers between two of the silvery webs, he reached into the brambles and produced a wrought iron key. He fit the key into the lock and turned, resulting in a satisfying click.

The door opened with ease. Maybe it was just well tended to. Or maybe the Thicket, as he'd called it, really *was* eager to receive him. Whatever the case might have been, it slammed closed behind us with equal intention. The sound reverberated into the ivy; the leaves swallowed up any noise that might have betrayed us.

This was an untidy residence, more reminiscent of a small forest than a garden hideaway. The inhabitants rejected all logic. Nightshades kept company with pepper cinnamon trees and sage bushes; blueberries flourished several months out of season. The strangest thing, however, was the light. I could still see the dusky sky above us, yet within Wilfried's secret spot, it was as though night had fallen.

Bugs chittered. The plants whispered to one another. The hairs on my arms stood to attention.

But I understood why the prince loved it here upon my first inhale.

"It smells like Yuletide," I whispered.

Which was not to say just spices and evergreens. No, it smelled like one *specific* Yule. The only one I could remember when nothing terrible happened. I closed my eyes, breathing in the strange air as I was transported to a simpler time.

The clean scent of ice filled my nostrils, like it was the first day of the lake being solid enough for skating. We could never afford any skates, but I loved to watch the others. It was all so clear in my mind: steam wafting from the rows of gingerbread Mrs. Rilkins placed on her open windowsill to cool. Trees strung with pine cone garlands. Candles lit at midnight.

"Mm," Wilfried hummed next to me, back in the garden. "It's the first day of spring, for me."

My eyes popped open. "What?"

He shrugged. "Always has been. That's my favorite time of year. Is Yule yours?"

"Yes," I said, my throat thick. "Well, I've always wanted it to be."

"The Thicket must know. I wonder if it smells different for everyone."

We didn't have time to ponder it any further. A bell tolled from the palace.

Wilfried frowned. "Supper."

"I can see why you love it here. I wish we could stay longer."

He took my hand. "We'll come back, soon as there's a chance to get away."

I smiled to reassure him, but as he locked the door behind us and we set off for the palace, I could not quell the sinking feeling that I'd never cross the Thicket's threshold again.

Later, tucked into the plush bed of a guest room, I longed to sort through the day, take apart my new memories, and reflect upon them. But no sooner had Elke closed the door than my eyelids began to droop.

The peace did not last for long.

I awoke to the sounds of my own terror. It was loud. Too loud. I had no idea how long I'd been screaming before I woke up. There was no telling how many people had heard.

At least, there wasn't for a moment. But then Elke burst into the room.

"I have summoned the prince, my lady. You need fret no longer."

I leapt from the bed. "Please, don't. This isn't something worth troubling him about. It was just a bad dream!"

It was too late. Wilfried was on her heels, his hair disheveled and a robe tied sloppily at his waist over his nightclothes. "Elke, you may go. I will attend to Miss Henoth."

"This really isn't anything to worry about—"

The maid wrung her hands. "Your Highness, it isn't appropriate for us to leave you with—"

"I stand in line for the Crown. I will decide what is or is not appropriate."

Elke's eyes went wide. "Beg pardon, Your Highness."

Wilfried softened then. "Trouble yourself no longer. You have done your duty. You may leave us now. We thank you for your discretion."

"Yes, Your Highness." She curtsied herself out of the room. Wilfried closed the door gently behind her before turning to survey me.

"Wilfried, really. It's nothing. I had a bad dream, that's all. I have them all the time." I climbed back into my bed, an attempt to prove that all was well.

"What about?"

"I promise, there is nothing of any interest in them whatsoever. Just my mind playing late-night tricks." I dug my nails into my palms to prevent my hands from shaking. "I will manage any screaming in the future. Don't worry, you won't be disturbed again."

"I am not worried about being disturbed. I am concerned that you are frightened. Please, tell me what happened."

I sighed. "I don't remember what was happening in the nightmare—"

I broke off as he took the liberty of sitting at the foot of my bed. "Tell me anything you can remember."

"You really wish to know?"

He nodded.

"You must promise you won't be upset."

"Gretel, even you cannot control the workings of your mind during sleep."

If I told him, there would be no walking back from it. If he knew, he would have a piece of me that was ready-made for fashioning into a weapon.

"Dearest . . . please." His words were more breath than sound, as if he spoke a thought aloud without intending to.

The endearment was my undoing. Though I was unable to quite make sense of it, I could no longer find it in myself to deny him. I relented.

"I only know that my brother was at the center of it," I began, staring at my hands to avoid his piercing gaze. "You've seen glimpses of how he is now, but what you don't understand is how different he used to be."

"So you've said before."

I nodded.

"I would like to understand."

I could do this. I could trust him. He was my friend, if nothing else.

I took a deep breath. "When we were growing up, he was my favorite person. He always looked out for me. He always protected me. But ever since the encounter with the Wood Witch, he's been different."

"Violent and cruel."

I nodded. "Incredibly so. But it is not just that. He's at war with the entire world around him and everything in it." I swiped at the tears spilling down my cheeks.

"How so?"

"He fights with our father and yearns for his approval in equal measure. He used to despise Ansel. Now I fear that he is becoming more and more like him. Worse, perhaps."

We were quiet as Wilfried took in my words and I continued trying to stifle my tears.

"What do you think caused this change?" he asked after a moment.

"I am not sure."

"You said he's only been different since the fight with the witch?"

"Yes."

"Maybe he regrets killing her. Maybe that is eating him up from the inside."

I curled my knees to my chest, the only defense I had.

My stomach churned. He deserved the truth.

"Wilfried, there is something I need to tell you. Something no one else knows apart from my brother."

"I am listening."

"Hansel didn't kill the Wood Witch."

Concern and confusion washed over his face. "She is still alive? Where is she? I will admit, I had never heard of any witch called by the name you use for her until—"

"No, she is dead." I left the bed so I could face away from him when I spoke the truth. "*I* am the one who killed her."

"Oh."

A heavy silence fell over the room.

He was quiet for so long, I eventually turned back, half expecting him to be gone.

He was still on the bed. A statue. A study in disappointment. It was almost worse than the revulsion I had initially anticipated.

I closed the distance between us and dropped to my knees, desperate for him to understand. "I had to. To save Hansel. To protect myself. He was tired from fighting. His sword had fallen. She would have killed us."

"Oh, Gretel. How horrifying for you."

"I know it was a wicked thing to do." I began to pace. "Even if she was a witch, I don't think she deserved to die. But I was terrified at the prospect of dying myself. Or worse, being left alone to live with my father without Hansel's protection. I didn't want to lose him to the Wood Witch, but now I fear that I have created a monster. I feel guilty for saving him *and* for wishing that I hadn't."

Wilfried came and took my hands in his. "You did what was necessary to survive. I cannot fault you for that. No one should."

He wrapped his arms around me and I let him. I would not deny myself that comfort.

A bitter joke bubbled up inside me and I spoke before I could reconsider. "You should be glad you aren't really going to marry me; imagine being forced to endure being awoken in the middle of the night, most nights, by servants afraid that I am under attack."

"It would be the lightest burden I would ever carry."

"If it were real." I spoke the words under my breath. I didn't want to acknowledge the ephemeral nature of this, but it was always there, gnawing at me.

He forged ahead in comforting me, as if I'd said nothing. "Gretel, you are not responsible for your brother's choices as to who he has become. He is his own man."

I nodded. Though I didn't believe him, I was too tired to argue.

He pulled me closer, settling his chin on my head. "Thank you for trusting me."

I nodded against his chest.

"Shall we . . . try to get some sleep again?" he murmured.

"I can try . . . Good night."

"I will remain here until you fall asleep."

I startled, tipping my head back to look at him. "Won't the servants talk?"

"No more than they already have. Besides, who are they going to tell? The king?" He smiled a little then and I returned it. It was the least I could do to thank him.

I climbed back beneath the covers and he settled himself next to me, propped up by two of the many pillows I had at my disposal. The entire side of my body nearest his buzzed with curiosity.

I was certain sleep would not find me, but he began humming a tune I didn't recognize. It was comforting all the same.

"That's a lovely song," I said, yawning, sleep tugging at me.

"My mother used to sing it over me when I was small."

"I like it."

"I could hold your hand as well," he ventured. "So the weaver of your nightmares will know that I am right here, that you are not alone and not such easy prey as they might assume."

In spite of everything, I laughed.

I snuggled down onto my pillow. "You're very good at that."

"Guarding you?"

"Making me laugh." My words were garbled by another yawn.

"If being king does not suit me, perhaps I can find a court willing to accept me as their jester." He blew out the candle next to my bed. "Sleep, Gretel."

In the darkness, I was braver.

"You can see if you're good at holding my hand, too."

His fingers found mine beneath the covers and he laced them together.

A feeling like warm light pooled through me.

His voice was the last thing I heard, singing softly as his thumb smoothed soothing lines over the back of my hand.

The next morning, I woke to an empty room. It was as though nothing remiss had happened. Wilfried met me at the door to walk to breakfast together, and although I was tense at first, anticipating that things might be awkward between us, he seemed perfectly at ease. He stopped me just before we entered the dining room, where the queen was waiting.

"I hope you know that I consider everything you told me last night to be in confidence. You need not worry that I will share any of it with anyone, including my mother. Your trust is not something I take for granted."

I swallowed the lump that gathered in my throat. "Thank you."

We entered the dining room together. The queen beamed at us.

"Good morning, my dears. Did you sleep well?"

"Yes, Your Majesty. My room was so comfortable, I fell asleep nearly immediately."

Wilfried kissed his mother on the cheek before pulling out my seat. "As did I, Mother. Thank you."

"Well, Miss Henoth," the queen said once Wilfried and I were settled across from each other. "I hope we've provided a positive glimpse into your future life here."

I replayed the feeling of Wilfried holding my hand in my mind and pushed away any thought of scarier things. "Yes, Your Majesty. Everything and everyone has been splendid."

"You'll have to come back before too long. It has been such a treat to have another woman around."

"It would be my pleasure, Your Majesty."

"And we must find a time soon for a proper engagement ball."

Wilfried caught my eye. I gave him a slight nod.

"We are at your disposal, Mother."

"Splendid." She smiled, then tucked into her eggs.

She will make a wonderful mother-in-law to someone.

I couldn't help but think of my own mother then. It was inaccurate to say that I missed her, since I could hardly remember her. I yearned for something *to* miss. Thankfully, the queen and Wilfried turned their conversation to matters of their social engagements for that evening and I was happy to observe while not actively contributing.

It was nice to have the quiet during my carriage ride back to the castle. I was grateful Wilfried had been so receptive to what I'd shared with him, but when he'd needed to stay behind to prepare for the dinner he was attending with his mother that night, I found I wasn't upset at the prospect of making the journey solo. I needed the space to reflect upon my time at the palace.

The sun was setting behind me when the carriage finally rolled up our drive.

"There we are, miss," Petyr said.

"Thank you."

I stayed seated, waiting with the carriage door open for several moments. Still, none of the castle's staff emerged to greet me.

The footman started for the castle door with my trunk in hand, but I stopped him.

"I can take care of it. I know you have a long ride back to the palace."

He hesitated. "His Royal Highness would not like me leaving you to fend for yourself, miss."

"Then he need not know of it." I offered what I hoped was an encouraging smile.

After a further moment of waffling, he gave a curt bow. "Much obliged, miss. Take care."

Once I'd dragged my trunk inside, I wasted no time sequestering myself in my room. It would be a few hours yet before I could leave for the village. I pushed my packed trunk in front of my door and retreated to my bed for a short nap.

CHAPTER TWENTY-ONE

Each day after Wilfried left the castle, I counted down the minutes until I could flee to Galwin. If spending time with Wilfried was a reprieve from the realities of my life, the village was a complete escape. Perhaps that was why I could push aside my misgivings about so quickly falling in with the witches.

But one night, everything took a turn.

I'd grown accustomed to at least the youngest girls flocking to me as soon as I entered the village, but that night it seemed that almost everyone was tucked inside their homes. Some adults gathered in whispering huddles on a couple of the porches, but the only sign of any of the children was a few eager faces pressed up against the windowpanes of those that had glass.

Instead of a passel of young children racing through the village center, there was only Katharina, frantically waving me over to the porch of the cabin she shared with her mother.

"Hurry and change, then come with me to the overnight sick cabin." Katharina thrust a bundle of the clothes she always lent me into my arms before slumping into the nearest porch rocker. I changed in record time and reported back to her. She was on her feet and moving before the door could swing closed behind me. I took off after her.

She wasted no time before revealing the matter at hand. "Have you had stoneground fever?"

"Yes, as a toddler. Almost every kid in our village fell ill with it one winter." I didn't mention that it killed my mother.

I jogged to keep up with Katharina. "Why?"

"Millie's baby has it."

I gasped.

Katharina nodded, her mouth a thin line as she stopped in front of the sick cabin. "Too young for the tonic. She's not getting better and Millie's near delirious with exhaustion."

"What's your mother saying?"

Katharina's face was grim. "She isn't. She's gone away to trade at a market two days' ride from here."

"What are you going to do?"

"*We* are going to heal this baby."

"B-but I'm—I can't—I've barely—"

She placed her hands on my shoulders, looked full and stern into my eyes. I suppressed the chill that crept up my spine. "No one else even knows how to *make* the tonic, Gretel. Everyone thinks you were led to us for a reason. You want a purpose here? This is your chance to prove it."

I nodded, numb.

When we entered the cabin that the witches reserved for those who had to receive treatment overnight, everything was grim and frantic. The baby's mother stood in a corner, silent tears streaming down her face as Katharina conducted a regiment of her mother's apprentices.

I ran through the ingredients for the tonic in my mind, in case there was something we could repurpose to help the baby. The fever was rare now, and the few cases that still went around were typically mild. Babies were the exception. They weren't strong enough to be dosed with the tonic until after their first winter. Such was the case with poor Millie's little daughter.

In his darkest moments when we were growing up, Ansel often ranted to Hansel and me that dying was our mother's punishment for getting involved with witches in the first place. Now that I knew more about both the witches and their healing work firsthand, I no longer believed the tonic bore any responsibility for her death. Still, doubts lingered. Was intervening a cross against fate? What if I gave baby Mills some other medicine and she didn't survive? Would I carry Millie's blame forever?

A handful of Orlantha's healing apprentices—those who had either no skill or no interest in herb work but still wished to provide aid—worked as a unit from the front room. They boiled and chilled water. Carried wood. Prepared bandages for other patients. Made tea.

I wove my way through their brigade and made my way to the back room, following the sound of the strangled cries from baby Mills.

"Miss Gretel!" Millie flung herself at me as soon as I walked through the door. Her eyes were swollen and red, the dark circles beneath them more pronounced than the night we first met.

Behind her, I could see her daughter's little body upon a high table. Katharina bent over her, dabbing her chest and forehead with cool, damp cloths. She looked up at me and her message was clear: Get Millie out.

"Shh, shh, Millie." I rubbed my hand in circles over her back. "It's all right. We'll take care of Mills, but you need to take care of you."

"I can't, I can't!" Millie wailed. "I'm not leaving her."

I held her face in my hands. "Look at me. Mills needs you to be strong. She's got a fight ahead of her. You don't want to end up in a sickbed right next to her, do you?"

She shook her head, hiccuping through her tears.

I curled an arm around her and led her out to the front room.

"Aster."

The blond looked up from the stove where she was stirring soup, took in the sight of Millie, and immediately understood.

"Oh, Ms. Millie. I'll make you some tea."

As soon as I'd passed her from my care to Aster's, I rushed back to the room.

Somehow, in that short time, Mills had taken a turn for the worse.

We worked for hours, trying every treatment Katharina and I could think of. But as redness worked through Mills's limbs and her heartbeat grew fainter and fainter, I began to despair.

Katharina paced the room. A terrible silence had fallen; Mills had no more strength to cry. I stared at a spot on the wall and racked my brain for new ideas.

"There must be something else, something we're missing," she muttered.

Her words triggered a memory I'd buried deep inside my consciousness without realizing it.

It was Hansel's first winter working full-time in the woods with Ansel. He'd stayed out too late, determined to surpass the quota of logs our father had set for him. When he'd dropped onto his pallet next to mine long after dark, I could hear his teeth chattering even over Ansel's snores.

The next morning, his body was riddled with fever. Not stone-ground, but no less terrifying. Ansel refused to call for a doctor.

"A waste of money on a soft boy."

And he would never stoop to seeking out help from the witches in the woods.

"Won't let 'em kill your brother like they did your mama."

Those were the last words he said before he trudged out into the woods for the day. Hansel had tried to push himself up, but he couldn't do more than brace his elbows against the blankets. He collapsed and slept for hours. I stayed home from school, watching him the entire time. Terrified that if I left, he would slip away just like our mother had and leave me all alone with the monster who'd sired us.

The room was growing dark when he woke, just long enough to grab my hand and croak five words: "Potato slices. In my socks." Then he closed his eyes once more.

His plea was nonsensical to my mind, but what other options were there?

Quick as I could, I sliced up a quarter of one of the potatoes we had in the cellar and slipped them into his socks. Then I waited, waited and prayed, and hoped I hadn't misunderstood him.

"We need potatoes," I said, breaking the silence that had fallen again.

"What?"

"Potatoes. They were a remedy of my mother's. They saved my . . ." I trailed off. I didn't want to speak of Hansel to her. "Potatoes will work. I'm sure of it. Trust me, please."

She nodded, one firm tip of her jaw. Permission to try.

I raced back to the front room, over to where Aster was still cooking.

"Give me your knife."

Wide-eyed, she did as I bade her. I snatched a potato from her pile of vegetables and cut it up into tiny chunks before ferrying the pieces back to Mills's sick room.

"You hold her socks open, I'll slip these in."

We both held our breath, first as we worked and then as we watched, waiting to see if our experiment would make a difference.

Several moments later, with a breath that took up all the oxygen in the room, Mills filled her lungs and let out her first earnest cry all night.

Katharina and I yelped with joy, pulled each other into an embrace, and hopped around in a small circle. Our eyes locked and the joy dancing in hers mirrored my own. At last we stopped, breathless and still clasping each other's arms as we heaved gulps of air into our lungs.

"Ahem."

We broke away, turning toward the sound of Aster clearing her throat in the doorway. "We heard noise."

"Mills has turned a corner," Katharina sighed, relief etched across her face.

"Oh!" Aster pressed her hand to her heart. "Thank the Spirits."

"Thank potatoes," Katharina deadpanned. Then, to me, with a look of approval that I'd rarely seen from her, "Thank Gretel."

I tucked my head. Unsure what to say, I turned back to our patient. Ran the backs of my fingers over her forehead. "Her skin's cooling down."

"Should I wake Millie?" Aster asked. "I finally talked her into lying down about an hour ago. She was out before she could even pull up a blanket around her."

Katharina shook her head. "No. Let her rest."

She turned once more to Mills, set about checking her health signs.

I watched from the edge of the sick room, taking it all in as the sky began to shift from dark blue to purple.

"How'd you know to do that? I thought your mother . . ."

"She did," I confirmed. "But I guess she showed my brother. He's older than me. That's what she did whenever he or our father got sick and they couldn't afford a doctor."

"Mm. My mother will be glad for you to share this with her."

"Guess we're all still learning." I fought, and failed, to stifle a yawn.

Katharina looked up. "Gretel, go home. You don't want them to catch you out."

I'd learned enough of her to know that she wouldn't turn away an extra set of hands unless she no longer had need for them. The baby's fate was still unclear, but far more hopeful than when first I arrived.

"All right."

She spoke just before I reached the door. "Thank you."

I turned to face her. "We're a good team."

She nodded.

We lingered for just a moment, until I tore myself away. I had a long journey ahead of me, and not much energy or cover of darkness with which to take it.

From the corner of my eye, I saw Katharina bend over Mills's tiny bundle and begin to whisper to the infant. I hovered in the doorway.

"Earth below you. Trees around you. Stars above you. Sisters with you. None shall harm you."

I swallowed around the lump in my throat and forced myself down the hallway. The witches called and murmured snatches of the blessing to one another often, but it took on a different tone now, spoken so soon after an almost-tragedy.

I murmured my goodbyes to the other girls as I left, donned

my own clothes once more, and set off for the castle.

As I made my way across the grounds, the movement of a third-floor curtain caught my eye. I blinked, and it hung still. I brushed it off as fatigue.

I was ready to fall into my bed fully clothed, eager to maximize the few hours I had before Wilfried would arrive for his daily visit. But I was not so weary that I had no fear of my brother. The last thing I did before surrendering to my bed was to place a chair in front of the doorway, so I would at least have some notice of any kind of disturbance.

CHAPTER TWENTY-TWO

My life fell into a comfortable pattern again for a couple of weeks after that. Visits from Wilfried. Sneaking out to visit the witches. The only drawback was that Ansel and Hansel seemed to be staying closer to home as well. I had a lingering suspicion that it was part of my father's aim to develop more of a relationship with Wilfried. But if the prince noticed, he showed no signs of awareness. Somehow, he always managed to steer us away from the company of my family swiftly and with tact.

One afternoon, we returned from the edge of the woods, where I'd shown Wilfried how to forage acorns, to find Ansel and Hansel together in the castle's front parlor. Queen Galen stood next to my father.

Wilfried and I bowed and curtsied before her.

"Your Majesty," I said, curiosity plain in my tone.

"Miss Henoth."

Wilfried led me over to a settee. "Mother, we were not expecting you. Is everything all right?"

"Of course, dearest. Lord Henoth simply wrote to me that he

had a proposal of interest and I felt it high time I see where you're spending all of your spare minutes these days."

"Her Majesty and I agree that it's past time for your engagement ball," Ansel declared.

The queen nodded, the corners of her eyes tight. "We wish our peers and subjects to know that all is moving along as it should with regard to your relationship and wedding."

"Since Her Majesty and you, Your Highness, have been so gracious to offer the palace for the wedding ceremony and reception afterward—"

"Well, it is tradition," Wilfried said, sharper than usual.

Ansel was uncharacteristically full of diplomacy. "Quite so, Your Highness, quite so. Nevertheless, I felt duty bound to repay your hospitality with a small token of my own. Thus, I requested of the queen that we might host the ball here, at our estate."

"To which I have agreed, with the stipulation that we shall preside over the festivities together," said the queen. "We wish the public to see our families as a united front, do we not?"

I stole a glance at my brother, who'd been silent for the entire exchange. His expression was passive, which in itself was likely calculated. But he did not say anything and so I could not object to his behavior. Meanwhile, Ansel and the queen looked far too cordial for my taste or comfort. I wanted to believe the queen was impervious to my father's questionable charms, but I did not know her well enough to have full confidence.

Nevertheless, I put on my own diplomatic smile. "Your Majesty,

I am honored, of course. Thank you for your continued graciousness toward our family."

"And I trust anything that you do, Mother."

We moved through the process of goodbyes.

"I will return first thing in the morning, alongside my son and the handful of staff I've chosen to shepherd this project with me." The queen looked at me as she spoke.

"We look forward to it, Your Majesty," Ansel said.

I looked around for Hansel, but he had quietly slipped out of the room.

As we all made our way toward the entry hall, I stopped Wilfried, holding him back as our parents continued forward. "May I speak to you for a moment before you leave?"

"Of course."

He followed me into a side room. "I do not like this cordiality that is arising between my father and your mother. I mean no disrespect to the queen, of course, but he is sly."

Wilfried's shoulders relaxed. "Ah, you need not worry. My mother only keeps the peace for your sake. Fret not, I am not the only one in our household who possesses clear eyes with regard to your well-being."

"You really believe so?"

"I know so. Whatever niceties with which my mother is engaging, I can assure you: They are on your behalf."

I remained unconvinced, but I had to trust him. "Of course. You know her best. Thank you for indulging me."

"Wilfried?" the queen called from the other room.

"I must go. Don't worry, we'll manage this together." He squeezed my shoulder and took off to join his mother.

The rest of the week went by in a flurry of preparations for the ball. I felt as if I didn't sleep more than an hour each night. There was always something to approve or try on or taste. It was almost like planning a second wedding, all while our first still had its own responsibilities that needed attending to.

At some point, I lost track of which was which and learned to just smile and nod alongside Wilfried. We must have appeared to be the most agreeable engaged couple in the kingdom. It was easy to be amenable when, underneath it all, none of our decisions were binding—for the wedding, at least. I made it through, drinking my body weight in tea and dodging any questions about my fatigued appearance.

The night before the ball, Wilfried and I finally found a stretch of time to relax. We'd just sequestered ourselves in chairs facing each other in a back corner of the castle library when one of the servants on loan from the palace for the festivities appeared.

"A package has arrived for you, Miss Henoth."

"Thank you, I will tend to it later." I yawned. "You may have it sent to my rooms if that suits."

"It has already been delivered to the parlor adjacent to your suite, Miss Henoth. I'm afraid, however, that I was instructed to inform you that it requires your immediate attention."

Following an exchanged look of relent, Wilfried and I hoisted ourselves from our seats and went to find out what was so urgent.

There was no package at all. The delivery was unwrapped and on display for us to see the moment we walked into the parlor.

An exquisite ball gown for me to wear the following night.

In the Crown's colors.

It was too much, too kind a gift from the queen when her reason for giving it was built on a lie.

"Please excuse me."

I ran from the parlor, holding back my tears until I reached the privacy of my own room. I flung myself onto my bed. But I made the mistake of not closing the door.

"Gretel, what is it?" Wilfried slipped inside and closed the door softly behind him. "If you don't like the gown, I am sure my mother would have no trouble securing an alternative."

"No, no, that is the last thing I want," I sobbed. "She has already been too kind."

He drew a chair to the side of my bed and sat.

"I don't understand, but I would like to."

His most common refrain. I'd lost count of how many times he'd repeated those words in the past few months, forever meeting me with patience.

I pushed myself up and faced him, snotty face and all. "Your mother has been so kind. *You* have been so kind. The staff members of both our households have worked themselves to the bone these past weeks to put the ball and the ceremony and the reception and this *idea* of my future in the palace together."

"Yes, it is a great deal of work, but—"

"And it is all a lie, Wilfried! They are all running in circles, because it is for nothing."

"Gretel, I—"

"I'm not upset with you and I am not ungrateful. I know the lengths you have gone to, to support me and keep me safe. My goodness, you've rearranged all of your days and managed to conduct so many of your royal duties removed from all the resources of the palace—"

"It was my choice and wish to do so—"

I held up a hand. "Please, let me finish."

He gestured for me to continue.

"I could never express how much your efforts mean to me. But, Wilfried, I saw that gown, with your family's colors, and it all became too much. I cannot continue pretending to your mother that this will all be worth something. Not when I know full well that someday—perhaps someday *soon*—you will break off this engagement and this entire pretense will all come crumbling down."

Defeated and spent, I buried my face in my hands. When I finally had the courage to look up in the ensuing silence, it was to find Wilfried kneeling before me.

"Marry me, Gretel."

"Sorry?"

"I mean it. Why should our engagement not be real? When first I suggested this arrangement, we were strangers. We're friends now, are we not?"

I nodded.

"My mother and I both adore you, as do the palace staff who've interacted with you. Even the Council is warming to the idea of another 'love match' in the tradition of my parents, instead of an arrangement for political gain."

"But I thought you wanted to be in love with the person you married?"

He was quiet for several moments as we each studied each other. I could not make out the meaning behind any of the emotions that flickered over his features in quick succession.

"Gretel." He took my hand. "I cannot imagine finding anyone with whom I enjoy spending time more than I do when I am with you. Though we find ourselves in strange circumstances, you make the prospect of the Crown's burden feel light. You are the only person of my acquaintance who has managed such a thing." His eyes were earnest, full of resilience and hope.

"I—"

Determination replaced his hopefulness. "And you will be safe, safe far from here."

A longing for his words to be true fluttered to life inside my chest.

"Even if we are only ever just friends," he continued, "that is a better marriage than many, especially among the nobility. I would never request of you that you say yes to such a binding agreement as this if you do not wish it."

I held my breath.

He clutched my hands now with both of his. "But you must know, Gretel: I do. I wish this with all my heart."

How could I refuse him? Even if it meant I would soon have to give up the second life I'd built my nights around—even if it meant losing Katharina and all the others—how could I say no? How could I push away the very offer of security I'd so longed for?

I could not.

So instead, I squeezed his hands in return and smiled through my tears. "I do, too. That is, yes. Yes, I will marry you."

"Actually marry me?"

"*Actually* marry you."

Then he was on his feet and we were hugging and he was spinning me around. And with each revolution, warring feelings rose within me.

I liked him. He had intrigued me from the moment we'd met. But with Wilfried, I had always believed that friendship was the best I could hope for. A life of safety was more than I'd dreamed possible before meeting him. And if he could offer me the gifts of both friendship and safety in exchange for me burying any inclination I had toward romance and a deeper desire to be loved?

Well then, I would accept his offer and I would not look back.

Twenty-four hours later, I stood before the closed doors to the ballroom. I was wearing the gown from his mother and reliving the promise we'd made over and over in my mind. In a moment, the doors would open and all of this would become actually, truly real.

I rolled my shoulders back and tried to pretend that someone had prepared me for this since I was born, that I hadn't been living in a one-room cottage less than a year ago, that I could make myself accept this new life. Because while it wasn't everything I dreamed of, it was far more than I'd ever expected to receive.

"Are you ready, miss?" the doorman asked, breaking into my thoughts.

I had to be.

"Yes."

The doors opened. I stepped into the room. Wilfried was waiting in the wings just on the other side, as he was supposed to.

"You look beautiful." He twirled me around, taking in the dress.

"Your Highness?" the doorman asked.

"We're ready," Wilfried said. He led me to the top of the staircase.

"Now presenting, His Royal Highness Prince Wilfried Claren Varnhagen and his betrothed, Miss Gretel Henoth."

The applause was polite and full. No matter how many members of the nobility might have resented that their own daughters or nieces or other assorted family members weren't gliding to the center of the room on the prince's arm, the prince and the queen were still well loved.

I let Wilfried guide me and allowed myself to float along the wave of—mostly—goodwill that surrounded us. We danced and danced and danced, pausing only to receive well-wishes on our upcoming nuptials, neither of us ever leaving the other's side.

"Are you happy?" Wilfried asked me as we floated around the room.

I lost myself in his open, vulnerable eyes. The kind of vulnerability I admired and longed to match.

"I am. I am happy," I whispered.

His shoulders relaxed. "We have so many nights like this ahead of us."

My heart leapt, thrilled at the promise in his words. I couldn't help it. Nights of beautiful gowns. Days of working by his side to improve the kingdom. A life beyond even the fairy-tale dreams I'd held as a child. Yes, it required trading the love I imagined in those dreams. But everything I would gain was worth it.

I beamed in the silence.

"And when we aren't on display for the world to see, nights of reading and coziness. Perhaps a dog." He paused. "Are you fond of dogs?"

"I think I am. We've never had one. There were lots of cats in our village. I liked them."

He lifted our arms and galloped us toward the center of the room as the musicians started playing a faster song. "We'll have one of each for good measure!"

Then he picked me up and spun me around for all the world to see.

It doesn't matter that it's mostly for show.

So I laughed and we whirled and I told myself everything would be okay.

There was a moment, just before midnight, when I met the gaze of my father from across the room. His face was pure greed and satisfaction.

I closed my eyes and imagined, for just a moment, what it might have been like if I lived in a world where my father was kind. A world where, when he looked at me, his eyes shone with unshed happy tears and his face beamed with pride.

Then I put that dream away, tucked it in alongside so many others, and focused on reality. I focused on the kind eyes of my fiancé—my dearest friend—and my *own* face beamed with pride for both of us and the way we'd concocted this plan together from the start.

I finally felt safe. At last, I was a part of something important, something strong, and warm, and dependable.

Without warning, panic pricked at me for the witches. What of Ansel and Hansel's plans for them?

Just as quickly as the fear rose and threatened to topple me, I pushed it down. After all, marrying Wilfried was my best chance at gaining enough authority in this world to stop my father and brother. I would hold fast to my plans and find a way to make sure we could all live free from fear of Ansel and Hansel.

Thinking of freedom, I had the briefest flash of a much different world, one where I ran away and lived among the witches and never married any man—even the kindest one I knew. I allowed myself one moment to imagine that story.

And then I turned the page.

CHAPTER TWENTY-THREE

Knowing that the wedding would now be real made everything easier. Where before I'd focused on resisting anything good because it was only a matter of time before it was snatched away from me, I now found that I was able to embrace the joy of planning my future.

Thus it was that I found myself back at the palace for my second stay and filled with more excitement than anything else.

Wilfried practically bounded down the palace steps to greet me. "Mother has turned half a wing of the palace into our own personal collection of showrooms. Prepare yourself."

"I think the ball prepared me for a lifetime of decision-making."

He made a show of hushing me. "Shh, not so loud. She'll hear you and be too encouraged."

We bantered back and forth the rest of the way. The queen was waiting to receive us as soon as we entered the first of the temporary showrooms. Wilfried hadn't exaggerated with regard to the extravagance.

"Ah, isn't it lovely to see you two laughing together," the queen said, smiling.

"Because historically we are known to be rather somber in each other's presence, Mother."

The queen raised her eyebrows. "You jest, but you'll need to keep that sense of humor. Wedding planning has splintered many a relationship before yours."

"We plan to approach this endeavor with the utmost stoicism," I said, mimicking Wilfried's stone-faced expression.

"Miss Henoth, are you joking at the expense of your queen?"

I bowed my head. "N-no, Your Majesty. Of course not. I apologize, Your Majesty."

"She is teasing you," Wilfried stage-whispered into my ear. "Unfair of her, in my opinion."

Queen Galen put her hand to her chest in shock. "Am I not allowed a little fun?"

It was easy to see from whom Wilfried inherited his antics.

"Not when it comes at the expense of my fiancée, Mother, no."

"I will endeavor to improve myself."

"That is all I ask."

He winked at his mother and they shared a smile. Not two seconds later, the queen's wedding planner marched into the room.

She was all business. "Now, first we must decide on the linens for the table settings . . ."

And that was just the start of it. The planner led us through a series of rooms and choices, so many I was certain a team of servants must have been transforming them from one setup to the next as soon as we exited for a different room. Even the palace couldn't have been that large. Despite the fact that it was exhausting, I enjoyed it. Wilfried and I worked well together, easily finding compromise on most decisions, and speaking in unison several times.

Until it was time to decide on the cake flavor.

The servants ushered us into yet another open room, then over to a table set with samples of almost two dozen cakes.

"This must have taken half your sugar stores," I joked weakly as I sank into the chair Wilfried pulled out for me.

He leaned over my shoulder. "I told you not to tempt my mother's flair for excess."

"I'll never question you again."

"Let's not be hasty, darling," he whispered just for me to hear.

A warm, gooey feeling sweeter than any confectionery swooped through me.

Six variations of chocolate, two types of imported citrus, and an unconscionable number of nut and fruit flavors later, I was ready to disavow the concept of food.

"I liked the hazelnut," Wilfried said.

I forced myself to smile through my fatigue. "Yes, so did I."

"Or we could do the lemon. That would be an interesting experiment."

"The lemon was refreshing."

"Yes, quite." A frown played at the corners of his mouth.

He stood and stretched his arms overhead, darted a glance at me before turning his attention to the ceiling. "Or vanilla might be a good familiar option."

"Everyone loves tradition," I yawned.

"Argh!" Wilfried raked his hands through his hair, pulling at the ends as he turned away from me.

I was suddenly no longer tired. My entire body was on alert. I froze, unsure why he was mad or how to fix it. I racked my brain for any words I could share to repair my mistake, coming up empty. I had never been the subject of his anger before and didn't know him well enough to manage his feelings.

His hands fell to his sides and his shoulders slumped. All the fight had gone out of him as suddenly as it came. "I am sorry."

"Wh-what is wrong?"

"You agree with everything I say."

"I am incredibly agreeable," I quipped.

My effort to coax a smile from him fell flat.

His expression was bleak as his eyes met mine. "That is exactly the problem."

"I do not understand."

"Gretel, I do not want a wife who functions only as an embodied affirmation of my own opinions."

His tone was not harsh, but disappointment wove through every syllable of his words, which was somehow worse. It hit me deeper than disdain or anger. Fear lanced through me: I was a stranger to this no-man's-land that camped in the valley between amiability and cruelty.

"Say something," he pleaded.

I stood, hands shaking. An attempt to place us on equal ground. "I . . . I don't know what to say."

"Tell me what you are thinking, *tell* me what you want!"

I raised my voice to match his. "It's harder to when you yell!"

His mouth popped open. It was difficult to say which one of us was more taken aback.

Then understanding washed over him.

In seconds, he was on my side of the table, reaching toward me.

I stepped back.

He held his hands up and retreated. "I don't mean to hurt you."

Across the room, the door opened, revealing one of the queen's advisers. "Your Highness, I am afraid we need your counsel on a report regarding the latest grain shipments to Dron."

Wilfried transformed into the royal version of himself. "Of course, Hockley. I won't be a moment. Wait for me outside."

"Yes, Your Highness."

"We will speak later?" he asked me.

I nodded.

He opened his mouth, thought better of it, then bowed his head to me before taking his leave.

I was alone.

I wandered over to stand before the windows that looked over the gardens. Traced my eyes over the paths we walked during my first visit here. Back when the mere notion of fighting with him had never crossed my mind.

Ever since he'd caught up to me in the woods and explained himself the night of Hansel's ball, not a single harsh word had passed between us. Yet I'd spent the past two months balancing myself on a razor's edge. Why? He was as different from Hansel and Ansel as a man could be, but the thought of crossing him terrified me.

Would my father and brother always haunt me this way? Would I spend my life anticipating cruelty even from those who were consistently kind?

"You two really do work well together."

I startled at the queen's voice. Her words reverberated off the walls. I turned and curtsied without thought, wiping away any stray tears with the back of my hand.

"Oh, Your Majesty, I did not hear you come in."

I met her in the center of the room.

"The prince has been called into a meeting. I was admiring your gardens," I explained.

"Miss Henoth, I will admit I harbored some reservations following our tea with your father and brother, but your solo visits here have proven something to me."

"Your Majesty?"

"You and my son truly are well suited to each other."

"Thank you, ma'am." I inclined my head.

Would she have said as much if she'd witnessed the end of our conversation this afternoon?

"I believe you will have an enduring friendship at the center of your marriage, which is rarer than it should be. That bond will see you through the darkest times. I know from experience."

"I've often heard tell of the great love you shared with the late king, but I did not realize that you were such close friends as well." I willed a smile onto my face.

She looped her arm through mine. "Oh, my dear, it was our friendship that made the love so rich."

Was she aware that friendship was the only thing our marriage would ever amount to? *If we can even manage that.*

It was difficult to believe she would feel so happy about the prospect of a long-lasting platonic companionship if she knew that it meant her son would likely never know a great love alongside it.

That night I was reading in bed, my heart still heavy from the afternoon, when there was a soft knock from behind one of the walls.

I set aside my book and waited.

There it was again. No, two knocks this time.

I curled my knees to my chest. Something or some*one* was

inside the wall. I reached for the candlestick on the bedside table to use as a makeshift weapon.

"Gretel, it's me," a voice whispered.

Impossible.

I prepared myself to face an impostor as a hidden door in the wall suddenly opened.

I stifled a yelp with my hand, then regretted it.

I should *scream.*

Had I just thrown away my one chance to call for help?

But then Wilfried stepped around the door.

"It *is* you! How?"

He held a finger to his lips and a hand out to me. I donned the robe and slippers next to the bed and followed him.

When we emerged from the dim tunnel, we were in the small room just off the grand ballroom. He beckoned me on, through the room and out to the terrace.

The terrace where we first met. We settled against the stone railing, looking out on the grounds instead of at each other.

"I worried your maid might hear us in your room," he offered as an explanation.

"The palace has secret passageways?"

"Of course. A relic of war. Now they're more convenient for . . . other uses."

"I see."

"I want to talk about this afternoon."

I pulled the robe tighter around me, the only protection I had.

"I apologize for frightening you." His voice was gentle. Too gentle.

Every unsettling feeling I'd shoved down hours ago came rushing up like spoiled food.

"I don't want to upset you." I choked on a sob. "I don't want you to regret this. I don't want to be a problem."

I moved away, hiding my face in my hands.

When he spoke, it was clear he hadn't moved any closer, that he was keeping a distance until I bade him otherwise. "You are the furthest thing from a problem."

"You say that now. What if you dislike one of my opinions in the future?"

"Well, we'll talk about it."

I faced him again, searching for any hint of condescension. I found none. Only patience. "And if we fight?"

"We can disagree without fighting."

I chewed my bottom lip. He could have spoken in French and it wouldn't have been any less comprehensible to me.

"Gretel." He dared a step closer. "I know that I will never understand all that you have endured. What I can promise you is that I will do everything in my power to ensure you never have to face anything of the kind here."

I studied my feet. If I looked at him, I would cry. "How can you be sure?"

He brought his hand up near my face but didn't touch me.

He let it be my choice.

I held my breath and leaned into his embrace. Unbidden, a sigh escaped me. Relief that I couldn't name. Despite my efforts, tears squeezed from the corners of my eyes. When they ran over his fingers, he didn't flinch or pull away. Simply brushed his thumbs across my cheeks and tilted my face until I was looking at him.

"We'll make mistakes. Together. We'll grow together. And someday, I hope I'll earn enough of your trust that you feel safe here. Always."

"Okay," I squeaked out as my throat closed up with emotion.

He pulled me into his arms and my bones melted against him. I'd almost forgotten how good it felt to be held like this.

Oh, if only I could let myself love you.

We stood that way until we were both shivering from the night's chill.

When we returned to my room, Wilfried insisted upon sleeping on the floor so he could be nearby.

"It worked last time. If nightmares plague you again, I'll be at your side before you awaken." He struck the pose of an assassin, ready to apprehend its quarry.

"You did do an admirable job last time."

He maintained his serious front. "See? I have a reputation to uphold."

Whether it was knowing that someone who cared about me slept so nearby, or because I was finally confident that I would be free from Ansel and Hansel very soon, I slept through the entire night for the first time in too many months.

Mrs. Chambers was standing in the center of the entryway when I returned home the next afternoon, hands crossed over each other. So still, she might have been a part of the architecture. The castle had an extra hush to it, a layer of murk compounded by the relatively few candles that were lit—too few, for this late in the day.

"Mrs. Chambers. I did not expect that you would be here to greet me."

She did not move.

I stepped back. Although we had faced off from time to time, she'd never been so overtly cold to me.

At last, she responded, though she remained in her place. "Your father and brother have returned to town for some important business. They plan to stay the night."

I did not wish to prolong the conversation; I stuck to the basic necessaries. "Do you know when they will return?"

"They are taking the carriage. I would wager they'll be gone at least through tomorrow night."

That meant I would spend all of tomorrow alone.

With profuse apologies, Wilfried had told me before I left the palace that he also had to deal with some urgent business a half-day's journey away. He would not return for two days.

"Thank you for informing me, Mrs. Chambers. I will have dinner in my room tonight."

She stepped aside for me to pass her. "I will have Polly bring you a tray."

"I have already prepared one, Mother." Polly breezed into the room as she spoke, her smile the first bit of true light amidst the gloom of the castle. "And I can keep you company if you'd like, Miss Gretel."

"Thank you, Polly. That would be nice."

Mrs. Chambers sniffed, but she said nothing. The brusque echo of her heels against the stones as she left the room was more than enough of a statement.

"Off we go, miss." Polly took the stairs two at a time, giving herself enough of a head start to reach my room ahead of me and have everything set up when I arrived.

I was slower. Loath to leave my traveling case behind, I negotiated it up each stair with no little effort. At the landing, I paused for a break near the servants' stairs.

The walls were . . . whispering?

Yes, I was hearing voices. But it was difficult to place them. I could make out snatches of their conversation, but not who spoke or what they were saying.

I set down my bag and tiptoed to the door, then pressed my ear against the wallpaper.

"Why should we alter our plans just because she has acted irrationally?"

I clapped a hand over my mouth to muffle my gasp. It was Hansel. Just on the other side.

He went back and forth with someone for several sentences, but the words were too muffled for me to make any of them out. I covered my left ear and pressed the right harder against the wood.

". . . simple fact: She is going to be queen." Ansel.

But Mrs. Chambers had declared so forcefully that he and Hansel had already departed for town . . .

They were moving farther away, their footfalls drowning out their words. Why would they be using the servants' stairs? I could think of few people with more disdain for such places.

"Gretel Henoth," Mrs. Chambers's voice barreled up the stairs.

All sound on the other side of the wall stopped.

"What *are* you doing?!" she continued. "To your room with you at once. If Polly cannot be trusted with your supervision, your father will be forced to find someone who can." It was strange to see her so changed. Though she was often sharp, she seldom spoke to anyone with such derision—certainly not anyone who wasn't a member of the staff. Despite the frequency with which she disapproved of my decisions, her old-fashioned respect for hierarchy had softened her criticism.

Until now.

I grabbed my bag and bolted to my room without another word.

Polly looked up as soon as I entered. Her expression morphed to one of concern as she took in my scattered appearance, noted my short bursts of breath. "Gretel, what is wrong?"

"I do not know," I answered honestly.

For I was dumbfounded by Mrs. Chambers's descent into such hostility. Confused by the apparent lie that my father and brother were already gone. Rattled by the snippets of their unsettling, unseen exchange that I still needed to decipher.

Yet as I handed my bag off to Polly, a desire to set all of it aside overcame me. For weeks I'd been pulled in all directions; here, at last, was the opportunity to spend a quiet evening with the person I'd known longest in this new life. The one I'd trusted on sight. I did not want to throw that away.

I forced myself to smile, let my problems slide from my shoulders into a box I would deal with later. "But I am certain it will keep. Let us not worry about any of it now."

I settled at the small table and tucked into the soup she'd set out for me.

"How was your stay at the palace this time?"

Strange. Comforting. Unsettling. Almost too good to trust.

I could not burden her with all that.

"Lovely. The queen and Prince Wilfried are excellent hosts, which was to be expected."

Noting my formality, she did not press further.

"How wonderful."

I wiped my hands before placing one over hers. "All of your lessons have been invaluable, Polly."

We both chuckled, each of us perhaps remembering what a disaster I was only months ago.

"Truly, Polly, I fear the prince would have dissolved our engagement immediately if you hadn't prepared me so well. To that point, it may never have happened at all without your guidance."

She squeezed my hand. "I am pleased to be useful."

"And *I* am pleased to think of all the wonderful years we have ahead of us. You'll love palace life, I am sure of it."

A shadow passed over her face as she sat back in her seat, folded her hands in her lap. "I will not be going to the palace."

"Of course you will. Wilfried has already assured me that I may bring any of the staff I choose. Frida and Annika will also come."

"Yes, because, in their positions, Frida and Annika will merely require training for a new household."

I shook my head at her, not understanding.

"You will not need a governess as a married woman, Gretel."

I could not name the sensation that washed over me alongside comprehension, but I did not like it. I crossed my arms, not caring if I looked like a petulant child.

"No." I pushed myself away from the table and paced. "No, I cannot leave you here."

"Do not fret, I will find another position."

"Another position where you will be treated abominably! I won't allow it, Polly. I won't. I will speak to Wilfried! I will speak to the *queen*! I know they would not wish you to suffer—"

She stood and caught me by my shoulders, stopping me

mid-stride and mid-speech. "This is the way things are done. If you are going to be queen someday, you cannot merely understand the ways of this world—you must accept them."

The only thing that stayed my tears was seeing the sheen in her own eyes. All the fight left me in one deep sigh of surrender; if this was difficult for me, how much more would it be for her? While I was living out my lavish princess dreams, she would be toiling beneath the thumb of new employers and yet another charge who was accustomed to seeing her as less than.

"Perhaps I am not fit to be queen."

Polly straightened her spine and fixed me with a firm look the likes of which I hadn't seen since our early lessons. "Then you must summon the wherewithal to rise to the occasion. Too many depend upon having a queen such as you succeed Queen Galen."

"What if I am not enough?" The question had plagued me since I first accepted Wilfried's real proposal.

She placed gentle hands on my cheeks and softened her gaze. "On our own, none of us ever are. But you are not alone."

Her words scratched something at the back of my mind, though I could not quite catch the shape of it. Before I could question her further, she'd turned away to clear the remainder of my supper.

"Now, to bed with you, before *someone* finds reason to come after us both."

I nodded and let her leave.

It was only later, after Annika and Frida had prepared me for bed and I was lying in my dark room alone once again, that I recalled Hansel and Ansel's conversation. The bits of it that I could hear, anyway.

I tossed and turned all night, wondering why Mrs. Chambers had lied and told me they were already gone.

At the first signs of light, I dressed and crept outside to check the stables.

The carriage was indeed missing. So were their horses.

Perhaps I'd been mistaken. Maybe I'd only overheard two of the male servants. The wall had muffled everything, after all. It was more than plausible that the barrier had also created a distortion of the voices.

"I was tired and confused last night. Nothing more."

Strangely, the fact that I was talking to myself did not do much to reassure me that all was well.

I snuck back inside, on alert for Mrs. Chambers to come storming across my path at any moment. But the castle seemed emptier than ever before. At this time of morning, I could usually hear the quiet hum of activity from the servants going about their morning responsibilities. Instead, there was an eerie silence. So thick, I doubted whether even a strong draft could break through the gloom.

I did not dare venture in search of breakfast. I needed answers more than food.

Emboldened by the strange quiet and the certainty that it would be empty, I set out for Ansel's office.

This round, I wasted no time. I dove right into his correspondence, looking for information that would make sense of my jumbled worries.

I did not have to search for long.

Nestled in between inconsequential reports regarding trade shipments, I discovered an agreement signed between my father and a mercenary. I sank to the floor to read it.

For weeks I'd pushed away the guilt that gnawed at me every time I visited Galwin and did not dilvulge the dangerous plans Ansel and Hansel were laying the groundwork to enact upon the witches come springtime. I told myself I needed to be in a position of power to do anything. I told myself I had time.

Time to spend in the escape of their hospitality.

Time to earn their trust.

Time to warn them.

Time to convince them I was not like my family.

With me set to become a princess, however, my father sought to push up his timeline. They would begin taking action against the witches late this winter into early spring

But the case they would build against the witches was only a foundation for their ultimate betrayal, which was to take place immediately after my wedding.

First, they would frame the witches for the crime.

Then they would leverage the prince's grief to convince him to issue a license to kill, harm, and steal from all witches. Which would, in turn, enable Ansel and Hansel to declare an all-out assault against them. All of it would be carried out under the guise of revenge.

I stepped back from the desk with shaking hands and unsteady feet, my mind reeling as I tried to absorb what I'd just read, in my father's own words.

They were going to kill me.

CHAPTER TWENTY-FOUR

I could not stay there. Propelled by terror, I saddled a horse, Snip, from our stables and set out for the palace.

I took nothing and told no one before I left.

Rain pelted down on me in sweeping sheets as our castle receded in the background. I regretted not grabbing at least a cloak, but what if those spared minutes were significant? If I'd taken the time to pack anything, that might have provided Mrs. Chambers with the opportunity to station herself outside my bedroom and delay me. I would suffer through the wet, chilly ride and hope that it paid off in the end.

Relying on muscle memory from my few trips to the palace, I spurred Snip onward. I just needed to make it to the palace. I would be safe inside its walls. I nudged the horse's sides as I flattened my torso over its back, until we were moving at a sustainable canter. The world became a blur.

The moment the palace gates came into view, peace washed over me. I was still afraid, but I clung to a renewed faith that I could solve all of this. I just needed help to do so.

I slid from the saddle and faced the guards with my head held high, resisting the urge to wipe the rain from my eyes. "I need to see Prince Wilfried."

The guards exchanged a look.

"Please, it is urgent."

I imagined they had never faced an issue such as the quandary I now presented. "How to respond to the future queen arriving at the palace's doorstep, drenched and lacking a chaperone" seemed an unlikely training topic. All the same, I would be a princess soon. Perhaps it was time I started acting like one.

"I have no desire to stand here and catch my death of cold. Both the prince and the queen would disapprove, I'm sure."

To my credit and theirs, they stood up to full attention. The guard on the left motioned me forward.

"Please, follow us, miss."

They escorted me inside.

The butler and housekeeper approached us in unison, but he quickly took a step back and surveyed the scene, leaving her to deal with me.

"Miss Henoth, Prince Wilfried has not yet returned from his trip. I assume this is an unexpected call?" The housekeeper frowned.

I thought Wilfried said that the staff all liked me . . .

"Yes, but please, I must wait for him to return."

She unfolded and refolded her hands, as if the very idea of my doing so caused her discomfort she was too professional to betray. "That would be most unusual. The palace does not make a habit of entertaining guests without proper warning."

"I understand, but this is urgent. I cannot imagine that the prince would wish for you to turn me away." I would do whatever I needed to avoid returning to the castle.

She glanced over her shoulder. The butler gave the tiniest shake of his head.

I did not wait for them to respond after that.

"May I have an audience with the queen instead?" I begged. "I feel confident she would like to know my business in coming here."

It was a desperate gamble. I could not be sure that her favor extended to me interrupting the middle of her day.

Still, she surely remembered how it felt to be a young, common girl standing on the precipice of marrying a future king. I hoped that memory would move her to take pity upon me.

The housekeeper did not seem pleased with the request. "I will alert Her Majesty that you have arrived."

"There will be no need."

All of us turned in the direction of the queen's voice.

"Your Majesty," we chorused, bowing and curtsying as one.

"Ms. Swithins, have you quite forgotten that remaining in wet clothes for a prolonged period of time can cause a chill?" The queen moved toward us, eyes on me though she spoke to the housekeeper.

"No, ma'am."

"Then I fail to understand why poor Miss Henoth is still standing here dripping on my floors." She waved in my direction, as if

Ms. Swithins might have simply not noticed that I was soaked to the bone. "Is it your intention for us to have a sickly future princess?"

"Of course not, Your Majesty," Ms. Swithins said, eyes downcast.

"Then do have someone fetch our guest, my future *daughter-in-law*, a fresh set of clothing."

Her words sent a tingle down my spine. She'd publicly declared me as close to family as possible.

The housekeeper curtsied. "Right away, ma'am."

"Now, Miss Henoth, is it strictly necessary that we speak this instant?"

If I answered yes, I would have an immediate audience with the queen, that was clear. But if I said no, I might be able to bide my time and prolong my stay at the palace. Or, at the very least, delay my return to the castle.

"No, Your Majesty. So long as I can stay, it can wait."

"Of course you can stay, child. That was never in question." She turned to the butler. "James, please have one of the maids draw a bath for Miss Henoth so she can change into dry clothing. Afterward, she and I will meet in my private sitting room."

"Yes, ma'am. Miss Henoth, follow me." James was better at hiding his disdain than Ms. Swithins was.

"Thank you, Your Majesty."

I lingered in the bath, contemplating my options and enjoying the tranquil solitude, so different from my constant nervousness in the castle. I had not prepared to share all the information I found with the queen before speaking to Wilfried. But if I wanted her to understand the extent of my situation, that would require telling her things about my life that even the prince did not yet know.

Wilfried, for whatever reason, did not share the same prejudices against witches that I had been raised with. Still, I could not be certain of the queen's views. It was entirely possible that she would call off the wedding once she found out that I had been associating with the witches in the village.

That was a risk I would have to take.

Once I was deemed suitably dry and refreshed, I joined the queen in her sitting room. We settled in with two cups of tea. I surreptitiously surveyed her over the edge of my cup but said nothing. I waited for her to address me.

"Now, Miss Henoth, please explain to me what is so dire that it moved you to ride all the way from your father's estate, unchaperoned, in the pouring rain?"

I curled and uncurled my toes in my shoes, fighting off the nervousness coursing through my body. "It's a bit of a long story."

"You have my leave to tell it."

So I did. I told her about seeing Katharina at the edge of the palace grounds on the night of Wilfried's birthday celebrations and escaping out onto the terrace with the intent to follow her, until I ran into Wilfried.

I recounted seeing her again behind the castle. I told her of the first time Hansel attacked me, my flight to the forest after. I admitted that when the fox appeared at my lowest moment, I allowed him to lead me to Katharina, then I followed her all the way to the village.

I acknowledged that I had, of course, been raised to fear witches and hold them in contempt. I confessed that, in spite of such conditioning, the witches I had come to know and respect were nothing like the stories. That I had, in fact, befriended them over time.

I did not reveal what Katharina had told me about the village's wards or their other protective measures, but I did suggest that I often wondered if the rumors about the witches were nothing more than that: rumors.

Finally, I revealed the truth about sneaking into my father's study and the revelations I'd uncovered by going through his paperwork and correspondence. I admitted that when I first spied upon him, he and my brother had intended only to harm the witches many months from now, and I thought I had more time. But now they were plotting to kill *me* shortly after Wilfried and I were wed and blame it on the witches to stoke more hatred against them.

The queen was silent.

I mentally counted backward from one hundred to keep myself from losing any shred of decorum and running from the room in fear of what she might say.

When I reached fifty, I could bear it no longer.

"I apologize for taking up so much of your time, Your Majesty.

I will excuse myself." To where, I was uncertain, but I rose as if I had an intended destination all the same.

The queen rose as well. "Gretel, follow me."

This was the first time she'd addressed me by my given name. I did not know if it boded well or ill, so I said nothing as I followed her through the sitting room and into her bedchamber.

It was a beautiful room, well-appointed in rich colors and fabrics befitting a queen. But I took almost no notice, because the queen was swiftly making her way toward another door on the opposite wall. She pulled a wine-colored key from the center of her bodice. The air shimmered with a new energy.

"You have trusted me with some of your secrets, and now I ask you: May I do the same? Can I trust your sense of discretion?"

I nodded mutely, not daring even to breathe.

She held the door open for me and I entered first.

The scent of rosemary and salt filled the air, cloaking a deeper aroma of the woods. Every surface of the many shelves and scattered side tables held a mix of herbs, precious stones and jewels, and vials filled with various tinctures. At the center of the room, an altar contained a small collection of portraits, dried flowers, and scraps of lace.

The door snicked shut behind us, breaking me from my reverie.

I turned to face the queen, eyes wide and mind whirling. "You are a witch."

CHAPTER TWENTY-FIVE

"Before I married the late king, I spent many nights in Galwin. I was an active member of the community of witches you know."

"Was the king aware?"

"He was. We fell in love first, when he was none the wiser. But I wanted a full love, with someone who knew the whole of me and embraced each piece."

"Which he did?"

"Yes. He never wavered for a moment. I believe that he always trusted me, but when he discovered that I could protect our home and cover over the residual fear he experienced after the war, that certainly helped convince him that my craft was not a negative thing."

"The peace I feel here . . . I've always felt safer here. Is it because you have . . ." I trailed off. I would let her say it.

"Wards? Yes." She motioned to two small stools and indicated for me to sit. "Magic is not the only reason you feel safe here, Gretel. You are also not among those who would harm you for their personal gain."

I shifted uncomfortably on my stool. Even now, it was difficult to lump Hansel in with our father. Acknowledging to myself the sinister person he'd become had been painful enough—it was worse hearing the implications from someone else. I shifted the direction of the conversation. "Do you still visit the village?"

"No. A few times, years ago, but never since the king passed. It is not safe. I would leave Wilfried in too vulnerable of a position if something were to happen to me."

"I imagine you must miss it a great deal."

"Yes. The witches themselves, especially. Orlantha is my oldest and dearest friend from childhood."

"Is that portrait of her?" I gestured to a miniature that sat on a small altar next to a portrait of the king.

Once again, the queen was silent for several moments. She stared at the altar for some time before speaking. "No," she whispered at last. Her voice was thick. "That portrait is of my sister, Viola. She and Orlantha were the same age, but she died when we were children. Stoneground fever."

"Oh, Your Majesty. I am sorry. What a terrible loss for you."

"Thank you, Gretel." She tilted her head back and pinched the bridge of her nose. "I've heard you lost your mother the same way."

I nodded, tears threatening. I did not want to cry in front of her. I needed to maintain the conversation, to give us both something solid to grab on to.

I gestured once more to the portrait. "That must have been before the tonic."

"Indeed. The loss of Viola was my impetus for joining the witches, in fact. I was determined to find or create a cure."

"You created the stoneground fever tonic?"

She nodded.

"But you must have been so young."

"I was seventeen the year the first doses went out." She was looking far over my shoulder now, transported back to a different time altogether.

"The year before you were engaged to the king. You were my age."

"Yes."

"Your Majesty . . . forgive me if I am speaking out of turn, but . . . well . . ."

"Speak freely, child," she ordered, not unkindly.

"I also had the fever, alongside my mother. We both took the tonic. You saved my life."

She studied me in silence once more. She appeared to weigh her next words with care, opening her mouth and then closing it several times without saying anything. At last, she cleared her throat, swallowing hard before finally responding. "You remember your mother taking the tonic? You were very small, I'm sure."

I shook my head. "My father told me. He thinks the tonic was responsible for her death."

"I see."

"But I do not!" I hastened to add. "Not anymore."

Her expression was somber. "I am sorry that we couldn't save your mother, Gretel."

"You saved me," I reiterated.

I considered the effect of her efforts, how the tonic was like a stone dropped into the waters of our realm, its impact forever expanding. What other ripples might the queen have created, if she hadn't married the king?

Frustration replaced my reverence.

"You changed the lives of so many. How were you able to walk away . . . for love? Think of all you could have accomplished!" A tiny voice in the back of my mind reminded me that I was scolding a woman who could have me arrested at any moment, but I was too vexed to heed it.

If she was taken aback by my response, she did not show it. "There are many ways to change the world, Gretel."

"Yes, but—"

"Though I am not able to live in concert with my sisters the way I did once, I have continued my work here, in private. I share my discoveries with Orlantha and the others through secret correspondence. In the meantime, I use my position as queen to maneuver the levers of power in other ways."

She sounded so confident, so assured of her position. I let her words turn over in my mind and tried to imagine feeling that secure. At least it was clear where Wilfried had learned his opinions on the witches.

"Wilfried once told me I did not need to fear the witches. I understand why now. Is everything I've been told a lie, then?"

"What have you experienced for yourself?"

"The exact opposite of my fears. I know not what to think."

"Is that so? Or are you simply afraid to accept your own thoughts, with no one to approve them for you?"

I gaped at her, unsure what to say and in awe. It was no wonder that Wilfried spoke his mind so freely. What would it have been like, to grow up with a mother so keen on me thinking for myself? Guilt gnawed at me for judging her just moments before. "The first night I met them, the little ones were all so excited that I was marrying Wilfried. Everyone in Galwin must truly admire you still."

"Making them proud has been one of my primary efforts during my time as queen."

"It has?"

"Ever since I ascended the throne, I have endeavored to gently steer public opinion in the direction of favor toward the witches."

"If the king agreed with you, why did he not just decree safety for them?"

"The king supported me, but we both knew something important that you must learn before you rule alongside my son."

"What is that?"

"You must sway public opinion before shifting laws or handing down mandates. We could have ordered our subjects to accept the witches into public society, but they were not ready for that. If the Crown moves against the will of the people, the people will move against the Crown. And then where would that leave those who depend upon our support—including the witches?"

I thought of the Wood Witch. Would she still be alive if the king and queen had made bolder choices? My own guilt and my judgment of the royal family teemed inside me. "What did you do instead?"

"I have done my best to plant seeds that might someday give people a reason to change their minds."

"It's slow work."

"It is," she agreed. "As will be whatever retaliation you wish to take against your father and brother. Right now, all you have is your word against theirs. We cannot take immediate or direct action with that."

Every hope I'd had that she might be considering helping me drained out of my body. "But—"

She held up a hand, halting me. "As a queen without a king, I cannot risk my Council determining that my actions are hasty or unfounded, motivated by emotion."

I slumped back in my stool. I understood then, though I did not want to. Before she was a queen, she was a woman. She, too, had to shape her choices around the moods of men.

I did not know what I would do now, but this much was clear: I could not ask her to risk her crown, maybe even her life, to help me. Nor would I ask Wilfried to do the same. I would have to make my way forward alone.

"Thank you, Your Majesty, for your confidence and your discretion." I curtsied and prepared myself to take the next step in this perilous journey alone.

There was still a little light yet. I would try to find my way to Galwin without crossing through my father's estate. Perhaps my little fox friend would appear once more to aid me. If I was successful, I would throw myself upon the witches' hospitality; I wasn't the first runaway they'd sheltered in exchange for a set of helpful hands.

When Wilfried returned from his trip, I would visit the palace one last time to explain and break off our engagement. I could not risk placing either of us or the witches in more danger through our marriage.

The queen touched my elbow as I made to pass her. "Are you saying goodbye, Gretel?"

I lowered my gaze and laced my fingers before me. "I believe that is best, Your Majesty."

"I did not expect you to give up so easily."

My head snapped up. "I thought—"

"That because I cannot do everything, I am willing to do nothing? This position is a constant balancing act, Gretel. You must learn this if you are to one day become queen yourself."

She stood and we were eye to eye. I held my breath, too afraid to hope again just yet.

"We will send word through my lady's maid for Orlantha and Katharina to join us here at the palace."

"Tonight?"

"In the morning. We should give them time to make arrangements for their absence."

I nodded.

She wrapped an arm around my shoulders and steered me back toward the sitting room. "For now, you and I will have a quick supper here, and then? To bed, for both of us. Tomorrow will be a long day."

CHAPTER TWENTY-SIX

Orlantha and Katharina arrived without fanfare through the servants' entrance at first light and were met by the queen's most trusted lady's maid, Lina. The four of us sequestered ourselves in the queen's chamber under strict orders of no disturbance and set to work at once.

"This is quite the predicament, Galen," Orlantha pronounced when the queen and I had updated her and Katharina.

The queen covered her friend's hand with her own. "We have triumphed over great dangers together before and we will do it again."

Only a few moments passed, but it seemed the two of them had an entire conversation with their eyes.

Orlantha turned to me. "Can you handle this, Gretel?"

"Handle what . . . specifically?"

"You have not told her what you are thinking?" The shock on the older witch's face told me I had missed something crucial.

"Told me what?"

The queen addressed Orlantha, as if I had not spoken. "I wanted to wait until we could work out the details together."

"The details of what?"

"You'll have to go back, Gretel," Katharina whispered. "To the castle."

At last, the queen faced me. "At least some of the time. You will be our spy."

"You can keep us abreast of where they plan to attack and when," Orlantha explained.

"So we can position ourselves to respond quickly in the aftermath of the attack," Katharina added.

"Even if I'm able to alert you, how will you respond? What will you do?"

Orlantha straightened her spine. "What we have always done: provide care to those in need."

"My most trusted maids and ladies-in-waiting will assist us," the queen continued. "Together, we will create a network of informants and messengers. You will not be alone, Gretel. I will send maids with you as well. They will be your go-betweens."

"I will not be able to visit the village?"

"I'm afraid it will be too dangerous. We cannot risk inadvertently leading your father or brother to us." Orlantha almost looked as if she pitied me. "The maids have more autonomy, and if questioned, they can say they are acting on business for the Crown."

Queen Galen laid her hand over mine. "I know this is a lot to ask of you."

It was the first time the queen had acknowledged the weight

of the burden I would assume. It bolstered me more than I would have anticipated.

"I can do it. If this is my part, I will play it."

The three of them nodded in support. My duties settled, we turned to laying out how the chain of communication would work and which of the queen's ladies and maids would oversee what.

In the case of an attack, the network would help transport some of the witches and their necessary supplies to the destination ahead of time. They would do what they could to mitigate the attack itself, while standing ready to provide immediate medical treatment and support for the victims. Thus, it would be nearly impossible for Ansel, Hansel, and their thugs to place the blame for the attack on the witches' shoulders.

Several times throughout the day, Lina knocked on the door with food and water, but we never ceased working. We talked all through the afternoon and late into the evening, anticipating pitfalls and working out every detail we could think of.

The midnight bell broke through our conversation and gave rise to a round of yawns from each of us.

"We shall need new candles soon," Katharina said as one of the stubs flickered out.

"For what?"

We turned as one toward the new, familiar voice.

The queen rose to greet her son and stepped in front of me. "Oh, Wilfried dear, you're home."

"Miss Orlantha. Kat." I could hear the sleepy smile in his voice.

Kat?

I leaned around the queen's skirts as she stepped forward to greet her son in the doorway. "You know each other?"

He peered over her shoulders as they embraced. *"Gretel?"* His voice was hamstrung between delight and concern.

Wilfried held his mother out at arm's length. "Is everything all right?"

"No, my son, but it will be."

Wilfried entered without being requested and joined us at the table. "What is going on, Mother?"

Orlantha gestured to me. "Gretel, I believe you should be the one to relay what brings us here tonight."

So I did. I explained how I met the witches and, much to my relief, he said nothing about me and the Wood Witch. Then I told him about sneaking around my father's castle.

I revealed Ansel and Hansel's plans.

I recounted how I raced to the palace as soon as I discovered everything.

"Gretel will remain at the palace through all of this, won't she? So she is safe?" Wilfried asked when I'd finished, looking to his mother with a searching, fervent expression.

I slipped my hand into his. "No, Wilfried. I will return to my father's home and pretend that nothing is out of the ordinary. I will become a spy for our efforts and provide information to your mother's network to carry to both the palace and the witches' village."

He sighed. "I can see how committed to this cause you are, though I fear it will be too dangerous."

"It is a risk I must take." I said, squeezing his hand. "Besides, Ansel and Hansel don't intend to harm me until after our wedding. I will be safe enough." I was attempting to convince myself as much as him.

He pulled our clasped hands to his chest. "I promise to help all of you in any way that I can. And if I cannot keep you out of harm's way, Gretel, then I can at least help you prepare to defend yourself."

"What, in combat?" I joked.

"Yes." He nodded earnestly. "With a sword."

The blood drained from my face.

The queen clapped her hands together, as if an idea had struck. "I will officially send word to Lord Henoth that I would like Wilfried to take up temporary residence at the castle until the wedding."

She turned her attention to her son, eyebrows raised. "I have, after all, been quite worried about how the frequent travel back and forth has been affecting his health."

Wilfried sighed with relief. "Yes. Yes! You have said as much many times, Mother."

A quick glance at Katharina revealed that she was listening with pursed lips and crossed arms, her eyes casting back and forth between Wilfried and his mother.

"Well then, we may all rest a bit easier about the matter of

Gretel's safety, if Wilfried is on hand." Orlantha smiled.

He turned back to me. "And we will be together, whatever may unfold."

Hours later, I said goodbye to Katharina and Orlantha alone at the servants' exit, so as not to raise suspicions.

"Be safe," I said, hugging them both. "I am sorry that you carry such dreadful news back to the others, but I have faith that we will make this right."

Orlantha tucked a loose curl behind my ear. "Goodbye, Gretel. I will speak protection over your name every day."

Katharina hugged me again. "We all will."

They slipped into the darkness just before dawn. I watched the shadows swallow them up and missed them already.

After breakfast, Wilfried and I set out for Ansel's estate on horseback, since the weather was fine and I needed to return Snip to the castle's stables. A bevy of servants, guards, and the maids the queen had selected to go undercover accompanied us in carriages behind.

Wilfried trotted up alongside me. "You are an accomplished rider! Why have we never ridden together before?"

Instead of answering him, I grinned at him and urged Snip to go faster, inviting the prince into an impromptu race. He laughed and joined me. It was a rare moment of reprieve for us both, one that I would cherish in the coming weeks.

That joy was short-lived. When we arrived at the castle's

entrance with our entourage in tow, Ansel and Hansel were waiting, ready to confront us. Mrs. Chambers stood behind them.

We dismounted and handed our horses off to waiting stable hands. Together, we stepped forward to face my father.

"Gretel, where have you been? We returned this morning to find out from Mrs. Chambers that you were missing." Ansel's rage simmered just below the surface, waiting for a private moment to be unleashed.

Wilfried stepped ever so slightly in front of me. "My apologies, Lord Henoth. My mother summoned Gretel with little notice the afternoon before yesterday."

"Be that as it may," Ansel said with forced, measured restraint, "And with no disrespect to Her Majesty, my daughter should have informed our housekeeper if such an invitation did appear so mysteriously that it was not even delivered by messenger."

I stared into Mrs. Chambers's cold, scrutinizing eyes. Once, I thought we might have been friends. But since our first interaction, she had operated in lockstep with my father, leaving no room for me. Since she could not find it in her to make me an ally, I would become a most excellent enemy.

"There was a messenger, Father. I received them when Mrs. Chambers did not answer the door. I searched for her for some time before I simply had to leave, lest I delay the queen. I cannot fathom where she should have been if not at her post." It was my best performance of innocence.

"Our apologies for the confusion, Lord Henoth. You will be

delighted to know that there is little chance of such a miscommunication happening again." Wilfried stepped forward and handed his mother's letter to my father. "My mother has declared that she wishes me to stay at your estate until our nuptials. She's grown rather concerned for my health with all of the traveling back and forth. It will be easier this way. You needn't worry about any additional trouble; as you can see, she has sent me with ample staff to mitigate any inconvenience."

A muscle on the underside of Ansel's jaw twitched. He smiled to hide it. "Hosting any member of the royal family is always nothing less than a pleasure for our family, Your Highness. You honor us with your presence." He bowed before retreating inside.

The foundational pieces of our puzzle were laid.

CHAPTER TWENTY-SEVEN

Upon returning to the castle, I uncovered that the first attack was set to take place three days after our secret council met to sketch out our plan.

Initially, the plan went well. To an outsider, our lives probably would have seemed largely unchanged, except for the fact that Wilfried no longer left at night. We rose early and spent as much time as possible out of doors or sequestered in the library. We traded walks for secret sword-fighting lessons and reading together for coordinating transfer of the information we provided to the queen's messenger network.

On the night Ansel and Hansel planned to begin the attacks, we were ready and at our stations.

I pulled my hood low over my brow as I made my way down the alley to meet Kat. The row of townhouses was used mostly by businessmen like Hansel and Ansel, who resided there during periods of a high volume in deals while their families remained in their manor houses and sprawling estates farther out in the country. During my preparations for doing battle with my father and brother, I'd discovered two key pieces of information: The address of this second home, and the schedule of when Hansel stayed there.

My gaze trained on the mouth of the backstreet, eager to spot Katharina's silhouette, I stayed alert for the sounds of opportunistic men. We did not have time for any troublesome detours.

In my hands, I clutched the remaining dose of the sleeping draught I'd slipped into Hansel's tea before the maid carried it upstairs. Just enough to make sure he slept through the night and couldn't race to the aid of his henchmen. Come morning, he would awaken to discover the first of his plans foiled. Gossip would filter through the mouths of the servants who rose before dawn. Word would spread of our would-be good deeds.

But only if we stayed on time.

Terrible assumptions wove themselves into my thoughts the closer I got to our meeting spot with no sign or sound of Katharina's presence. Perhaps it was foolish to have sent her to the front door to distract the maid. What if she'd raised too much suspicion and Hillen summoned the authorities? How would I explain to Orlantha that I'd led her daughter right into a certain jail sentence?

The fear was so loud in my mind that I did not notice the hand that reached out from behind a half-rotted wine cask until it was clasped firmly around my wrist and yanking me into the grimy shadows. Another covered my mouth before I could shout.

"Shh."

Relief coursed through me. I nodded and Katharina stopped restraining me.

"I was worried. I didn't see you," I whispered into her ear.

"As intended."

Her breath smelled like the cinnamon bark she chewed during long nights working in the medical cabin. I smirked into the darkness. She could pretend she wasn't just as nervous as I was, and I would let her. Unlike me, this wasn't her first venture into espionage, and I was more than willing to let her lead.

The church bells in the square chimed midnight.

"Let's go." Katharina tugged on my cape and scurried from the shadows, her own bobbing hood concealing her bright copper hair.

During the following half hour, we wove our way through the labyrinth of Cannickton, keeping to the edges of less-trafficked streets. A light snow muffled the clash of our bootheels upon the cobblestones and washed the air clean as it fell. With the promise of our plans before us, the damp chill that drifted into the crevices of my cloak shook me awake and bolstered my courage.

At the edge of the square, I retrieved Snip from where I'd left him at the public stable, taking care not to awaken the young lad on duty. I swung myself into the saddle, but Katharina hesitated when I offered my hand to help her up.

"I've got a strong grip, I promise," I teased.

With an almost imperceptible shake of her head, she stepped farther back.

I studied her. This was the first time I'd ever seen her falter.

She was always the one forging ahead, clearing a path no matter the obstacles.

"A-are you scared? Of horses?"

The question seemed silly as soon as I asked it. Katharina was fearless, in my experience. No matter how stressed, she simply popped a new piece of cinnamon bark into her mouth to chew and kept going. Which was why I was so surprised when she reluctantly nodded.

"But you've spent your life in close commune with animals."

"Horses are big. And unpredictable." Defense laced every word.

Her eyes blazed. She considered this a weakness in herself, I could tell. Something in me softened, my spirit instantly chastised. I knew what it was like to feel exposed, flawed. I didn't want to wield superiority as a cudgel like Hansel so often did.

"I won't let you fall." I held out my hand again. "I promise."

A muscle in her jaw ticked. "If you do, I'm taking you with me."

"Down I'll gladly go." I'd rather risk a trampling than her displeasure.

With a sigh, she took my hand and let me pull her up behind me.

Her arms wrapped tight around my waist as she burrowed her face between my shoulder blades. A swoop that had nothing to do with fear lurched through my belly.

Behind us, the sounds of groups leaving parties and gatherings trickled out of open doors. There was no more time to waste. Somewhere, Pia Strickton and her mother were no doubt amongst those managing their goodbyes as they turned their thoughts toward bed.

I clicked at Snip and gently squeezed his sides with my calves. Katharina yelped as we started moving, her voice muffled by the fabric of my cloak, but we could not hang back any longer without risking the upset of everything we'd planned. We crossed through the unmanned gates and took to the main road that led into the country, leaving the sounds of town behind. The forest grew denser the farther we went. With only the moon and a handful of stars to light our way, we set course for where the others would be waiting for us.

After a time, the distant sounds of other travelers bound for home fluttered to us across the breeze. As we left the main road and took to the wood trails, I urged Snip into a gentle trot to make up for lost time.

The moon was creeping high overhead when we finally reached the cluster of trees that bordered the edge of the Strickton estate. A candle burned in the window of the gatehouse down the way, but no one stood guard that I could see. No doubt Ansel had paid them off.

I looped Snip's reins around the trunk of a young beech and helped Katharina slide back to the solid ground. She whistled a soft starling call, the signal that it was safe for the others to emerge from their hiding spots.

I remounted and waited. I would stay until Katharina was with them.

One by one, Orlantha and a dozen of the other witches materialized from the shadows, their steps soundless.

"What delayed you?" Orlantha whispered.

"Nothing worth discussing," Katharina countered before I could speak.

I bit the inside of my cheeks. It was absurd to find humor in anything about this night, but I couldn't help it.

Katharina's expression was stubborn to a point that her mother left well enough alone.

I cleared my throat. "They'll be here soon. There were several carriages not far behind us before we left the road."

The energy of the group changed. Orlantha shifted into the resolute attitude I'd witnessed many times while assisting her and Katharina in their work.

"To your places," she ordered the others.

Fully returned to herself after the riding ordeal, Katharina gave me a quick wink before disappearing. "Earth below you."

"Trees around you." Orlantha clasped my hand before joining her daughter.

"Stars above you." I returned her squeeze, then watched her vanish.

Then Snip and I took off, deeper into the woods in the direction of Ansel's castle. I had to get back before the attack. I had to make sure Ansel believed I was abed when everything went awry.

"Sisters with me," I said to myself for the first time as I raced into the night.

None shall harm you. I wasn't brave enough to finish the blessing out loud, but I hoped the thought would be enough to shield us through the morning.

Annika and Frida's familiar whispers woke me a handful of hours later. Taking care not to alert them to my being awake, I shifted to my side and watched them through slitted eyes. They moved through the motions of rebuilding my fire as a well-seasoned team. I was accustomed to sleeping through their morning routines, so I'd never noticed before.

Free from the surveillance of authority, Annika was warmer with her counterpart. Gentler. Frida thrived in the glow of the other girl's kindness. A pull of recognition tugged at the back of my brain. The air between them was familiar.

What—who—do they remind me of?

Huddled now over the hearth, Frida stopped speaking and Annika followed suit, a comfortable silence replacing their chatter as Annika fed Frida pieces of wood.

When the fire was roaring once more, Annika helped Frida to her feet. Their fingers remained tangled for just a moment longer than necessary. Annika brushed a stray strand of Frida's hair back into her neat braid. Frida blushed.

My own skin grew warm. Even though it was my room, they didn't know I was awake. I was intruding upon a private moment. I just wasn't sure what kind.

Whatever was happening, I didn't want to interlope any longer.

"Ahhhaaa." I made a show of yawning, sweeping my arms overhead and rustling around beneath my covers as I smacked my jaws together, clearing any lingering dryness in my mouth.

Annika and Frida, to their credit, did not spring away from each other. Frida simply shifted away from Annika and continued stoking the fire.

Annika smoothed her hands down her apron and faced me. "Good morning, Miss Gretel."

I scooted into a sitting position, rearranging my pillows behind me.

"What were you two talking about?"

Frida looked over her shoulder, first at me, then Annika, before brushing the soot from her hands. She was stalling for time.

I studied the more staid maid at the foot of my bed. She was worrying her lip. I'd never seen Annika unnerved like this. Especially not when the three of us were alone, free from the watchful eyes of Ansel, Hansel, and Mrs. Chambers.

It was Frida who broke the silence. "We don't like to frighten you, miss."

"Frighten me?" Incredulity laced my words. If only they knew the scores of fears I'd faced in these past months and weeks.

Annika drew close to the side of the bed where I was perched, Frida right on her heels.

After a look I couldn't quite decipher from Frida, Annika finally said, "The witches are astir, Gretel."

Frida gasped and I nearly joined her; Annika had never used my first name alone before, despite my cajoling her to do so.

"What do you mean?" I kept my voice level.

"There was an attack last night," Frida whispered.

Anticipation flickered in my belly. Gossip had traveled just as fast as the coven and I had hoped.

I clutched both their hands, playing my part. "Was anyone hurt?"

Frida nodded, eyes wide and somber.

But in Annika's expression I glimpsed dark satisfaction.

"What happened?"

The clock in the hall outside my room chimed seven times.

"Oh, we best get you dressed, Miss Gretel." Annika's deference for custom returned.

Frida urged me out of the cocoon of my bedclothes. "We'll tell you as we do."

Together, they prepared me for the day and recounted what they'd heard.

On their way home from a party in town, the Strickton carriage was accosted by an unidentified group of men. They succeeded in knocking the driver and footman unconscious.

"But no sooner had they opened the door to the carriage," Frida said, her voice pitching higher with urgency, "then the witches descended upon them from the trees with a rallying cry."

"They fought off the assailants, saw the Stricktons safely back to their estate, then disappeared into the woods again," Annika concluded.

My heart thudded against my ribs. It was all just as we'd planned it.

"So the witches didn't cause any harm?" My voice was muffled as they pulled a warm dress over my head.

Frida smoothed out the skirt over my underclothes. "Not so far as we've heard tell."

"How strange."

Annika nodded, her mouth full of hairpins.

If only I could have told them everything without jeopardizing their safety in turn. They should know that it wasn't strange at all. That we'd been lied to all our lives about the witches.

Except the one who tried to kill you. And Hansel.

I pushed the thought away. I still hadn't summoned the courage to ask Orlantha or Katharina or any of the others about the Wood Witch. If they blamed me for her death, what would I do? How would I fight against my father and brother and their nefarious plans without the witches' help? And how would the witches fight against my father and brother without my spying?

What if they would seek vengeance upon me?

No. I could not even consider it.

"No one can make heads nor tails of it," Frida said.

Annika made a noncommittal sound. "Perhaps we have misjudged them?"

She slipped the final pin in my hair and stepped back to admire her handiwork. Wilfried rapped upon the door at that exact moment. Three sharp strikes against the old wood, followed by two soft ones. It was our secret knock, though the girls were used to it by now.

"She's nearly ready, Your Highness," Frida called.

After a final nod of approval from Annika, I hastened to greet my fiancé.

He was leaning against the wall when I opened the door, head tipped back and eyes closed. A rare moment of rest. These past weeks—of planning our wedding, of plotting the battle we were fighting against my family, of overseeing my sword training—had run us ragged. Nonetheless, warmth flowed through me as I drank us in. We were tired, but we were whole. Stretched to our limits, but making progress that mattered.

I laid a gentle hand on his shoulder, reluctant to rouse him. Instead of startling, he nuzzled his cheek into my palm.

A different kind of warmth spread through me.

Immediately, I pushed it away with the same kinds of reminders I always gave myself to keep my feelings in check.

We are only friends.

He is merely comfortable with me.

This is just the closeness of our working together running its course.

I told myself these things over and over, the phrasing so familiar to my mind, they were almost chants.

And yet, even had someone stumbled into the hall and forced a need for inches of discretion between us, I would have sooner removed my shoulder from its socket and left him my limb than willfully pulled my hand away.

We stood there suspended, just long enough for my arm to grow numb.

Until Wilfried pulled himself off the wall with a groan, tucked my hand appropriately into the crook of his elbow, and led me downstairs.

Outside, we walked briskly and in silence until we reached the stable.

The stifled yawns and bleary eyes of the young hand who fetched our horses were the product of Wilfried's handiwork; I wasn't the only one who'd tipped a sleeping draught into tea the previous night.

We thanked the boy and set off, slowing near a secluded brook in the far reaches of Ansel's estate. Confident that the gurgle of the water would cover our voices, we filled each other in on our nights. After he'd administered the draught to the stable boy on duty, Wilfried had ridden to the palace for a rare evening at home. One where he was seen by multiple members of staff, so his every minute was accounted for.

"I believe the tide of gossip may already be turning in our favor."

Wilfried raised his eyebrows. "Do you now?"

I nodded. "After last night, even Annika said she thinks the witches may have been misjudged."

We dismounted and walked the horses deeper into the forest

in search of a place open enough to train, but with a fair amount of tree cover, to shield us from prying eyes should anyone wander by.

"My mother feels certain that shifting public opinion is essential to our cause." Wilfried handed me his horse's reins.

"She has good reason to," I said, looping both sets of reins around a nearby tree surrounded by grass for grazing. "The aristocracy wield power and might, but the lowborn shape the superstitions that all our lives are built around."

He handed me a practice sword and we squared up across from each other. "Why is that, do you think? Why rely so much on rumors and unproven ideas?"

I shrugged. "Necessity."

I settled into a sparring stance, shifted my boots until my weight was perfectly balanced. Looked into Wilfried's eyes and leaned into the gap of life experience that would always stand between us, no matter how close we grew. "When you do not have money to insulate you from the horrors of the world, stories become both bread and blanket."

The next attack came with little warning, the details buried in code we had not cracked within Ansel and Hansel's correspondence with their coconspirators. We were not prepared.

By the time the witches and I arrived at the village they'd attacked, several of the garden plots were already aflame, the fire licking through rows of crucifers and gourds that were due to be harvested. Our brigade went to work immediately, the most experienced of the witches calling up water from the nearby creek, while the rest ran back and forth, filling up buckets. We had to stop the spread of the fire before it reached any of the small homes that peppered the area. Most importantly, we needed to make sure all the villagers were safe and out of harm's way.

"Come with me!" I gathered a group of girls a few years younger than me and herded them toward the homes nearest the fire. The sun was still too low in the sky to shine through any of the shutters' cracks; the smoke was not yet bad enough to have woken any of the occupants. It would be too late if we didn't alert everyone quickly.

When we reached the first cottage, I circled the girls up. "Go house to house, wake them, and tell them there is a fire. Help however you can."

"Where should we take them?" asked a teenager clutching the hand of a smaller girl with matching hair and dimples.

"I imagine they'll make for that hill." I pointed to a shadow I could just make out in the moonlight. "If they need guidance, tell them that's the safest place."

One of the newer orphans piped up. "What if they want to go help with the fire?"

"Only adults. Only if they've no children. Keep the families together."

All three of them nodded.

"Off we go."

And off we went, lanterns bobbing before us. Though we used traditional, non-spelled ones outside Galwin and the forest, the dark of the night erased our shadows and made the lanterns appear as if they were floating all the same.

Within minutes, the village became a hub of fear and quick action. As I raced for the hill alongside several families, a baby in my arms, I glanced back toward the fire. The witches had made progress. But they'd have to stop summoning water directly from the creek and rely on only the bucket brigade now that the villagers were racing to join them. It was safest for our community that way. No way around it, when the alternatives were risking our exposure as witches or forbidding the locals from helping and inviting their blame if we were ultimately unsuccessful. Still, I worried that our efforts would not be enough.

And all I could personally do was wait. I sat on the hillside with the children and many of the adults. The nearness of the forest was my lone comfort.

For hours, the others fought against the flames. As the sun rose, the final embers were put out. Rays of light cast the ruin of the night into stark relief, exposing the hard reality: Almost none of the crops had been saved.

One by one, those on the hill staggered down to reunite with their kin, bleary-eyed and bedraggled. But safe. For we'd soon confirm the frayed threads of good news to which their community would cling: No lives were lost in the fire. No homes, either.

Eventually, they'd turn to thank the mysterious strangers who'd alerted them to danger and fought by their side.

We would already be deep in the forest by then.

Not content with destroying the crops of one village, Ansel and Hansel next set our old cottage on fire. Or rather, a band of their cronies did. It was clever, in a cruel way; our peers and neighbors would be less likely to assume the Henoths were behind an attack on their own former home.

Ansel attempted to plant a theory that the other witches were seeking revenge against Hansel for killing the Wood Witch.

Unlucky for him, word was already traveling fast that the witches had helped put out the fire in the first village. What was more, they'd left behind medical aid supplies for burns and smoke inhalation.

And so it unfolded for the next several weeks.

At every attack on a village or noble family, the witches were stationed and at the ready to help.

Whenever I could, I snuck through the back passage of the castle, using the unlocked entrance from the servants' staircase to gain access to my father's study. I made copies of every piece of correspondence that would prove his undoing, painstakingly duplicating his writing until my hand would cramp too frequently to allow me to continue without a break.

Meanwhile, Ansel and Hansel's brigade expanded from arson to petty thefts at markets and on festival nights. Those were more difficult to anticipate and harder to prevent, but the people of the kingdom were less likely to pin such crimes on the witches, low-level as they were.

Determined to prevail, my father then moved on to accosting the homes of lower-ranking nobility. Each time, the witches sounded the alarm for the occupants, just before their guards were bribed or rendered unconscious.

The tide was beginning to shift as more and more people in the surrounding areas received help from the witches. Reports trickled in of conversations where peasants and nobles alike mused that perhaps the negative witch stories they'd heard growing up were simply exaggerated or misinformed.

I watched as my father's irritation at being thwarted over and over multiplied and poisoned him.

Time passed. Winter fell away and we found ourselves on the precipice of early spring, poised to welcome it at the queen's Midnight Masquerade. Much had changed since my first palace ball as the prince's betrothed. This time, Wilfried did not need to spend half an hour bolstering my confidence so I was steady enough to face the crowd.

Instead, I entered the ballroom with my head held high. Few present knew it, but we were at the helm of changing the direction of our kingdom for the better. I had earned my place. I no longer had to fear that our engagement would one day crumble in the wake of Wilfried falling in love with someone else.

We made our way once more through the crowd. For the first time, I did not take any praise or criticism of me to heart. I had more important gossip to tend to. I let their more personal comments slip over me like water upon oil and tuned my ears for commentary upon our efforts with the witches.

"Our kitchen maids say those villagers whose gardens were burned up are still walking out their doors to find food left for them."

"No idea who it came from?"

"Not a whit."

"Could be the witches. I heard tell they helped extinguish the fire."

"Oh, pishposh. Nobody saw any of them once the last flames were put out."

"I'm only relaying what I've heard."

I fought back a grin as we reached the center of the room and took up our positions for the first dance.

"Why do I feel as though you're scheming?" Wilfried asked.

"I am simply relishing in the fruits of *our* already-enacted schemes."

"Public disfavor for the witches does seem to have decreased." He looked over my head to scan the room. "Just as their favor for you *in*creases."

I brushed off his compliment. "That is not as important."

"I disagree. You are positively regal, especially these days, and

I think everyone should acknowledge it." His grin would have won over even Mrs. Chambers.

"Fine," I laughed, "I will allow it."

The rest of the evening unfolded with ease. At last, I was comfortable enough to mingle at Wilfried's side, instead of us mostly keeping to ourselves.

Just before midnight and the toast to usher in spring, I needed a moment to myself.

"I'm going to take some air."

"Do you want me to come with you?" Wilfried murmured.

I did, but I didn't want to take him away from his eager subjects. He needed all the opportunities to foster goodwill among the people that he could get. "No, I'll be all right. Stay here and enjoy yourself."

I slunk to the edges of the room, eager to avoid any further conversations before I could make my brief escape. I let out a sigh of relief when I reached the balcony.

Relief that was too short-lived.

As soon as I stepped through the doors, someone grabbed me by the arm, pulled me into the shadows, and clapped a hand over my mouth.

CHAPTER TWENTY-EIGHT

"It's me," Katharina whispered into my ear.

My entire body relaxed and I slumped against her.

Just as quickly, I pulled away and rounded to face her. "What are you doing here?"

"I wanted to see this part of the palace up close." She shrugged, as if that was a reasonable explanation for risking so much.

"Someone could have caught you! Besides, you've seen plenty of the palace before. Tell me the real reason."

"That's all there is to tell." She wouldn't meet my eyes.

I'd been skeptical of her before, but never suspicious. Until that moment. "I don't believe you."

She threw her arms up with a huff, then crossed them over her chest. A cage—or a fence.

"Fine," she said, looking at the sky. "I wanted to see you."

"Oh." My voice was small, hardly more than a breath. That was the last thing I'd expected her to say. Could she see my heart battering against the skintight fabric of my bodice?

"Don't make a big fuss out of it."

"I don't have to; it already is one. This is dangerous."

Across the grounds, the bells of the tower atop the church began to strike midnight.

I gasped. "I have to go. I'll miss the toast."

I turned away, then stopped.

"Meet me back here when the bell tolls two."

With that, I lifted my skirts and dashed back inside.

Not two hours later, while the rest of the palace slumbered, I met Katharina on the terrace. The moon was high and full overhead. I'd decided that I would sneak her into my room through the passageway Wilfried had shown me. That would keep us out of view of the night guards, while ensuring that if anyone looked in on my chambers, I would be able to answer through the door.

"Come with me," I told Katharina. It was strange, having our roles reversed like this. I was used to following her orders. We took the stairs two at a time.

To her credit, she was so quiet, there were several times I had to look over my shoulder to make sure she was still following me. She didn't say a word or make a sound until we were ensconced safely in my room. After I closed the passage door behind us, she was still careful to whisper.

"You know the palace well already."

"Not so well. Wilfried visited me through that one once."

She raised a brow and my cheeks warmed. "Not like that."

"No? Are the two of you not madly in love?" Her words dripped with sarcasm.

I didn't meet her eyes. Only Wilfried and I knew the true nature of our arrangement. To breach that would put both of us in jeopardy.

"Of course we are," I blurted. "But he is a gentleman."

She sniffed in such a way that suggested she didn't not believe me, but said nothing further.

She walked slowly around my room, taking in everything, taking note of the smallest details revealed by the candlelight. "You like all of this?"

"Of course. Do you not?"

"It's pretty. I could never live so separated from nature, though." She sat on the edge of my bed. "I wouldn't feel like myself."

I joined her. "I think that's why Queen Galen maintains such extensive gardens."

"Not the same."

"No, but she's making the best of her circumstances. She has to."

Katharina picked at her nails. "You don't, though."

"Pardon?"

She grabbed my hands, her expression radiating with a fervent openness I wasn't used to from her. "You haven't married him yet. You still have a choice."

"I don't understand. A choice for what?"

"You don't have to get married."

A laugh choked out of me. "Do you have a fever? This marriage is going to save me, Katharina. Why would I not follow through with it?"

She scooted closer to me, laid her hand gently upon my knee. "You have other options for safety. You could live in Galwin."

My heart stuttered, beating in starts and stops. She spoke as if she'd witnessed my most private thoughts, the questions I only fully entertained in the darkest and most solitary hours of the night.

"You're very presumptuous."

"Am I? Or am I simply observant?"

"I love Wilfried. I will marry him. I don't require any other options because I've made my choice."

"You think you'll be happy, locked up in this palace?"

I stood, moved around to the side of the bed to create distance between us. "I won't be *locked* up. I like it here. And I have plans—*we* have plans, Wilfried and I. We're going to change the realm for the better."

"You really think—"

I held up my hand for her to stop. "It is late and I do not wish to quarrel."

Her natural guard slid back into place and she regarded me with a cool stare. "Fine."

"You should stay here," I continued. "I'll sneak you back out in the morning."

"I'll need to send a message first."

She walked over to the window and traced symbols I didn't recognize with her finger onto the glass, leaving echoes of fingerprints behind. A heartbeat later, a large crow alighted on the sill. She put her lips to the glass and whispered something. The crow tapped its beak lightly against the window twice, then took flight.

"Well, that was incredibly normal." I still wasn't entirely accustomed to the ways of the witches. There was so much to learn, I wondered if I ever would be.

"It is for me." Her voice was sour.

I nodded, then crossed past her to retrieve a spare night shift from the wardrobe, which I tossed to her.

While I busied myself with turning down the blankets, she changed, then we both climbed into the bed.

"Good night," I said.

"Night." Disappointment laced her tone.

I fell asleep faster than I expected, with dreams plagued by the what-if that Katharina had planted, the long-fought doubts of my own that she'd given voice to.

CHAPTER TWENTY-NINE

Katharina and I both stirred at the first sign of light creeping through the cracks in the curtains I'd pulled tight the night before to ensure that no one witnessed our shadows from the grounds below.

I had no chance to process anything before suddenly we were both fully awake, lying on our sides and looking at each other. We'd maintained our distance through the night, a clear stretch of the bed open between us. Except, at some point, our arms had migrated.

As we lay there in silence, staring, I suddenly sensed the warmth of her pinkie brushing against mine. I snatched my arm back. Aware of how erratic that must have seemed, I camouflaged my movement by feeding it into a full roll out of the bed and onto my feet.

Katharina was still, her mood unflappable and her thoughts unreadable, as ever.

"Did you sleep well?" she asked, tone even.

It was a direct attack on my own turbulent heartbeat.

I nodded, not trusting myself to speak.

I needed to get her out of the palace, for her own safety.

And mine, my jittery brain croaked.

"You must go, before the rest of the palace wakes and one of the other overnight guests catches you."

She cut her eyes to the maid's costume she'd taken off and thrown over a chair the night before. "How would they mark me apart from any of the other palace maids?"

I cast about for a reasonable excuse.

She smiled, self-satisfied. "Exactly. I'm going back to sleep. These beds are comfortable."

She burrowed back beneath the covers and set off fires in my brain. This was absolutely the opposite of the path I'd intended to take.

"You can't!" I hissed.

She sighed with such force, it briefly puffed up the part of the blanket that was draped over her head.

This time, I latched on to the first reason I could think of. "They—if they think you are employed here, they might make a request of you, and then what would you do? The palace will face rumors of infiltration, the queen will have to reinforce security measures, our entire operation will be compromised, all because you wanted to sleep in—"

"Enough!"

Her palms appeared just above the duvet in an act of surrender. "I can't rest with you carrying on, anyhow."

She climbed out of the bed and this time *I* sighed—with relief.

I turned around, waiting for her to change. The sun was rising, quickly. Soon, I would be looked for. We were working against multiple timepieces.

"All right, I'm ready for you to smuggle me away."

I didn't waste another minute. Back through the passageway we went.

When we reached the little room on the other side, I barreled on through to the terrace door, but she was no longer behind me. I ran back inside.

"Katharina!" I hissed. "We have to go!"

She was peering through the curtained partition, into the ballroom. She popped her head back in. "What is it like to dance in there? With a full band of musicians?"

I rubbed my temples. Had anyone ever been so interesting *and* irritating?

"Are you *trying* to get us caught?"

"I'm just asking!"

I closed the distance in three strides. "Someday, when we aren't under immediate threat, I'll tell you all about it. But we have to make it to that someday first!"

I grabbed her hand and pulled her to the door. Mere months ago, I would have marveled at the very concept of questioning or crossing her.

Keeping a firm grip, I rushed us across the terrace, down the back stairs, around the stone wall, and—

Right into the sight line of Wilfried.

"No!" I yelped under my breath.

I jumped back and threw my arm across her waist, flattening us against the wall.

"Have you gone mad?"

"It's Wilfried!" I whispered.

Neither of us spoke quietly enough. Or perhaps it was my first outcry that alerted him to our presence. In any case, breaths later, Wilfried strode around the wall, dueling sword up and eyes on alert.

I squeezed my eyes shut against the inevitable.

"Gretel?"

I opened one eye. And immediately considered closing it again. He was standing right in front of us.

Then, with yet another sigh, I chose to face my fate.

His sword was lowered, at least.

But he was staring at my arm still stretched across Katharina's waist. At our hands, still joined.

Something twisted in my stomach as I reclaimed my body parts. Heat climbed up my face. Bile threatened to consume my throat, though my gut was empty.

"Gretel, what is going on? We were meant to meet for your training session a quarter of an hour ago. When I called upon your rooms, your maid said your bedchamber was empty, so I came here thinking you might have woken early, but—"

"I did!" I cut him off, desperate to speak before Katharina could. "And when I came down, I stumbled upon Katharina on the terrace. She, um . . ." I trailed off. I was lying to him before I could think to tell the truth.

"—I came to deliver a message from my mother, Your Highness, and inadvertently startled your fiancée," Katharina said, covering for me.

I should have come clean right then, confessed to the risk I'd taken by hiding Katharina in my room. But the expression on his face when he'd registered our closeness loomed in my mind, and I was too afraid.

"Yes!" I agreed.

Wilfried's brow furrowed. "Why did you not use the kitchen entrance and pass on your message through Lina, as we've previously established?"

She didn't miss a beat. "I should have, Your Highness. My apologies. I saw Gretel in the distance when I came through the trees and I wished to bid her good morning. I thought to give her my mother's report directly. I was foolish."

For a moment, none of us spoke. Then the clouds lifted from Wilfried's face and he was amiable once more. "I understand. After all, who among us has not been overexcited to see our Gretel at least once? I trust you'll stick to protocol in the future."

"Of course, Your Highness." She dipped her head for good measure.

"Now, what news from your mother?"

Katharina blinked several times.

"The message you came to impart?" Wilfried fished.

"Oh! Yes. She wanted you all to know that the gossip she hears at the markets continues to improve in our favor."

If Wilfried found this a thin reason for taking the risk of visiting the palace, he did not say so. "Splendid. Gretel remains steadfast in her role as spy, though it feels promising that she's uncovered no recent correspondence indicating the threat of a further attack."

"Our efforts must be working in multiple ways," Katharina said.

I forced myself to smile and nod.

"Well, please offer your mother and the others our regards. Gretel and I have training to attend to."

"I will, Your Highness. Good morning to you both."

She gave me a quick hug. "Think on what I said," she breathed into my ear.

I locked eyes with Wilfried over her shoulder, spotted the tightness at the corners of his mouth, forced myself to show no reaction to Katharina's words.

Nevertheless, they would haunt me in the days to come.

CHAPTER THIRTY

Later that morning, some of Wilfried's advisers requested he spend the afternoon in conference with them. I leapt at the opportunity to return to the castle by myself, assuring Wilfried that I did not mind. Though I appreciated the extra safety his presence at the castle brought, my chances for time alone had become increasingly rare.

I arrived with as little fanfare as possible, leaving my bag with the footmen and setting out for my room before the rest of the castle was notified of my premature arrival. I took the stairs two at a time and nearly broke into a jog down the hallway to my room.

When I opened the door, Annika and Frida were standing in the center. Their faces were inches apart, and their bodies close enough that I could see no space between them. Far enough away from any of the furniture and fireplace that I could not determine their purpose.

I cleared my throat to alert them and they sprang apart.

"Oh, Miss Gretel!" Frida's cheeks were bright pink, her eyes wide. "You are home early!"

"The prince had business to attend to."

"Welcome back, miss." Her smile was so tight, the sound of her teeth grinding carried across the room.

"Thank you. I apologize for disturbing—"

Annika spoke for the first time, cutting me off. "No apology needed. There was no disturbance."

"Quite right. I was just about to bring some of your linens down to the laundry." Frida pointed to a full basket waiting near the door.

Annika motioned toward the hearth. "And I shall build your fire, now that you've returned."

Maintaining an atypical distance from each other, the girls went about their duties. I was rooted to the spot, bewildered, until the sound of the door closing behind Frida shook me from my reverie.

I moved to sit at the table nearby. For a bit, Annika and I existed in silence. I reviewed the moment I'd entered the room over and over in my mind; it scratched at some other memory, but I couldn't place which one.

Until, suddenly, I could.

It reminded me of earlier that morning, when Wilfried found me with Katharina.

It reminded me of Aster walking into Mills's sick room while Katharina and I were celebrating the baby's turn for the better.

It reminded me of a dozen other moments that I'd tried to forget and refused to examine. I brought them together to consider next to Katharina's admonishing plea from that morning, that I consider breaking off my engagement to live and work alongside the witches—alongside her.

"Annika, do you think you'll ever marry?"

She snorted, then covered it with a tight cough. "No. I do not."

"And Frida?"

She stiffened. "I do not know."

"You knew each other before your placement here, yes? Polly said Mrs. Chambers hired you together."

She set one last log in the grate, finally turning to face me. "We've known each other since we were girls. My parents and her father served in the same household."

"Did you work there as well?"

"No," she said, sitting back on her heels. "We left home as soon as we could."

"Together?"

She nodded. "This is our second placement since then."

I tried to catch her eye, to no avail. But she did not make an excuse to leave the room. I took my chances and crossed to sit next to her.

"Why are you so confident you'll never marry? You are still young yet."

She looked at me then. Really looked. Every bit of her face was armor, except her eyes: soft and open, like she was trying to tell me something in a silent, pleading language.

I took a deep breath and walked onto a precipice, hoping

she would join me. "Do you and Frida share more than a friendship?"

If I had blinked in that moment, I would have missed her sliver of a nod.

But my eyes had remained wide open, so I didn't miss a single instant.

We did not speak for several minutes.

It is possible.

"I will not say anything. I only ask because I . . ." We'd reached a shore I could not cross without embroiling her in danger. "That is . . . I have made a . . . friend. During my time at court." It was a partial truth. Enough, I hoped, for her to understand.

Her expression shifted to one of pity.

She took my hand, and it was such a deviation from her characteristic observation of the rules that governed our lives, I almost gasped.

"Gretel, you must marry the prince. He is the only chance you have for safety in this world. The only chance any of us have."

Her words curdled my insides. Not because I did not intend to heed them, but because she was right: If I did not marry Wilfried, she and Frida could not join me at the palace as my lady's maids, as planned. I would be placing all of us at risk.

I squeezed her hand. "Of course. Of course, I will."

She slipped her hand out of my grasp and returned to finishing the fire.

I sat in front of it for a long time after she left, looking into the flames.

From the moment I'd accepted Wilfried's "real" proposal, I had never considered any alternative.

But now a different, equally real path lay before me, and my heart burned as I turned away from it.

CHAPTER THIRTY-ONE

". . . keep thwarting us. We can no longer abide their impudence in hopes they will relent."

My father's voice halted my progress.

He's supposed to be in town.

I'd grown accustomed to knowing which times were best for me to collect information to pass to the queen's network. Clearly, I'd become too comfortable in my assumptions.

I pressed myself flat against the stone wall of the hallway that connected the servants' wing to the forbidden wing of the castle. I fought the temptation to hold my breath and made myself inhale and exhale as slowly as possible to maintain silence. A treacherous strip of light fell across the path before me, illuminated by the open door ahead and as damning as the voices around the corner.

They weren't supposed to be here, I repeated to myself.

I was meant to be able to slip in, record their latest plans, and return to the other side of the castle with hours of the evening to spare.

"We'll have to go farther afield. Expand. That way, the

witches won't be able to reach us in time to subvert our plans." Hansel spoke with a tone that was too loud, too assured for my liking.

"This is sooner than we'd anticipated. Do you think the men are ready?" If Ansel was admitting deference, that was a sure sign they were desperate.

"They'll have to be."

"Do we have the necessary supplies?"

"Our men have gathered enough oil to saturate the entire village. We'll act while they're sleeping."

A pause as Ansel considered. "Very well. Give the order to lay siege to Bricht and set the place on fire once you've collected anything valuable."

"No survivors?" Hansel confirmed.

Dread snaked down my spine. Even now, it still surprised me that my brother could speak of violence in such a casual tone.

"If possible. We want the devastation to be great enough among the villagers that those who've shifted their support toward the witches will be ashamed to speak for them."

Chairs scraped the floor as they presumably pushed away from the desk. "It is settled," Ansel declared. "In two days' time, we will raze Bricht until nothing remains but ashes."

I covered my mouth to keep from screaming. We would have to move immediately for there to be any chance of us reaching Bricht in time to help evacuate the village. Extinguishing an oil-based fire of that size would be all but impossible; we needed to ensure that the villagers were moved to safety in advance, or most of them would perish in the fire.

I hurried back to the other side of the castle and sought out Hannah, one of the network maids. Once I'd dispatched her to notify the queen, it was time to find Wilfried. I needed him on my side for what I planned, or it would never work. We didn't have time to waste.

I found him waiting for me in the library and motioned him to my side.

"I need you to follow me outside and go where I go. I cannot explain right now, but please trust me."

His eyes were wide but certain. "Of course."

I breathed a sigh of relief. "Thank you."

He placed his hand in mine and off we went. Through the back gates and around the hedges, never slowing down, though my breath grew labored and Wilfried struggled to keep up.

Once we reached the edge of the back lawn, however, his attitude changed.

"Gretel, wait. Where *are* we going?" he demanded between gulps of air.

I kept pressing forward, pulling him behind me. "We have to go to Galwin. Something terrible is going to happen and we need to warn them."

"We can utilize the network."

"We don't have time."

"Gretel, they can move as quickly as we can. You know what my mother said about—"

His grip slipped from mine and I rounded on him. "I am going, with or without you. You can choose to come with me, or stay, but I cannot waste another moment."

I ran into the woods and, to his credit, he followed me with no further objection. When we reached the village, the energy was so somber, it stopped me in my tracks.

The little girls were no longer playing or braiding their hair. Nor were they peeking from behind windows, like the night of the stoneground fever case. Everyone was at work, the village a churn of preparation for looping tragedies. Witches entered and exited buildings with arms full of supplies or the ingredients to make them. Everyone shuffled from one action to the next. They must have been plagued by perpetual exhaustion and fear. My heart ached over the new burden I was about to place on them.

I searched for Katharina among those currently outside. When I found her, I motioned for Wilfried to stay quiet and made my way around the edge of the village, looking for the most discreet path to my friend. At last, we made eye contact and I waved her over to us.

"Gretel! Wilfried? What are you doing here?" Dark circles rimmed her eyes. I imagined she'd shouldered much of the workload herself during these past weeks, working tirelessly alongside her mother.

"There's going to be another attack."

Her shoulders relaxed. "Well, of course. We expected so, unfortunately. But we are prepared."

"No, Katharina," I said, taking her hand in mine. "It is far worse than anything we've witnessed them attempt thus far. They are going to lay an entire village to waste a half-day's travel from here. They're purposely trying to make sure you aren't able to reach them in time."

"When?"

"Two days."

"We must tell my mother immediately." Her gaze rested briefly on Wilfried, standing just behind me. "Come with me around back."

As soon as we informed Orlantha of the latest developments, our pace and workload doubled. The entire village was called to attention. Everyone abandoned any task not directly related to the preparation efforts. We slept in shifts. Soon, members of the maid network appeared with extra provisions and a spare wagon provided by the palace. The next thirty hours passed in a blur, but when the sun rose on the day Ansel and Hansel planned to attack, we were ready.

Twenty of the most experienced witches, including Katharina and Orlantha, set off in three wagons. One was loaded with supplies, the other two would provide transport for fleeing villagers. They would hide in the woods near Bricht and wait for the opportune moment to help bring people to safety. The network maids were dispatched back to my father's castle and the palace. Those returning to the castle would provide reasons for Wilfried's and my absence.

Once everything was as settled as possible in Galwin, Wilfried and I boarded our own wagon, disguised in farmhand garb. We would travel an hour or so behind the witches, prepared to provide backup assistance as needed.

When we arrived at Bricht that night, everything was too quiet. Something was wrong. Wilfried tied the horses up to a tree and we crept toward the village's edge. As we drew nearer, an overwhelming feeling of loss washed over me.

"Are you sure we came the right way?"

"Unless our maps were inaccurate . . ." He looked back over his shoulder, as if searching for a wrong turn, or a sign that would point us in the right direction.

The village was empty. Half-rotted and returning to nature in such a way that suggested it had been abandoned for several years, at the very least.

My mind reeling, I replayed the conversation I'd overheard between Ansel and Hansel. The perfectly worded sentences. The clear outline of their plan. The repetition of the location they intended to attack. No shorthand. No variation in volume. No closed doors or other attempts at secrecy.

"It was all a trap." I feared my knees would buckle beneath me.

Wilfried steadied me with his arm. "Are you sure?"

"Look around! There's no one here but us. And the witches, if they're still in their hiding spots. Ansel and Hansel must have wanted us to be stuck out here, out of the way, so they could carry out something even worse than what they pretended to have planned for Bricht. We need to find Orlantha and come up with a new plan. If we hurry, maybe we can make it back home in time to figure out what their *real* move is."

A rustle of noise near the woods caught my attention. I turned just in time to see two torches fly into the trees, to hear the first screams from the witches I now considered friends.

I ran to the woods without another thought, searching the area for the band of roughs my father had employed, but there were none except for the two henchmen responsible for setting the fire. They were retreating back down the road on horseback. Alone. There had never been a brigade, or an oil supply, or a plan to destroy a village—only a plan to decimate the witches, to destroy me.

"There's water and buckets in one of the wagons!" I yelled to Wilfried above the din of the flames and cries for help.

We ran faster.

Wilfried peeled away from me to go in search of the water. I ran on toward the screaming. My eyes teared up from the smoke. My lungs were tight, my mouth gritty.

I found Orlantha next to one of the empty wagons, unconscious from smoke inhalation. I propped her against my chest and dragged her back, inching toward the trees' edge. We were so close to the clearing that I could see the moldering houses of the village when someone wrapped their arms around me from behind. I was so startled, I dropped hold of Orlantha and stumbled forward several paces, nearly tripping over her body.

"Hello, sister. I see you failed my little test."

I gasped. His voice was rough from the smoke, his face shrouded by the hood of a cloak, but it was unmistakably Hansel.

"I *told* Father you were working with the witches."

"How?" I rasped. *How does he know?*

"It all made sense as soon as I figured it out. The strange disappearances on your part, for months now. The perfectly timed appearances of theirs. He didn't believe me, of course.

"No, your falling for my trick of leaving the office door unlocked so you could access private information wasn't enough for him. He convinced himself it was all a coincidence. Didn't think you bright enough, truth be told."

I was rooted to the spot, my body paralyzed by fear, the way it always betrayed me when confronted by him. He began to circle me, forcing me forward with each loop around, until my back was pressed up against a tree and I had nowhere else to go.

"He needed to see you crowned queen, after all. He wouldn't be satisfied by any measure of wealth or power that I could help provide him. No, he needed to control the realm, with you as a royal puppet."

When I broke into a coughing fit, he covered my mouth to stop the smoke from escaping. My body convulsed pathetically as my vision grew blurry.

"But I knew." His breath was hot against my ear.

"And now, I don't need his little plans. No, this fire will burn down several miles of this part of the country by morning. The devastation will be so great, I no longer think we'll need a princess's death to force the Council's hand. People across the realm will be *clamoring* for a ban against the witches."

He abruptly stepped back and I choked as I gasped for air.

"And since we no longer need the Crown's power, we no longer require a princess for our purposes. I'll tell Father you died in the fire, of course. Trying to save the very witches who are only in danger because you couldn't leave well enough alone. If you had kept to your own business, none of them would be here right now."

I watched in mute terror as my brother unsheathed a jagged knife and raised it over me. I covered my face with my arms, the only defense I had. Then, suddenly, he was pitching forward, slumping to his knees before falling on his face. A slight trickle of blood leaked from his skull.

My arms fell limply to my sides. Wilfried was standing before me, a large rock held aloft in his hand.

"Are you okay?" he gasped.

I'd never been so thankful to see him. "Y-yes, I think so. That is, I am uninjured."

He helped me up. I could tell he wanted to look after me, but we didn't have time.

"Did you find the water?" I was already in motion, moving to pick Orlantha up from where she was still lying on the forest floor.

Wilfried lifted her feet while I grabbed her shoulders. "Yes. The witches are making headway on controlling the fire. Most of them are relatively unharmed, just shaken."

Together, we carried Orlantha to safety and then went back into the fray to help the witches contain the fire. Someone had found a creek nearby and a water brigade had assembled. For hours and hours, we fought back the flames. Several times, a spark caught on a new area and it seemed we would not be successful. But with the sunrise came a renewed hope; with the added light, we could see that we were making progress.

When we'd finally put out the last of the flames, it was clear this part of the forest would take years to recover. But the fire was gone. I wanted to collapse with exhaustion and relief, but we had to press on. Our long day had only just begun.

As soon as it was safe to do so, the witches consolidated and piled the remaining supplies and themselves into one wagon to flee back to the village without worrying about separation. Wilfried had tied Hansel to a tree as soon as he could be spared during the fire efforts. He went to make sure that the knots were tight enough to hold my brother until we were far away, and added a second gag in the form of a handkerchief for good measure.

We left him there, unhooked the horses from our wagon, and took off in the direction of the palace.

The queen was waiting for us at the side entrance. She led us immediately to her sitting room.

I stood before her and bowed my head. "Your Majesty, I have been found out. The fire was an ambush, a trap laid by my brother to prove to our father his suspicions that I was working with the witches."

She did not answer me right away, turning instead to address her lady's maid. "Lina, have all of our maids and staff, including Polly Chambers, been moved from the Henoths' estate?"

"Yes, Your Majesty."

"Thank you. Please see that a room is prepared for Miss Henoth and then return for her."

Lina curtsied. "Your Majesty."

"I took precautions," the queen said when Lina was gone. "No matter the intent, I knew that an attack of this kind and scale could not bode well for any of us after." She took a seat on one of her couches and gestured for Wilfried and me to do the same opposite her.

"What do you intend now, Mother?"

"We will operate from here. The maids will have to rely on gossip to best ascertain and anticipate the time and location of likely attacks. They will continue to inform the witches as they are able."

I interjected. "Your Majesty, with respect, we cannot afford to wait any longer to expose Hansel and Ansel for their actions."

"I am afraid that is all we can do for now, Gretel."

Frustration bubbled up within me. I was weary of this dance. "But then what was the point all this? More people support the witches than ever before. Why did we spend all this time, all these resources—"

"Providing aid to those in need? Preventing Ansel and Hansel from doing their worst? Miss Henoth, dozens of families have been spared their homes, their health, even their lives, all because of the work we and the witches have done together."

"But it has been months!" I stood and faced her down.

She reviewed me with a calm that had been honed through nearly two decades in power. "Yes, *only* months. Change takes time. We will not win every battle. True, many have come to our side of reason, but far more are still bound by superstition and bias. We cannot be rash, painful though that is."

"People will be hurt. Some people might die!"

"Can you imagine how many would be harmed if we brought forth upheaval to the realm?" She joined me in standing, though her expression remained serene. "Do you know how many people there are like your father and brother, who bide their time in the shadows and would see everything burned to the ground for their own gain at the slightest provocation?"

I wanted to be strong; I wanted to be impenetrable, like her. Instead, tears choked my still-raw throat, removing the fight from my words. "How can you bear it?"

"A day at a time. One decision at a time. We must be strong and patient, Gretel. For now, you both need baths and rest. We will of course have you stay here with us from now on. I recognize that it is not possible for you to return to the castle. Guards will fetch your belongings later."

So I'll be safe, while everyone in Galwin remains exposed.

It hit me then. She would never take direct action against Ansel and Hansel, or anyone else who posed a threat to the witches. She would never think it was safe enough, supported enough.

All this time, we'd simply been treading water, placing patches over symptoms instead of addressing the root cause. If nothing changed, we would surrender the witches to an indefinite cycle of fear and hiding. If I stayed, one day I would be the one expected to don an air of unflappable stoicism while I made choices that provided only the barest of solutions.

"I apologize for my impatience, Your Majesty. Fatigue and my emotions got the best of me. Thank you for your continued hospitality." I inclined my head in a gesture of submission. "I will, of course, trust your wisdom and guidance as we proceed. I am ready to go to my rooms, at your leave."

Wilfried's touch was light on my back, his voice soft. "I have a few matters to attend to with my mother. I will meet you in your rooms after both of us have had an opportunity to freshen up."

I looked into his blue eyes and resolve steeled within me. He was the perfect son, the consummate prince. His heart was in the right place, but he would never cross his mother. With a nod to Wilfried and a curtsy to the queen, I allowed Lina to lead me from the room.

CHAPTER THIRTY-TWO

I lingered long enough to take a bath and change into clean clothes, knowing they were the last I was likely to have for some time.

When I was confident that Lina believed I was just relaxing, I armed myself with the sword and knife Wilfried had used for my training. Then I snuck out of my room and down to the stables. I wasn't sure how long Wilfried would remain speaking with the queen. I needed to move quickly.

I chose one of the milder, older horses. One who could find his way back home when our business together was done. "Hullo there, Biscuit. We're going on a little adventure." I offered him an apple I'd smuggled from the wagon Wilfried and I had driven back.

"Gretel, don't do this."

I turned and Wilfried stepped into view. Evidently, the answer to my question of how long he'd tarry with the queen was *not long enough*.

I focused my attention back on Biscuit, smoothing my hand over his nose. "I can't stand by and do nothing. I won't sit here, safe in the palace, while my friends and other innocent people are in danger. Not when I have the power to stop it."

"If we cannot take them down with the might of the Crown behind us, what will you do alone?"

"What I should have done weeks ago. My brother wants nothing more than to see me dead, and I am more than certain that my father now shares that wish. I will lure them to the woods and see to it that they can no longer hurt anyone."

He placed his hand upon my shoulder and turned me to face him. "Surely you do not mean—"

"That is all I can say. The more I tell you about my plan, the more in danger you will be."

"Please, just stay here for the night. How much difference can one night make?"

"A great deal of difference, in my experience. Much of my life has been shaped by the events of single, disparate evenings, strung together like pearls." I pushed the images of those nights when he played a starring role from my mind. I could not afford to indulge those memories.

"Wait until morning and I am confident that we can negotiate with my mother. I do not think she realizes the intensity of your feelings." He took my hands in his. His calluses brushed against my skin as warmth spread through my fingers.

I squeezed his hands back. "I have tried waiting. I have tried patience. They did not work."

"What if I can promise that I will convince her to take the

kind of direct action that you've requested in the past?"

"I have full faith in you, but I can see that your mother's decision is firm."

He cupped my cheek in a sudden and sure motion, his fingers fervent and careful all at once. "And if I tell you that I love you?"

All the air fled my lungs. Amongst the hundred declarations and pleas I'd anticipated, this had not appeared as even a possibility.

He brought his other hand to rest against the base of my neck. "I love you, Gretel. I think I began falling in love with you the moment we collided on the terrace. You are the first real friend I've chosen entirely for myself. You are the most resilient person I know. You face terror every day and run toward it with eyes open. Even now, you risk everything for those you care about. But I am begging you, if you care for *me*, please refrain. I do not wish to lose you."

A fevered pitch kicked up the pace of his words. "Once we are married, I will become king. I won't have to be careful and accommodating like my mother. Nor will you. Because we will be together. And side by side, we will transform our kingdom into a land where the witches—where *all* people—are safe.

"But we—" His voice hitched on a dry sob. "We cannot do that if you die fighting your family alone in the woods."

It was all mapped out before us, reflected in the shimmering pools of his eyes. A glittering future that mere days ago I would have leapt toward. He'd laid his soul bare without a trace of self-consciousness, and yet he considered me the brave one? I wanted nothing more than to hold his heart gently with one hand while giving him mine with the other.

"I cannot deny that I hold true feelings for you, Wil. I have for longer than I was willing to admit before, even to myself."

I took a shuddering breath. "I wish that I had been honest. With myself, with you. I wish I had been a different kind of brave. I wish I'd spent all the days I've known you exploring the truth of how I feel—the depths to which we might have gone if only I'd spoken sooner."

I wiped away his tears and he covered my hands with his, holding them to either side of his face. I brushed the tips of my fingers over the curls that formed at the nape of his neck. I tried to absorb the feeling into my very skin so I would not forget: For a moment, this was ours.

"I do not know how I would have survived these months without you," I confessed. "You are everything good and true in this world. You have helped rebuild my ability to trust, which I believed was beyond repair." He closed his eyes and leaned his forehead against mine. A tear slipped down his nose and landed on my cheek.

"I know that you will be a good and just king," I whispered in the breath of space between us. "You will usher fresh ideas and dreams into our realm and I would love to stand by your side and do that work with you. But I, I—"

He pressed his lips against mine and swallowed up the words I could not find.

And I knew, however long or short my life might be, I would never again deny myself the gift of speaking up and asking for what I wanted. His hands were certain and his lips were tender, and knowing that I could have met them months ago made my bones ache.

Biscuit whinnied and startled us apart.

"But you are saying goodbye." He breathed the words into my mouth, finishing the sentence I couldn't bear to speak.

"I have to. I must help them. I must do what is right, even if it breaks my heart or puts me in danger." I stepped back from him. Our arms dangled awkwardly, unsure of their purpose now that they were no longer reaching for each other.

"I could never bear a life of lavish comfort otherwise, knowing what the cost would be."

"No, I don't suppose you could." His mouth had thinned to a line of pain, but there was a sheen of pride in his eyes. Even now, he chose to see the best version of me.

"If you truly care for me, please let me go and do not follow."

"I do. I will. I understand." He was the one to take a second step back. But then he leaned forward and caught my hand with both of his, and I was in as much danger of staying as ever.

"Gretel, this I swear: I will do everything in my power to minimize the harm caused to the witches and any of the families who are targeted while your plan unfolds. Whatever it may be, I trust you. I promise you shall always have a friend in me and in the Crown."

I threw my arms around him. I wished I could bring him with me.

"Go, quickly, before it is too late," he said against my hair.

I ripped myself away from him then. If I lingered another moment, I would never leave. I swung myself into Biscuit's saddle and took off for the forest, crying the entire time.

At the threshold of the woods, my fox waited for me. I dismounted, gave Biscuit a pat, then sent him back toward his home.

Once again, the fox led me on an unknown path. We wove our way through the trees and bushes as the night grew darker and frost appeared before me with each exhale.

We came upon a lonely cottage, glittering beneath the moonlight with jewels that seemed deeply embedded from its outer walls or rooftop.

Behind me, the forest path itself shone with idyllic flowers and all manner of welcoming fauna. It was the inverse twin of the path to Galwin, designed to welcome humans, to draw those who would harm me closer.

It was as though the cottage had conjured itself to conspire with my efforts to lure my brother and father. As if I knew it already, as if I were greeting an old friend.

I took up residence in the cottage and waited.

I spent my days practicing the craft I'd learned from the witches and marking myself through my sword drills. I thought of Wilfried with every swing, every parry. I gave free rein to my tears. I wished him well. I missed them all, the royals and the witches.

Weeks passed.

Each sunset, the fox brought me a parcel with food from Galwin. Each morning, a crow alighted upon the windowsill with bits of parchment carrying news written in code.

The attacks had died down. The other witches had withdrawn into hiding once more. Rumors swirled that a solitary witch had taken up residence in the old abandoned cottage in the woods, not far from the palace. Gossips began to inquire about the recent absences of the would-be princess from society events.

I relished the day I heard the first tale about me. It was a day closer to my family's reckoning. I took comfort knowing that the fabrications would keep away all those with whom I held no quarrel. Meanwhile, they were bait for those I wished nothing less than harm.

I wondered if Ansel and Hansel were themselves biding their time, waiting for the stories about the cottage witch to spin into lies wicked enough that they would justify seeking her out with the intent to harm her. Did they know that I was the solitary witch of whom the rumors spoke? Or did they not care where I had disappeared to, now that I could no longer advance their agenda for power?

In the end, whether they knew the truth or no, neither of them were able to resist the invitation to a witch hunt.

CHAPTER THIRTY-THREE

They arrived in the middle of the night, as so many monsters do. The jangling of the knob and straining of the door on its hinges alerted me to their presence. I retrieved the dagger from beneath my pillow and the sword next to my bed. The fox sat watchful before the hearth. I stood guard next to him.

"Let them come to me."

At my command, he leapt upon the handle. The door flew open and a gust of wind pushed through the cottage, though the candle flames did not so much as flicker.

"This is the end for you, witch," Ansel grunted.

"Perhaps."

Ansel flinched at the sound of my voice.

His gaze lifted to meet mine, eyes round with shock. "So . . . it *is* you."

I said nothing. They slammed the door behind them and stood just over the threshold, surveying my small home.

"Some things stay exactly the same." Hansel sighed.

"And some things change," I countered.

I struck before he could anticipate me. My brother barely

raised his sword in time. Even still, the force of his weapon colliding with mine reverberated through my entire shoulder. Too much time had passed since I'd faced a proper opponent. I gritted my teeth and moved to block his next attack.

Ansel hung back, cowering in a half-crouched position by the bed, letting his son take all his blows. Typical.

Keeping my gaze steady upon Hansel, I called upon the protections I'd learned from the witches. I let myself slide into the muscle memory of Wilfried's lessons. I infused every movement with my own rage at my father and brother's cruelty and greed. I brought my best to every step, every swing.

Hansel, however, was hardly trying.

He expects me to relent. He does not think me capable of facing him to the end.

The realization clouded my judgment for just a breath. I took one wrong step. Hansel's blade grazed my upper arm, tearing a hole in the sleeve of my nightdress. I gasped and he took advantage of my distraction, knocking the sword from my hand. It clattered to the ground. We stood suspended in time for a moment. Then an expression of arrogant triumph melted across his face and my blood leapt to a boiling point.

"Watch out!" Ansel rasped from the floor where he cowered.

But he was too late.

With a howl of rage, I pulled the dagger hidden beneath my opposite sleeve and launched myself toward Hansel. His jaw fell open. For the first time, he viewed me as a true opponent. Freed from the weight of a sword, I was faster than him, and a consistent step ahead.

I kneed him in the groin and glee coursed through me as he reflexively loosened the grip on his weapon in a move to shield himself. Before he could recover, I grabbed the sword with my free hand and pinned him to the ground.

I held my dagger to his throat and positioned the sword's point over his heart, prepared to end our battle for good.

"Gretel, don't."

The fear in his eyes was so familiar it stayed my hand. It was a look I'd only ever seen him give one person, and I had never imagined I would be the second. It was the terror of a little boy. Trapped, with nowhere to go. It pulled me back, back into a narrative I'd all but forgotten.

Let me tell you a story . . .

A voice whispered in my mind. A voice that sounded like my own, from a time far, far away.

And all at once, I remembered.

CHAPTER THIRTY-FOUR

Once upon a time, there was a Brother and a Sister.

He was only eight and the Sister three when the girl and their Mother fell ill. While the Father worked in the woods, the Brother nursed them as best he could. Until the day the Mother grew desperate and sent the Brother into the woods to find a cure from the Wood Witches, whom the Father distrusted and the Village despised. The Brother soon returned with two witches in tow. They arrived just before dawn, as so many miracles do.

"You must choose," one of the cloaked figures said with remorse.

"We have only enough left for one of you," confirmed the other.

"My daughter," rasped the Mother, before she closed her eyes to sleep.

In the wake of losing their mother, the Brother and the Sister became inseparable.

When the Father grew angry and violent in his grief, the Brother shielded the Sister.

Despite the early sadness of their lives, the Brother and Sister found joy wherever they could. In chores that were transformed into games. In wisdom that masqueraded as stories. The Brother taught the Sister to read, passing on knowledge through the small collection of books the Mother had left behind. Lack grew their imaginations and want fed their dreams.

One day, a peddler passed through their village. Taking pity upon the two poor children, they offered each a piece of candy. The Brother devoured his treat on the spot and ran off, eager to resume playing, but the Sister lingered near the stranger.

The peddler leaned down, their face concealed beneath a hooded cloak, and shared a secret with her.

"Save this candy for when you need it most. It is meant *just* for you. Take care that you do not let it fall into the hands of others. When the time comes, bury the candy at the edge of the woods and it will lead you to a new world. But you must tell no one."

The Sister promised to keep the secret and save the candy.

Years went by. The Father became meaner and the Brother walked in his footsteps, eager for the Father's approval.

The Sister kept her word, made sure the candy was hidden and safe.

One night, after the Father left the Brother beaten near to a pulp, the Sister knew it was time.

Under the light of the full moon, she buried the candy at the edge of the forest and waited for her salvation to appear.

Moments later, a fox walked out from the trees and right up to her.

Before she could react, the fox opened its mouth. On its tongue lay a bright red jewel the exact same shade of the candy she'd buried.

The fox led her through the woods to a beautiful cottage covered in more jewels. Inside, she found a note explaining that the fox's magic supplied one jewel each day, which it would faithfully bring to the cottage's occupant as a means to provide a living.

The Sister returned home and determined she would share her secret with the one person who mattered most to her in all the world. She could not bear to leave him behind, even if it meant breaking a promise.

The next morning, after the Father went into the woods for the day, she told the Brother about the candy, the cottage, and the fox.

The Sister revealed that she intended to leave. She could no longer bear living with the Father anymore, and wanted the Brother to come with her to the cottage, where they could be happy and safe.

But the Brother shared none of the Sister's joy or optimism. He took her news as confirmation that everything he'd done to protect her was not good enough in her eyes.

He put his foot down and told the Sister he would not go.

"You need to be happy with life here. This village is all the world holds for people like us," the Brother declared.

She pleaded and pleaded with him, but the more the Sister

pushed back, the more irate the Brother became. He was certain that she took him for a fool.

He refused to go with her, convinced it would stop her from leaving.

Afraid that her Brother would only grow to become more and more like the Father, the Sister escaped their home that very night and set off for the cottage by herself.

This time, when she reached the cottage, she discovered she was not alone.

I watched my memories unfold like a storybook in my mind's eye, as everything came flooding back. I gasped when I reached the cottage, saw the woman standing before the door, waiting for me.

"You found your way," Orlantha said.

Gretel nodded.

"Do you seek a new life?"

Another nod.

"Come with me." Orlantha extended her hand. "There is much for you to learn."

Gretel took a step toward the stranger, her heart filling with trust and hope that she could not explain. But just before she reached the woman, Orlantha gasped.

"You did not do as you promised. You revealed our secret."

Gretel looked over her shoulder to the source of Orlantha's horror.

Hansel stood at the edge of the clearing, an axe in his hands and rage painted across his face.

"Witch," he accused, his gaze intent upon Orlantha.

I knew how the rest of the story unfolded; Orlantha must have escaped back to Galwin once Hansel left her for dead and dragged both me and the cottage's riches back to Ansel's hovel.

He'd beaten a witch that day.

But not this time.

CHAPTER THIRTY-FIVE

"Gretel, please."

Hansel's gasping plea brought my consciousness back into the present with such forcefulness that I nearly fell over and lost my advantage.

His chin quivered like he meant it.

But I had the full story now. I'd been right to escape to safety once upon a time; given the chance, Hansel *had* become just like Ansel.

"Gretel, I'm sorry."

I sneered at his lying face.

This time, I had learned my lesson.

This time, I would end this cycle of violence. Forever.

"Let me tell you something, brother." I spoke loud enough for Ansel to hear.

"Anything."

"I remember."

He cried out and thrashed beneath my weight. Clamping my hand firm over his mouth, I denied him his voice just as he had long stolen mine.

With a final wail of fury and sorrow, a lament for the sweet boy I remembered as my brother and the kind man I had once hoped he'd become, I raised my dagger and thrust it through his heart.

Then, with the blood of his only son still dripping from my hands, I pounced upon the coward in the corner I'd once called Father, freeing the world from my original tormentor at last.

CHAPTER THIRTY-SIX

I emerged from the cottage cloaked in sweat and blood to find her standing there, serene as when we'd first faced each other in the same place nearly a year before.

"You came back for me?" I croaked as I stumbled toward her.

"I came to see you choose yourself, Gretel." Orlantha's voice was calm, steady as the breeze that stirred the branches of the trees around us.

I stared at her shoulder, pictured the tangled scar that lay beneath the layers of her clothes. "I am so sorry."

"As am I, for many things."

"I should never have told him. I should have listened to you."

"You were willing to risk yourself for the hope that he might be healed. I cannot fault you for that. It is a trait I believe you inherited from your mother." She tucked a strand of hair behind my ear. "You look just like her, you know."

I hung my head. "Have I let her down?"

"I did not know her well enough to say what she would have wished on this day." Orlantha crouched until we were eye to eye once more. "But I know this: She fought to save your life so you could live."

I studied her face, looking for any trace of instruction, any hint of what she thought I should do, how I could best please everyone around me.

Instead, in the face of her neutrality, my own desires were suddenly clear to me; for the first time, my internal voice was louder to me than anyone else's.

I did not know what waited—for the witches, for the realm, for any of those I cared about. But there was only one place I wanted to be when the unknown came for us all.

"Is it too late?" I whispered.

Orlantha's face softened as she straightened to her full height.

I followed her into the forest, along unfamiliar paths that led to those I'd grown to see as dear friends.

When we emerged from the tunnel at the edge of Galwin, the sky was beginning to shift from deep blue to streaks of periwinkle and rose. Only one lantern hovered in the center of the square below the hill, standing sentry with a lone figure.

I forced myself to walk with measured steps, prepared for her to reject me. But when I drew close enough for her to see, Katharina's face broke into a smile brighter than any sunrise.

Before I knew what to think, she was running. Running toward me with her arms outstretched and her hair billowing behind her. We collided in an embrace of tangled limbs and tears.

"I'm safe," I rasped.

"You're home," she whispered, her cheek pressed firm against mine.

"For good."

ACKNOWLEDGEMENTS

Writing this book was the culmination of decades of life and work, so I have many people to thank, if you'll bear with me:

First, my incredible editor, Talia Seidenfeld. Thank you for this adventure and for creating such a safe space for me to take risks. I'm so proud of the work we've done together.

Second, Marietta Zacker, the dearest, fiercest, and funniest agent in all the land. What a *quest* we have been on since 2017. There's no one else I would rather wear all the hats with than you.

Thank you to Maithili Joshi, Melissa Schirmer, Jessica White, Lara Kennedy, Hannah Calderazzo, Maddy Newquist, Maeve Norton, Aimee Friedman, David Levithan, Kristin Standley, Amanda Book, and Rachel Feld for all your hard, wonderful work bringing Gretel to life. It is such a gift to be in good hands like yours.

To Andrew Briedis, for twelve years of deep friendship and creative collaboration. You are the best thing the internet has ever given me. You jump, I jump. And to Darby Bozeman for a friendship that feels like casting a spell—I'm so grateful we're on this author journey together.

To those who've passed on:

Zack Allen, my Matthew Cuthbert and Anne Sullivan rolled into one. Thank you for saving me.

Grandma Ruth, thank you for teaching me how to read and being my biggest cheerleader every day I knew you.

Kati, thank you for letting me force you into elaborate, scripted games and a Spice Girls cover band with regimented rehearsals, when you would've preferred to just run around and play.

Brandon Gibson, thank you for all the joy and story and ongoing bits you brought into my life. I know you've charmed everybody up there, including the stars.

Tyson, thank you for standing guard and teaching me that cycles can be broken.

Arissa Gaekle, thank you for teaching me how to be resilient and persevere, no matter the odds or circumstances.

Thank you to Dennis Perkins for your enduring friendship and steadfast example of commitment to a mission. Also to Jenny Ballard, Sien Moon, Caroline King, and the generations of KCT staff, families, and children who have time and again reminded me of the value in art by and for young artists and their peers.

Thank you to Tim Federle for taking me under your wing when I needed it, taking me seriously always, and convincing me to jump when you knew I was ready, even if I didn't. Hunter Arnold, thank you for bringing me into the fold and teaching me so much about making art happen.

Thank you to Grandpa Lee for my name and love of details, and for all the sacrifices you've made. And to all of the families that provided ports in a storm as I was growing up and needed shelter and support. You know who you are, and I'll never forget your kindness.

Thank you to Sandy Hughes, Connie Francis, Jill Robbins, Leann Dickson, Madam Melanie Kennedy, Katie Alley, and Ginny Thurston for making sure I survived high school. To Casey Sams, Kenton Yeager, Kate Buckley, Edward Francisco, and Smokey's Food Pantry for making sure I survived college. And to Yuliya for helping me heal and thrive in adulthood.

Thank you to so many chosen family members, friends, and colleagues for encouragement, laughs, venting, support, and wisdom along the way: Jason Blitman, Bryan and Darby Bozeman, Nicole Davis, Cheyenne Ferguson and Mitchell Pearce, Lauren Irwin, Hannah Jones, David Levy and Keith Schumann, Tatra Luke, Angie Manfredi, Maggie Marks, McKinley Merritt, Elle Nelson, Jodi Picoult, Ash Poston, David Ratliff, Becky and Rick Riordan, Shelly Romero, Rob Rokicki, Amy Sapp, Arya Shahi, Rachel Strolle, Team GZLA, Joe Tracz, Austin Witt, Bezi Yohannes, Beth Young, and Ada Young.

Shout-out to the *The Lightning Thief* musical team, the Riordans, and all the Percy Jackson fans for five years of dream jobs. Special thanks to Merel, Tiannah, Tessa, Apple and Kiwi, the Dutch demigods, Katie from Australia, and whichever one of you made that canvas with printouts of your favorite @LTMusical tweets. I hope my books can someday inspire a fandom with even a tenth of y'all's passion.

Thank you to Jake Richards for *Backwoods Witchcraft*, which helped me create Galwin. And to Alix Wery and Bárbara for your French expertise. Thank you to Paris Paloma for writing music that became the conduit for Gretel's and my rage.

Thank you to Tori, Chelsea, Bran, and the entire Union Ave Books team for all your support over the years. Also the Paysan and Remedy staffs for keeping me in breakfast sandwiches and coffee.

Thank you to every reader, reviewer, and bookish person who's celebrated *Witchkiller* and lifted me up.

And finally, if you see yourself in the dedication for this book: You will make it through and you will become so much more than what you've survived. I'm rooting for you, always.